Second Hand Stops

The Van Buren Series, Volume 1

Katie St. Claire

New World Publishing, 2015.

Character model April Berry as Julia Malone.

© JT Smith Photography, 2015.

Dedication

Second Hand Stops is dedicated to everyone who has ever felt alone, abandoned, or misunderstood. Each of you possesses the greatest gift known to man—hope.

I'd like to thank my family, especially my husband Chris, who supported me throughout this journey and kept the home fires burning. Cherish and protect your inner light, because with perseverance, anything is possible.

In the words of Julia Malone,
"No one has the patent on me!"

Contents

Prologue

The dreary clouds cast shadows across the sky and heavy rain soaks me to the bone. A bald man stinking of smoke leads the way toward an old brick manor.

I'm terrified by his determined expression and he drags me by the hand, stumbling behind him on the stone driveway. Coattails fly behind him in the wind and I yearn for the warm car idling in the distance. The man's eyes are less than reassuring, and his touch devoid of warmth or caring as I trip across the uneven cobblestone. I'm positive he's delivering me to my death.

The man raps at a thick wooden door, and the echo reverberates in my head. I don't know whether it's the uncertainty of fate, unfamiliar surroundings, or a sopping wet coat that makes me shiver. Perhaps it's all three. When the door creaks opens on decades-old hinges, I'm relieved. A plump woman with soft features greets me with a gentle voice in my head.

"I'm Lillian, welcome to the manor. Reputation has

it you're a handful and I should keep an eye on you." The woman seems mild and my breath evens out a wee bit after that.

The bald man nods and turns to leave. He scurries through the rain and back to the warm, black car. The last sound I remember is tires crunching on gravel; it's a sound I'll connect with this moment forever. Somehow, their slow departure appears guilty—one last appraisal of the crying girl on a stranger's doorstep.

The dripping teddy bear is as pathetic as the uncertainty of my future. Lillian is kind and leads us to a cavernous room with thick wooden beams at the ceiling. Flickering blue flames crackle and pop in a stone hearth, warming the wide open room. Lillian wraps a thick crocheted blanket around my shoulders and sits in an antique rocking chair beside the fireplace.

Her voice rings out in my head.

"Several other children are coming to the manor so we won't be alone for long— you have so much to learn here." She gazes my direction and waits for a response.

"Do you have any candy?" I'm serious, but Lillian *slaps a hand over her mouth, trying not to laugh.*

"Candy you say?"

"Yes. It's been a shite of a day." I cuddle into my blanket.

"Oh dear lord. You're a handful aren't you? And yes, I have plenty of candy." She stokes the fire with an elaborate black poker. *"We need to clean up that mouth of yours. How old are you again?"*

"Three and still counting." I sigh with exasperation. How hard is it to dig up chocolate?

"Three." She grins at me. *"Candy it is, then."*

Chapter One—The Elixir

My father abandoned me on the doorstep of an old English manor when I was three. I have a hazy recollection of a long, black car driving off while hot, salty tears stung my face. I'm Julia Malone, but can't remember my father's name and wouldn't recognize him on the street if he showed up tomorrow. Time whittles away memories until they become nothing but vague recollections at the back of your mind.

Abandonment is a soul wound, leaving in its wake doubt and suspicion where once there was innocence and trust. In my experience, memories cause headaches and chest pain. Certain days it feels as if my heart might beat through my ribcage and I clutch at my chest. It's a habit now, even after fifteen years.

The mistress of our manor let us choose our own names when we first arrived. Lillian Perriman is a squat, gray haired woman with a warm heart and sharp tongue. Her quick temper is legendary, but she's the only mum I've ever known. I still remember the day I chose my name, thinking long and hard how I wanted the world to view me.

1

"Okay, you little bundle of curiosity." She'd said, studying my mop of unkempt red hair. "What do you want to call yourself?"

Creating your own name is a challenge when you're three and since I'd always liked the sound of Julia, it was the only logical choice.

"I want to be Julia. It's a lovely name." I had scrunched my brows up real tight, thinking of a proper last name for Julia. The sounds of words are magical and I'm conscious of how they flow together when people talk. "Malone. I want to be Julia Malone."

After announcing my chosen my name, it became clear Lillian gave me a gift that day. My sense of helplessness vanished, and for the first time, I had control over something in my life. Everyone else in the room exchanged looks, quieted their giggles, and kicked each other under the table. Who cares what anyone else thinks?

I live with five telepathic housemates and we're the same age. Certain ones are nice, but a few are a pain in my butt.

"You can talk with your mind, too? Bet I'm better. You're just a stupid girl." The boy with shiny black hair folds his arms across his chest, challenging me to disagree.

Nic, Sebastian, and Dutch Maye came to the manor,

and Lillian introduced them as brothers.

"Well, boys, it looks as if you're in need of new names, ones you've chosen yourselves. What do you say?" Lillian stirred boiling soup and waited for their response. They stood motionless with uncertain expressions, glancing at each other. I watched the scene unfold from the kitchen table, enthralled by their reactions.

"We get to pick our own names?" One child's deep aqua eyes were expressive. I remember being impressed by that, even when I was small. He didn't have a lick of pretense and turned to the other two boys, shrugging his shoulders.

"It's May, so that's a good last name. And I want to be Nic." There were whisperings between the three of them and he continued. "This one here wants to be Dutch. The other one wants to be Sebastian. He had a cat named Sebastian, you know." Nic slung an arm over each boy's shoulder and they became the invincible three.

"Fair enough, Nic Maye. Oh, and we can't forget Dutch and Sebastian. Those are fine names for handsome young lads." Lillian winked and then busied herself slicing bread. It's amazing I remember so much of that day, but maybe it's because of my unusual abilities.

The three brothers are nothing alike, but as close as

3

any orphans could be. Nic is my best friend, and over the years, the two of us developed a deep bond. Sebastian torments me for reasons I've yet to unravel, but I love him just the same. Dutch is the sweet, sappy poet in the group and acts more girlish than actual girls do. He's as sensitive as they come. In the summer, the days are long, and he sits outside writing poetry, and sketching. He always sketched me prettier than I am, and I was grateful for it. I never felt attractive or fit in anywhere. That's why Nic calls me goose.

Lyra Twerth is the only other female in the house besides Lillian and me. She arrived the same day as that nasty boy with the jet-black hair and dark eyes. She chose her name from a character in a cartoon series, and it's ridiculous if you ask me.

"Lyra Twerth. She kicks tail on Girl Power." She had announced, inspecting her fingernails and biting at the cuticles.

"Okay, you're Lyra Twerth but watch your language. And you, young man?" The expression on Lillian's face changed when she addressed the black haired boy. Her demeanor shifted from controlled, to uncertain.

"Lincoln." He stated in a flat tone, staring at us after the announcement.

"Lincoln. That's an interesting name. May I ask how you came up with it?"

"I'll be the first president of the United States someday. Abraham Lincoln wasn't the first *real* president." His defiant glare unnerved every one of us in the room except Lyra.

She and I are as different as oil and water, and like the elements, we just don't mix. Her attitude problem goes well beyond what I consider off kilter.

Lincoln, or Linc for short, chose the last name Sackinstock. He made it up after helping Lillian stock the pantry with sacks of potatoes the day of his arrival. He's weird, and when I say weird, there's something inherently wrong with his brain. I try to stay clear of him, but to the all-around catty Lyra, he's catnip.

* * *

The dinner bell clangs, calling us to a family meeting which promises to change our lives.

"This is it. You ready to have your life changed forever?" Nic sets his book aside, parroting Lillian's words.

"I'm eighteen and it's a little early to have my life changed forever, don't you think?" At least that's what common sense dictates.

Lillian prattled on this topic for a week, and I'm

tired of hearing the word *elixir* in our everyday conversations. I can't wait to be on my own without Lillian monitoring my every move, but it's impossible to wrap my mind around an elixir that prolongs life.

"I want to have a family, grow old, and die like a normal person. Who wants to hang around after their friends and family have passed?"

"Everyone wants to be immortal. Don't you want to live forever?" Nic bumps my shoulder.

"I want to travel the world and die when I'm old. Call me moronic." I trek toward Rose Hall, my mood bored and foul. Nic is lagging behind so I snatch his hand and we pick up the pace.

I think about the home that I've grown to love in the sleepy countryside of England. It's serene here, with a landscape that's lush and green. Most of our neighbors have quaint English cottages, many of them with red or violet flowering vines that climb the outbuildings. They add bursts of color to the land every spring and summer. I'm fond of the wispy purple wisteria, with its drooping habit, and hearty grape vines with clusters of deep purple fruits that ripen at the end of autumn.

Gardening isn't a hobby in Chipping Campden; it's a way of life. Our bricked manor has mismatched pots of lavender, bee orchid, and foxglove scattered over the property.

"Julia, you need to bring those pots inside the manor. A chill settled in my bones last night, and it's getting ready to frost. Would you do that for an old woman?"

"You know I will." I watch her wipe dirt covered hands on an old gardening apron. She waddles through the back door and is gone.

Lillian likes our flowers in pots so we can rearrange our yard whenever she changes her mind, which is often. We bring the flowers indoors when frigid weather arrives and I'm in charge of their care all year.

There's a great big world waiting for me to take it by storm, or at least a small squall. I can't hide in the sleepy countryside of England forever.

***

Rose Hall looms ahead, vast and dim. Rows of lit candles flicker on the fireplace mantle and I check them off one by one in my head. It's a compulsive habit, and helps me relax when I'm nervous, which is darn near every day. The old, creaky, hardwood floors scarcely make a sound under my feet as I creep along trying not to bring attention to myself as we enter the hall.

Pine hangs heavy in the air, its rich heady scent making me long for the outdoors. Our fascinating group of misfits is milling about the room and I have the urge to flee before they suck me into their black holes. My ability to spot the nuances of body language is uncanny, and I nailed everyone's personality from the start. In fifteen years, not one of those pot lickers has deviated from my initial assessment.

Rose Hall is nothing short of extraordinary and the first things I notice are whitewashed fieldstone walls, stark next to the hand-hewed beams at the ceiling. My attention often strays upward during family meetings and Lillian accuses me of daydreaming when my head lolls to the side. I guess it's a dead giveaway I'm bored out of my skull.

It's better to ponder the architectural elegance of the manor as opposed to listening to a dull recanting of my everyday existence. The curtains I picked out show their age, a dusty smell lingering despite pine candles burning on the mantle.

When I was eight, Lillian let me tag along to a local tailor and allowed me to pick the brocade fabric. Now it hangs from four, twenty-foot windows in the hall.

"Which fabric stands out, dear?" She studied me while I glanced from a masculine checkered pattern, to the rose fabric that caught my attention and held it.

"The one with the flowers," I shouted, jumping around the shop. My decision was quick at the time and I shudder at how time has slipped away. Ten years to be exact, and now we're adults.

Sebastian, the absolute bane of my existence, pushes past me as I make my way toward the fireplace.

"Move your caboose, Malone." He lives to torture me with his incessant teasing. He's the rebel brother with a dark brooding side and slings an arm over my shoulder. Sebastian behaves as if he doesn't care much but if you ask me, it's all an act. Choppy, dirty blond hair hangs across his eyes and he stares at me through chunks of it, and then swipes the nuisance off his forehead.

There's more to Sebastian than meets the eye, but I haven't figured him out yet. He studies my every move, refusing to avert his gaze when I catch him. It's intimidating, and he unravels me like the skittish little basket case I am. His constant one-upmanship with Nic for the alpha male position in this house gets old and I want no part of their stupid sibling rivalry.

"Quit being such a bloody wanker." Nic elbows Sebastian out of the way.

He's my best friend and I'll love him until the day I

die—maybe longer. Try as I may, I can find no fault other than he doesn't love me the same. It's not a fault per se, just an observation. Nic has an insane sense of humor and a crazy habit of turning every situation into a comedic opportunity. It cheers me up when I'm sad or just flat out overwhelmed.

I have this crazy fantasy of me chattering away while Nic leans over to shut me up with a kiss. So far, the fantasy has remained a figment of my overactive imagination but it keeps me from being bored out of my mind.

Lincoln sits next to Lyra, shooting the rest of us a stone-faced glare. When he arrived at the manor a week after Nic and his brothers, his disturbing, quiet demeanor gave me the creeps. I'm positive Lincoln is plotting world destruction. He keeps his telepathy on lockdown with everyone except Lyra, ten shades of apathy and sarcasm rolled into a snotty little ball of shocking black hair.

Now we're eighteen. Lillian says it changes everything. Does this mean she's tossing us on the street to fend for ourselves? I've thought of my future and cross *super model* off the list since confidence is a prerequisite. I have a hard time imagining myself as anything special. Everyone says I'm gorgeous. So, define gorgeous; I can't.

Sometimes I stand before my bedroom mirror, gazing at the willowy body and piercing green eyes, and try to figure out society's definition of beautiful. I see nothing but imperfection in my sharp nose, and auburn hair and don't stand out like the striking English actresses on the telly.

The six of us are telepathic and read each other's thoughts. Lillian taught us to block telepathic intrusion, but it was a painful lesson I'll never forget. When we read thoughts, it leaves people with a throbbing headache. It was trial and error at first, but we perfected the skill with practice. It took years.

"Let's get this freak show on the road already." I brush Sebastian off my shoulder and sit Indian style in front of the fireplace because the flames always hypnotize me into a calmer state of mind. Sometimes, I check out, picturing myself on a beach while Lillian complains about her arthritis, the weather, or our behavior.

"Come on, you little terrorists. Quit dragging your butts or I'll send you arse over tea kettle." Lillian taps an impatient foot on the hardwood floors as we find our seats.

I've recorded her funny expressions in the pages of my journal, and one of my favorites is when she's *busier than a cat carrying smoke*. The visuals they create make

11

me smile, and my sick sense of humor makes funny little pictures in my head. I imagine Lillian sending Lincoln face first down a flight of stairs, followed by his insufferable crony, Lyra. Nic and Dutch laugh with inside jokes and I keep to myself, lest I become their next target.

"What's the reason for this stupid meeting again?" The words roll off Lincoln's tongue in a defiant tone as if he's sneering.

He turns to Lyra for approval and she smirks so I roll my eyes at their loathsome friendship and imagine swatting him off his chair.

"Shut your trap Sackinstock." Sebastian shoots Linc a warning and I can't believe he's Nic's brother for as different as they are. He has balls of steel.

I'm happy he put Lincoln in his place, but I avoid eye contact. The guy always hooks me with his unnerving stare. I peek over at Nic and he offers a reassuring smile that feels like a warm, comfortable blanket. Lillian's voice pierces the room when she speaks.

"Lyra had her eighteenth birthday this week. That's the last of you. We've discussed the details for weeks now, and you'll be receiving your inheritance along with the first dose of elixir." No one flinches because she's talked about it for years.

Lillian tried to pass this mysterious elixir off as one of the greatest gifts in history, but considering the state of the world, who wants a long life? I raise my hand and ignore Lyra's nasty scowl. She could melt the eyeballs from a person's skull with her condescending glares.

"Do we *have* to take the elixir?" I pout.

"Is this a stall tactic young lady?"

"I don't want to prolong my life and who wants to be a guinea pig for something we know nothing about? Am I the only rocket scientist with half a lick in this house?" I'm pushing my luck and I know it. *They can have their long drawn-out lives on this messed up planet, but I'm out.*

"You don't have a choice in the matter." Lillian's expression stiffens and her cheeks might crack if she doesn't stop frowning.

"No kidding? I can't opt out, so what else is new? Can I have my own darn thoughts to myself for once?"

"Not in this house you can't." Her telepathic response is terse. She never could curb my penchant for the occasional cuss word.

It rocks living with a house full of mind-readers—rocks like no tomorrow. I imagine our nightmare of a life once we're unleashed on the *real* world.

Ginger-blue flames crackle in the fireplace, and

scents from burning peach wood is rather hypnotic. If it were any other day, the flames might lull me into a peaceful coma, but today it feels as if I'm bubbling away in a witch's cauldron.

"Inhale, Julia, you're the master of whacked out situations."

Lyra elbows Lincoln and he turns to study me with his normal expressionless stare and she with loathing. I avert my attention and catch Lillian moving toward a stained wooden box set upon a pedestal. She produces an old-fashioned skeleton key from her apron pocket and holds it in the air with a theatrical flair. It captures our attention. Good old Lillian, she holds the patent on dramatization.

"Julia, Nic, Lincoln, Sebastian, Dutch, and Lyra," our names roll off her tongue with enunciated syllables, effectively quieting our chatter.

She inserts the key and there's a faint hitch followed by a loud releasing click. The top of the box opens to reveal six vials of amethyst liquid in four-inch illuminated cylinders. The tension in the room is conspicuous. My inappropriate giggle echoes inside the hall, the way some people laugh at funerals. Lillian glares until my throat constricts. *Hey, it was an accident. I'm nervous.*

"Find something amusing, young lady?" Her watery gray eyes lock with mine, and my throat is as dry as sandpaper.

"I'm just anxious." Air hisses through my teeth like a leaking tire.

"Well then. As you know, the elixir prolongs life. Experts at your benefactor's lab have named it substance x, but it has no scientific label. These same experts have something in the works for the elixir. Let me be the first to inform you it's *extraordinary.*" Her lips melt into a thin, flesh colored line, and she reaches for one of the amethyst vials.

"They discovered the elixir... um... well, that's not important." A vein bulges at the side of her forehead, her pulse pounding with every erratic heartbeat. "When I call your name, step forward, and drink your vial. We've discussed how everyone might have a different reaction to the elixir so don't expect it to be a walk in the park. Are there any questions?" She raises a brow, and the hard lines of her body shimmer in and out while my eyes water. It must be nerves.

I try not to panic because it makes me hyperventilate and pass out. There's movement to my left

15

and Nic makes his way toward me on the floor. His expression is intent, as if to say *don't you dare*, so I keep my gaze up front.

If I go first, and if it causes a dangerous reaction, at least everyone else will be safe. I jump to my feet, raising my hand.

"I'll take the first vial." The words fly from my mouth before I can stop them, and my fair skin shows every fleeting emotion. Nic grabs my arm, and judging by the expression on his face, he's pissed.

"Not such a good idea my dear, sweet, impetuous goose," he whispers in my ear, locking eyes with Lillian. She has a hand on her hip, and a nasty scowl pickling her face.

"I'll go first," Nic pipes up, and she nods in agreement, beckoning him forward with a silver-tipped fingernail.

Lillian's choice in nail polish makes her look a witch, so we need to talk about her misguided fashion sense. Nic brushes past my shoulder leaving me impotent and overruled, and I grit my teeth, frustrated and scared. The white-washed walls close in and the room spins. Everyone has control over me, except me. This oppressive manor makes me want to run and never turn back.

Resigned to defeat, I drop to my butt and stare at the rows of flickering candles with angry dancing flames. My nails are already gnawed off so I check around to see if anyone else has fingernails I can chew. *Really Julia? You have 'now' lost your bloody mind.*

Lincoln scoots up and blows his hot, putrid breath on my neck. "Looks like big bad Nic saved the day again, huh?" He needs to brush his teeth because he smells foul, and his mere presence makes me want to punch him in the throat.

"Oh, shut up," I snap, pushing him off my shoulder.

My body tenses as I focus on the vial of liquid Lillian hands Nic. He tips it toward his mouth and gags. After a ferocious coughing fit, he leans over to rest his hands on his knees.

"Nic?" I shove Lincoln out of the way, and Lillian holds her hand up to stop me. As usual, I don't listen.

"Something isn't right with Nic. This can't be a normal reaction." I ignore her hand in the air and place my arm around his shoulders while he controls his breathing. When I glance back at the others, they're intent on the scene, but no one bothers to help.

"Don't rush up at once you cowards." Their inability to take action disgusts me and I dismiss the lot of

17

them as incompetent. Even Nic's brothers sit there as useless as paperweights.

"He'll be fine, Julia. The elixir causes different reactions and we've gone over this a hundred times." Her expression is stoic and I can't believe she isn't upset over the severe reaction.

"With all due respect, he seems nowhere close to fine." I lean in to capture his face between my hands. "Nic, look at me. How can I help?" His eyes are bloodshot, and he straightens his back with defiance. Tremendous heat radiates from his body.

"*Geez*, Nic, you're burning up. What's happening?" I whisper.

"My insides are on fire, but I'm okay." He blows out a huff of air and stares at the rest of our group through watery eyes. "You're up, Lincoln. Hope you choke on it." I slap a hand over my mouth and smile through parted fingers. He's back.

"I don't think so Nic. Ladies first." Lyra bulldozes her way up front, hands on hips, and legs parted. I imagine she thinks she's Wonder Woman. Truth is she's a ridiculous brat with a head full of jet-black hair, and sloppy mismatched clothes. You'd think someone blessed with Lyra's genetics would take pride in her appearance.

18

She snatches a vial and ignores me when I shake my head back and forth in warning. *It's her darn funeral.*

We wait for her to swallow the radiant amethyst elixir, and she convulses the same way Nic did moments ago. The liquid snakes through Lyra's body, illuminating her veins. We search Lillian's face for a reaction and find nothing but a calm exterior.

"Everyone will have a different response to the elixir and violent reactions are rare, but possible. Please stay calm." Her voice trails off as Lyra chokes and coughs, her body contorting.

"She needs help!" I knock Lillian out of the way and try to calm Lyra as she thrashes on the floor.

"You just hush!" She pushes me back, her cheeks red and blotchy. Angry raised hives creep up the sides of her neck.

Linc takes the ensuing ruckus as an opportunity to create chaos of his own. He slips behind me and yanks my hair back, his teeth grazing my neck in a mock vampire bite. Nic erupts like Mount Vesuvius and fists fly before anyone neutralizes the fight. Lincoln swings his lanky arms and misses, still clumsy from a summer growth spurt. Nic rams him backwards and everyone scatters when Lillian shouts for the boys to stop.

"Enough, you bloody little hellions." Her high-pitched voice echoes in the cavernous room, but I stay out of the action this time. Their ridiculous, testosterone driven cockfights are commonplace these days. I've been in the middle more times than I want to admit.

Lillian slams her cane on the floor and demands everyone's attention. Nic freezes mid-swing and Lincoln lets his arms dangle by his sides. Lyra's body tightens, and she hits the floor with a thud, her thick black hair pooling on the deep, stained hardwood. The rest of the group rushes toward her limp body, afraid to breathe, much less utter a word.

Shadows of dancing firelight cast a bizarre glow on her motionless frame and make her lifeless body the color of death. We stand there frozen in silence, wondering if she's dead.

***

Lyra's eyes slide open after several heart-stopping seconds and we collectively inhale at the same time. The rest of the group inches back, but I'm frozen in place, both hands covering my mouth. Lyra's once piercing blue eyes are now an inky shade of black with no discernible pupils. She pushes off her hands to a sitting, then standing position, and returns our stunned reactions with animosity.

"What's wrong with her, Lillian?" Nic moves in to examine Lyra and I can tell he's both curious and repulsed at the same time.

"It's not what we expected to happen, but—" She stops as if hiding a dreadful secret.

"What? What *is* the expected reaction?" I grab Lillian by the shoulders. Lifeless eyes meet mine, and her shoulders sag.

Those darn imaginary fingernails scrape along my spine when her eyes widen at something behind me. That sinking feeling of dread settles in the pit of my stomach and I turn.

"Fancy meeting you here." Lyra taps my shoulder and the sight of her dark glassy eyes sends chills up my back.

"Your eyes…" I point as a thin sheen of sweat forms on my forehead.

"Are the color of my soul. You like?" Her tinny high-pitched laughter makes my skin crawl and I step back. She was God-awful before, but the elixir stepped it up a notch.

"Relax, drama queen. I feel fabulous." She twirls in the center of the room like a crazed fairy, basking in our undivided attention.

21

"You're next, pretty-proper-princess." She informs me in a lilting, mocking, tone.

"I am not drinking that poison." I turn to Lillian, expecting mercy. Instead, she meets me with spitfire determination and newfound resolve in the face of this mad science experiment.

"I'm afraid it's required by your benefactor."

I blanch at the weak-willed reply and wonder how my loving mum could turn on me without a moment's hesitation. An unknown substance from God knows where and I'm ready to drink this nightmare in hopes of a long life?

Run, Julia.

Sebastian pushes that damnable hair from his eyes, barges up front and center, and addresses everyone. Here we go.

I recall the day Nic, Sebastian, and Dutch arrived at the manor, although my memory has somewhat faded. They held hands everywhere they went and the days of adorable little boys are gone forever. When I snap back to the present, I refocus on Sebastian's ridiculous display of authority. He doesn't know a thing about the elixir.

"We knew this day was coming and none of this," he motions and spins in a circle, "should come as a shock

22

to any of you. Grow a set." He rolls his eyes at the group and rests them on me. "Why don't you enchant us with your bravery and go next, Julia." He runs a hand through his hair and smiles, but the gesture doesn't reach his eyes. He lives to torment me, I swear to God.

"Bugger off, Sebastian." I walk until we're nose to nose and dare him to mess with me. This isn't the time or place.

"I'm not taking any of your crap, Mr. Maye." My response is venomous.

He reaches out and cups the back of my head, intent on kissing me, so the tip of my toe meets his shin in a merciless act of self-defense. Sebastian bows his head in deference. He can't retaliate because I'm a girl.

"Just as I thought." The tenacity in my response makes him grin.

"Miss Malone?" His retreat from my head is swift and I don't censure my language.

"That's right you bloody wanker, back off."

People best learn they can't mess with me and learn it fast. I inch toward the box of horrors, knowing there's a vial of amethyst liquid with my name on it. Nic steps in, slipping his hand to the small of my back and urges me forward. When I glance back, Sebastian glares at his

brother, and I freeze, but Nic's voice reassures me
everything will be okay.

"You can do this." His confidence ignites my
resolve but I still don't know why we're doing it. This isn't
even our plan, but it's our lives and bodies. At eighteen, we
should be able to say no.

You know what? I *am* the brave one; I'll always be
the brave one. Impetuous and stormy, mercurial and
confusing—but brave. I swallow the vial, closing my eyes
while the stillness has everyone in the room holding their
breath.

When I open my eyes again, Dutch jumps in the air
with a fist pump and everyone breathes a sigh of relief
except Lyra and Lincoln. He's blank faced and apathetic,
and she chews the ends of her hair. Hey, I never said she
was normal, just gorgeous. Sebastian doesn't have the
decency to avert his gaze, even for a second, and I know
one thing for sure: there's a distinct emotional division
between the six of us.

My insides burn like hell just as Nic described, and
my skin tingles, along with the backs of my eyes. A part of
me is terrified to check the mirror and find my eye color
has changed. There's a freestanding oval mirror next to a
peeling cedar chest in the back corner of Rose Hall. Its

ancient legs hold the answer to my question as I peer into its reflective surface.

I'm met with the most brilliant pair of emerald eyes, surrounded by a darker ring of jade. My once sparse lashes are thick, black, and opulent, making my eyes appear greener and brighter than the jewel. I reach for the mirror in case it's an illusion. My shoulder length auburn hair, which has always been unmanageable, is as smooth as glass.

"This can't be real." I release the breath I'd been holding. Nic leans over my shoulder, and for the first time, I notice his eyes have turned the most impossible shade of sapphire I've ever seen in my life.

"Side effect?" He touches my hair, and I'm as limp as a rag doll, burying my nose in his shoulder.

"I thought I'd end up a monster, living with the side effects forever." My relief drips on Nic's shoulder until his shirt is a soggy mess.

He pulls me in for a hug, leading us toward the fireplace to watch Lincoln, Dutch, and Sebastian drink their elixirs. Lyra is perched on the couch like a bird, a devious smirk curling her lips at the corners. It's impossible not to notice how unusual she's acting just minutes after her near-death experience on the floor. The elixir sure as hell didn't fix her attitude problem though and I'll never get used to those eyes.

Minutes tick by, and my quiet apprehension makes it difficult to breathe. Dutch has the same reaction as Nic and me, but Lincoln and Sebastian have the same dark reaction. Their eyes turn from bright blues to deep black spheres.

For the first time in forever, my mind goes blank. This didn't go as planned. The six of us stand at attention, staring at the mistress of our manor and wait for God knows what.

Lillian's eyes cloud over and she resigns herself to an overstuffed chair in the far corner of Rose Hall, sagging into its cushiony depths. Thick brocade curtains swallow her diminutive frame while she stares straight ahead, unblinking. Now what?

Chapter Two—Endowment

I grind sleep from my eyes with a long stretch and contented squeal. Last Saturday left a sour taste in my mouth and I still have flashbacks of us stumbling back to our rooms after drinking the elixir. Lincoln, Sebastian, and Lyra are acting weirder than usual and it's as if the elixir personified their dark personality traits.

Sure, it's unsettling to see three blue-eyed friends staring back at me with fathomless black spheres—but it's more than that. Lyra's former indifference morphed into seething hatred, and Sebastian's obsession with me is dark and disturbing, but Linc seems downright diabolical.

I've been avoiding them as much as possible because their sudden changes are too much to handle just yet. Everyone thinks I'm acting like a drama queen, but their indifference and willingness to play the part of sheep worries me.

My legs dangle over the side of my bed. This foggy old brain should signal my body to move but I'm caffeine deprived and void of that morning perk. The bathroom taunts me along with my bladder, and with coffee surging through my veins, I'm sure I can drag myself a few feet to the door.

"Nic, you awake?"

He stumbles into my room with a hot cup of coffee and I ruffle his matted brown hair.

"You look no better than a steaming pile of dung this morning." We laugh, knowing it's not true. His eyes are without a doubt, the most incredible color I've ever seen.

"I brought you a cup of *rouse the dead*." Nic always anticipates my needs and I love him so hard it hurts.

Rouse the dead is my pet name for coffee. His disposition is bright this morning, and he hands me the cup. I blow on the surface before taking a sip because a burned tongue has the propensity to ruin one's day. My love for Nic is almost a part of me now, and because it's too hard to explain, I don't even try.

"You're my best friend in the whole world and I still don't know what I did to deserve you." He gathers my tangled hair and holds a handful to his nose.

"God knew he added just a pinch too much dork to the Julia recipe. He sent me to keep your arse out of trouble. That's what." He pats me on the knee and my heart

28

soars. I've always been familiar with his thoughts but he's masterful at blocking emotion.

"Julia?" Lillian shouts from the bottom of the stairwell, diverting my attention from our conversation. She never uses telepathy, and it annoys the bloody snot out of me. It's not as if I need the extra exercise.

"You stay put." I motion to Nic and jog to the stairwell to see what she wants.

As usual, he doesn't listen and follows me across the hall. He's not deterred by my dirty look and grins at me in his footed pajamas. Sometimes, I want nothing more than to wrap myself in his arms and stay there forever. I'm absurd—in case anyone should ever wonder.

"Yes, Lillian?" I cock my head to the side, my raised brow a dead giveaway I don't appreciate her intrusion.

She's wearing that blasted apron again. I swear the darn thing could walk on its own.

"How are the arrangements coming?" Deeper meaning always lurks behind her innocuous questions.

"The menu is finished, but we haven't figured out seating arrangements for the back yard." Nic is underfoot again and makes me to trip at the bottom of the staircase. He shrugs after I shoot him a withering look.

"Remember, we have a family meeting tonight. Everything will make perfect sense." Her docile expression is misleading, and she tries leaving on that note.

"Don't you see the question mark hanging above my head?" I grab her apron strings so she can't walk away.

"Of course I see it; it's huge." She stops in her tracks. "Stop worrying before it ages you, dear. The elixir can't cure a neurotic disposition." My face heats up, and she waddles off humming one of her obscure and annoying tunes. And with that, I'm dismissed.

Our annual autumn party is in two days and I'm in charge of food preparation. Lillian gave Nic grill duty and seating arrangements. Lincoln and Lyra have no duties whatsoever and my last nerve twitches at the thought of them resting on their lazy arse laurels. I grab Nic's arm and lead him toward the kitchen, bristling at the idleness of my insufferable housemates.

"We need more coffee, and holy hell you were certainly a boat load of help back there."

"Sorry." At least he has the decency to appear sheepish through his impossibly thick lashes. My insides melt, but I pretend he has no effect on me. "And clean up that mouth of yours before the party. We don't want anyone thinking Lillian raised a house full of future

sailors."

"Oh, ha ha."

Our kitchen glows in the early morning sun, with slivers of light bouncing off copper pots. It sprays brilliant prisms of color onto the pale, terra cotta walls. As we chat over a good cup of coffee, my nemesis strolls in looking as if the cat chewed her up and spit her out.

"There you are." Lyra's irritating voice makes me itch to run for cover, but I meet her phony smile with boredom. My posture screams, *tick me off again and I'll squash you like a bug.*

"Yes, Lyra, whatever can I do for you this fine morning?" I sigh. No part of her is normal anymore.

Sensing good and evil is easy, but the waters get muddy when decent people do awful things. There's always been something wrong with Lyra, but her personality changed after she drank the elixir. You'd think fifteen years together, and we would be as close as sisters, but it never happened. She stuck with Lincoln, and their relationship made no sense to anyone.

The changes are undeniable, and even Sebastian acted unusual by the fourth day, the transformations noticeable to everyone in the house. Lillian still refuses to talk about that night even though I pester her non-stop. She stares straight ahead, tightens her lips, and wrenches her hands in that old stained apron I despise. I'm getting her a new apron for Christmas and hiding that one so she can never wear it again.

"Are you going into town?" Lyra dances around as if she has to pee, but normal was never her style.

"Yes."

"Can I come?"

"No."

She huffs at my clipped response and before I can explain why she storms from the kitchen. Lyra never asks to go *anywhere* with me and the request is unusual. Nic shrugs his shoulders and pours two fresh cups of coffee, handing me one.

"Do you think we'll keep the autumn party tradition once we're married?" His question blindsides me.

I stare, unable to respond. What did he just say? Fourteen years of being best friends and he never even said I love you.

"Wham. Just like that, huh?" I'm confused and his eyes crinkle with amusement.

"Well, yeah. Aren't you planning on getting married someday?" My pulse shoots through the stratosphere and Lincoln wanders in the kitchen. I want to scream at his atrocious timing.

Then it hits me. Nic isn't talking about marrying me; he's referring to marriage in general.

"Lyra's in a fine tizzy this morning. Did you threaten to put make-up on her or something?" Linc's smirk makes me want to whack him in the snout—with a shoe. Those two come from the same demented peapod, I swear.

"Back off, Lincoln. She's not in the mood for any of your crap." Nic bristles.

"Back off or what, Maye?"

Nic's fists clench at Lincoln's use of his last name. Unlike Lyra and Linc, we chose normal last names. Lincoln Sackinstock and Lyra Twerth just don't leave the same taste in your mouth and I don't care who you are; they're ridiculous names.

"You guys need to grow up and act your age. We're supposed to be on the same team here." This day already has me irritated, and it just started. Nic's fists relax and Lincoln's antagonizing smirk fades with a slow burn. It wouldn't surprise me if Linc plunged a knife in our backs. I'm positive he'd have no qualms in doing so. His hair is as black as his soul but unlike Lyra, I've yet to find a redeeming quality.

33

"Same team, right." He parrots, throwing attitude Nic's direction.

"Your one-upping each other drives me crazy. Can we get through tomorrow's autumn party without your girlie drama?" I take a deep breath and grit my teeth. Lincoln glares at Nic one last time and saunters off with arrogant disregard.

"Don't let him get to you. And girlie drama? You're funny, goose." He moves near, his closeness causing my heart to skip a beat. Nic doesn't know how much I adore him, and I'm wound tighter than a piano wire imagining our futures together—or not.

"What's wrong?" He lifts my chin with his index finger, studying my expression.

"What? Nothing, *sheesh*."

"Then why are you blushing?"

"How the bloody hell would I know? My skin does crazy things when I'm upset. You and Linc knocking heads makes me want to chew through the straps. I'm ready to check myself into a home." He'll never know it's because I'm hopelessly in love with him.

"Anyway, I have to tackle this seating nightmare, but if you need me I'll come to town with you." He drains the rest of his coffee in one gulp and rinses the cup, not bothering to make eye contact with the offer.

"No. I've got it under control." I'm sick of him viewing me as a ridiculous little girl who fawns over him. "Sorry. What I mean is—" I can't make my brain work, and he finds my mental malfunction amusing. Nic pushes at the edge of my mind and frowns when he meets the resistance.

"I'll do it myself, but thanks for the offer," I mumble.

Nic walks out of the kitchen with his hands raised in defeat. He says *girls* are impossible to understand. As complicated as we are, I understand myself just fine. Guys make zero sense.

"See you later?" He shouts over his shoulder.

"Yeah, later. Thanks for the offer though; I appreciate it."

Appreciate? I palm my forehead when he's out of sight. *I can't believe I used the word appreciate. How much more forced can I sound?*

***

It takes longer than expected to find all the ingredients on my grocery list, and everyone is waiting in Rose Hall with anxious, drawn faces. My stomach turns sour.

"Julia, you're late. Go put the food away." Lillian's voice is brusque and impatient and she's pacing the floor as if her panties were on fire.

The visual makes me grin and I head toward the kitchen to put everything away. Chamomile tea calls because something tells me it's needed. I'm not known for an even-keeled disposition.

Inhale... exhale.

When I return, everyone stares as if I've committed capital murder, and Lillian eyes me with irritation before continuing. I didn't think they'd start without me, but what else is new?

"Sorry I'm late." Scooting into the nearest seat, I avoid fidgeting by folding both hands into my lap. Lyra and Linc smirk, their hostility expected. Nic is oblivious, and Sebastian licks his lips, biting the lower one with innuendo. I want to sock that wanker in the head for being so crude but control myself for Lillian's sake.

"It's time to meet your benefactor. Each of you came to the manor as a small child." Lillian takes a steady breath, pale from excitement or emotional overload. "Your benefactor granted each of you a sizable endowment, which I can now sign over in your names." Again, she takes another wheezing breath.

What's with the drama? I glance at Nic but his full attention is on Lillian, which makes me pouty and disagreeable.

"I've established trusts for each of you, and you're now *millionaires*. Your benefactor will assist in finding penthouses in New York, so you can work for him as interns."

Did every ounce of oxygen just evaporate from the room? I reach for my best friend's mind. *"Is she frakking serious?"*

"She sounds serious to me." Nic's response is immediate.

"Who leaves money to a bunch of kids? It makes no sense."

Sebastian interrupts. *"Shut up. I'm trying to listen here."*

"Sorry, but get out of our heads then." He's a royal pain in the butt, always intruding on our telepathic conversations. Then I notice his ridiculous outfit of purple tie-died jeans and a plaid shirt. *"Dude, are you serious?"* I shake my head, laughing at his outfit but Dutch asks a question that gets my attention.

"Who's our benefactor and why leave millions of dollars to a bunch of kids?" He's right; it makes little sense.

Linc stretches out and raises his hand. It's not so much that he raises his hand, but his body language is rude, and flusters Lillian. The wanker never bothers unless he's contrary, or fixing on a fight.

"Yes, Lincoln?" Her curt tone is laced with threat.

"No need to buy me a penthouse. I volunteer to sleep with Julia. In fact, it would be my sincerest pleasure to share her bed. Sorry Sebastian, did I just steal the demented thought right from your head?" His shoulders shake and he has the nerve to rally us for approval. If inward snarls had a color, mine would be a bloody shade of red right now.

"What the hell is your problem?" I shout.

"Lincoln, one more remark like that and you're grounded." Lillian snaps and I imagine slapping his smirk to the floor and stomping on it.

"No worries, goose." Nic's shoulders tighten, assuring me there won't be an altercation. Thank God for small favors. The conversation becomes background noise as my mind races with exciting and terrifying possibilities. Lillian distracts my endless array of thoughts with a question.

"Julia, do you have any objections?" Everyone turns to stare and I scramble for clues as to the current topic of conversation.

"Um... I don't see why not." I hope it's the right response.

Great, what did I just agree to? This could be serious.

"It's settled then." Lillian taps her cane on the floor to quiet our whispering.

"I'm sorry, but what's settled?" You'd think someone tattooed the word *dunce* across my forehead.

"Nic gave up his endowment to stay with you." She repeats, and my stomach does ecstatic somersaults.

A warm sensation washes over me and I sink further into my chair, meeting Nic's awkward expression with doe eyes. It's time to raise my mental guards. My exterior is a clean slate, but on the inside, I'm grinning like the cat that ate a whole cow—another favorite expression of Lillian's I keep in my journals.

A dark shadow flits across her face and we wait for the rest as she clears her throat to get everyone's attention. Her tone is cautious.

"Over the years you've become accustomed to having access to each other's thoughts. Most interactions have been at the manor and I tried to protect you from the outside world. This will soon change." Her gaze darts toward the ceiling as if divine words and inspiration might appear from thin air. She finds nothing, and sadness settles into her eyes.

"You won't understand these new experiences. It's possible you won't like people much anymore but learn to adapt. It's *imperative* to blend in with the others."

Why can't I breathe? It's as if she's sending us to an execution.

"Or we'll become science experiments? Is that what you're saying?" Sebastian's question brings new ideas to light. He's defiant and strong-willed. Half the time I want to punch him, and the rest of the time, I want to eavesdrop on the inner workings of his mind.

"Lillian, can I ask a question?" I take a deep breath.

"Yes dear, what is it now?"

"Why did Sebastian, Lincoln, and Lyra have adverse reactions to the elixir and the rest of us didn't?"

Her expression darkens. "I'm not at liberty to talk about the details, Julia. Please see me in private." She requests, and for the first time I sense her misery.

Whatever she's hiding, it's serious. Lincoln and Lyra ignore the conversation, strange because they *live* to pounce. They're glued to their seats, unaffected by the turn of events.

"We'll talk about living arrangements later but concentrate on New York because that's where you're going. Money is no object." Silence ensues, and the air feels dense and heavy. Everyone is wide eyed and speechless. This benefactor, whoever he is, has serious wealth.

Lillian offers nothing more, and we're perplexed and confused.

"You're dismissed." She taps the cane and everyone scatters. I wait for Nic outside the great room, and poke Dutch as he walks by the door.

"Easy there, killer." He winks, but Nic stops with an unreadable expression on his face.

"Come to my room later?" I whisper, making sure no one can overhear. "We need to talk. This is crazy."

"Roger that. Something isn't right with this picture." He dashes up the staircase toward our bedrooms and I lag while everyone else goes different directions. Sebastian stops and looks back before ascending the steps. His penetrating gaze freezes me in place and I'm holding my breath again. Just as fast, he turns and darts up the stairs.

My curiosity is more than piqued. I make a beeline toward Van Buren Library while Lillian's attention is focused elsewhere. We'll talk logistics later.

Chapter Three—Journal

The doors to the library click open and I will the hinges to stay quiet. I slip into the vast room, inhaling the scents of leather and dust from old books. Using Van Buren Library without permission is against manor rules, but I'm always the problem child even though I mean no harm.

I flip the light, and it casts a dim, rose-colored glow across the library. The hardwood floors have a high gloss finish and Lillian's desk sits in the center of the room on a whimsical, rose patterned rug. It softens and contrasts the dark cherry shelving. Her rug is the only feminine feature in this masculine chamber, making me wonder who lived here before the seven of us arrived.

I dart toward the west end of the library where thousands of books line the walls in endless rows. The leather-bound volumes in rich hues scream affluence and the pungent scent of leather, paper, and ink matured over the decades makes me lower my lids and inhale.

Nothing compares to the heady smell of old books to make my chest expand with the sheer luxury of it. But,

I'm not here for sights and smells, and I reel my dreamer's mind back to reality.

I grab a book off the shelf but I'm not impressed by the title and return it. Lillian's desk drawer is opened a crack and my heart leaps at the prospect of finding something scandalous.

With the stealth of a cat, I pad across the slippery hardwood floors until I reach the desk, noting the silence. There's an old notebook with *Groceries* scrawled across the top in capital letters. This isn't much of a find, so I brush the nuisance aside and rifle through the various contents. A folded letter slips from the notebook, and jackpot. I snatch the letter as if a map to a pirate's treasure.

January 1, 1842

Dearest Lillian,

I hope this letter finds you healthy and missing me somewhat. I know the archeological dig will take a few weeks to finish but I had hoped to see you before your birthday because a wonderful surprise waits.

Please tell me of the mysterious liquid Henry Van Buren claims is the fountain of youth, and his crazy plans for the world. I declare, he's the embodiment of insanity, but I know you're loyal.

I love you, my wife. Please be well and come home soon.

With love,
Charles Perriman

***

My hands tremble as I stare at the year; I'm waiting for it to change into something in the mid-1900s. The date is impossible. It would mean Lillian is over a hundred and fifty years old. It can't belong to *the* Lillian Perriman, head mum of our manor.

I dismiss it as ridiculous. She can't be over a hundred and fifty years old. There's discussion of an archaeological dig. What happened to our parents? The sharp echo of heels on hardwood floors has me panicking so I shove the letter inside the notebook.

The clicking stops outside the library door and my heart freezes mid-pump. I duck under Lillian's desk, pull my legs in tight, and hold my breath as the door creaks open.

"That's odd. I remember turning this pesky light off." Lillian steps inside and I watch her shoes approach.

I'm so cooked. De-scaled, deboned, and fried in a pan.

My head is woozy from holding my breath for so long and she stops in front of the desk and then retreats from the library clucking to herself. The lights click off and my breath rushes out in a cough. *Oh thank God.*

Minutes tick by and my heart stops lurching enough to get out from under the desk. What to do next?

"Ah, bloody hell, I'm here so I might as well make use of it." After an executive decision, I seize the notebook and stuff it under my shirt.

Groceries, my butt.

I leave the drawer just how I found it, and sneak toward the door, eerie shadows casting life-like figures on the wall. A sudden scurrying sound almost gives me a heart attack until I realize it's just a mouse. There's nothing but silence when I press my ear against the door. It's time to get out and run like hell, and to my relief, the darkened hallway is empty. After catching my breath, I dart up the staircase and slam face first into a solid male chest.

"Going somewhere my lovely?" Sebastian purrs.

"Yeah, what's it to you? Get out of my way you heathen." Irritated, I push against his arm but he refuses to move.

"Not so fast, Cat Woman, what's under your shirt there—a notebook?" His eyes widen with feigned shock.

"I don't know what you're talking about so get out of my way." Before I can escape, he presses my back against the wall and I don't sense Nic anywhere.

Where's that handy telepathic connection when you need it?

"Nic can't hear you. He crashed." Sebastian says, so darned sure of himself.

"Get out of my head or I'll scream." I push against his muscular chest, but he blocks me between his arms. I'm no match for his strength.

"Such a wildcat you are, Jules. You know he's the wrong guy for you, right?" His face dips closer and I jerk my head to the side trying to avoid his advance. There's a noise behind us and it's not Mother Nature.

"What the hell?" Nic growls.

Sebastian steps back and I stumble forward, relieved for the awkward interception. He pivots in a slow manner, his cocky smile spreading. Here's my knight in shining armor once again, and it boils my blood. I stamp my foot and cross my arms like an ill-tempered child, not caring how preposterous I look.

"What do you think will happen when Lillian finds out you accosted me in the hallway?" I hug my arms tighter to my chest with an implied *harrumph.*

"What do *you* think will happen when she finds you've been trolling through her off-limits library?" He trumps me with ease, a slow smile spreading across his face.

"Touché—I guess we're both sworn to secrecy, then." Two can play this game. My spine straightens with annoyance and Nic rolls his eyes.

"You're such cute little firecracker," he whispers in my head.

"Am not." My cheeks heat.

"Are too." Nic insists.

"The love banter is nauseating." Sebastian interrupts, leaning against the wall, annoyed by our effortless connection.

"Get out of my head!" We shout at the same time and Nic is somewhat startled. It's obvious this argument is heating up before it cools down so I brace myself for ridiculous male posturing.

"Dearest brother," Sebastian counters, his voice as smooth as ice, "You never staked a claim on the lovely Miss Malone. She's fair game." His defiant tone says I don't have a choice in the matter.

"That might be true, but she made it clear she's not interested in you or Lincoln." Nic loves his brother, but things are heating up.

"You called?" Linc appears and I slap a hand over my mouth to avoid screaming with frustration.

We stand in the hallway locked in battle while the notebook burns a square in my chest. Maybe I can sneak away while these testosterone junkies duke it out. I need to indulge my curiosity and bickering housemates aren't high on my list of priorities.

"You know what? I'm sick of this alpha male showdown." I declare, "We have the autumn party tomorrow, so if you boneheads will excuse me." Without another word, I duck into my bedroom, taking care not to slam the door and bring more attention to the fight. Why can't those moronic boys terrorize Lyra for a change?

Exasperated, I slip the confiscated notebook from my shirt. The word *groceries* glares back at me and shouts *lies, lies, lies.* Sebastian knows more than he's letting on, which makes me eye the door and speculate how he could have known I had it.

After ten minutes, they're still squabbling in the hallway. Nic's voice raises an octave now and then and I glance to the door, wondering if I should intervene. Soon, none of this teenage idiocy will matter and we'll be living in New York City doing God knows what. I flip the cover and read. No, it's not a grocery list at all; it's a journal.

Thursday:

Julia is much too curious for her own good and she'll land in a crock of boiling water someday. Still, I can't curb her love for the unknown. Sebastian is intense. He can go either way. He's taken a liking to Julia, and Nic doesn't approve. I need to tell them before it's too late, but not right now though. Lincoln is so dark. His inner nature scares me and I wonder if the decision to give him the elixir was a wise one. They can turn; it's happened before. I hope there's a shred of decency in his nature. Lyra will come around in time. That girl strikes my funny bone.

Friday:
Claude recommends giving the elixir to all of them. We've never predicted outcomes with any measure of success. Henry still isn't aging as one expects, and his laboratories continue working on a reformulation, but they need fresh eyes. On a genetic level, the children are superior. I don't know, it's unnatural... and I've started tapering off on the elixir despite Claude's protests.

Wednesday:

Jack is doing well. He's not aging but how awful to trade your soul for immortality. The world will never understand, and we can't risk Henry Van Buren's brilliant vision for the future. Our children's mind powers are strong—much more developed than we had anticipated, especially Julia. The Van Buren family is mad brilliance that walks the edge of genius.

I'm astonished by Lillian's thoughts and fall backward on the bed, closing the notebook. Lillian led each of us to believe that we were the only ones with telepathy. I fling an arm over my forehead and stare at the ceiling. My energy reserves are depleted, and I don't feel like returning the notebook to its rightful place.

Lillian skips days in her journal so I doubt she'll notice its absence in the midst of our annual festivities. I slip the journal beneath my mattress, detecting a sudden chill in the air.

***

Sun pours through my bedroom window, obscuring my vision and it takes a minute to realize where I am. I spring into action, realizing I'd fallen asleep in my clothes. There are items still needed for the party and I'm biking into town this morning. After a huge dogfight between the boys last night, I decide against Nic's company.

Nicolas Maye whatever shall I do with you?

Why would he give up his endowment if he didn't have feelings for me? My mind wanders in places better left unvisited and the best cure for confusion is a long bike ride through the countryside. I need to escape from my nightmare week of elixirs, fights, and worries over a mysterious benefactor.

After clearing the manor gates with no one noticing, I bike toward town and enjoy the idyllic scenery of my beloved England. The wind tickles my cheeks and I'm content at last. Then it hits me in the face like a fist.

The stench of cow manure from a nearby field infiltrates my nostrils and burns my eyes. Our neighbors fertilize their uncultivated land hoping to grow crops someday, but so far, we've seen nothing but dirt and manure. The Chesterfields are likely insane, or take sadistic pleasure in irritating their neighbors.

When I reach the old cobblestone streets of Chipping Campden, I hop off and walk my bike the rest of the way. My heel catches on a stone, bringing forth unladylike expletives. I look around the market to see if anyone noticed, but good thing no one did, or they'd get a dose of my sailor mouth.

My irritation subsides when I spot a group of brick structures ahead. Café tables sit atop quaint cobblestone lined streets, and it reminds me, this will always be home. Even if they transplant my body in New York City, my soul belongs to England.

Wistful thoughts recede and I return to my current reality of elixirs, endowments, and strategic jumps halfway across the world. I'm nervous about moving to New York to spread my wings. Lillian says it will be the adventure of a lifetime but I imagine it's much like walking through a giant spider web and dodging black widows. Truth has a funny way of creating a tapestry of little white lies that form a deep and unforgiving blanket of deception.

I shake it off, not wanting to ruin this perfect moment as I stroll past an old stone building covered in ivy. The haunting whistle of trains in the distance is familiar, and I inhale the yeasty, intoxicating perfume of fresh bread from a nearby bakery.

Need chai tea, stat. Holy Hannah, it's hot and busy here today.

I glance around the square, dreading the swarms of people with their overwhelming thoughts and emotions. The marketplace is buzzing with shoppers and I meander from business to business, careful not to touch anyone. I read minds through touch—unless it's Nic or the rest of our crazy crew.

After twenty minutes of pondering the produce, sweat trickles between my shoulder blades and I notice the sun creeping upward. When I finish shopping, a friendly vendor places the items in my basket and I pedal toward Café Boroughgard.

I'll find relief at the bottom of a coffee cup; I always do. Many a problem can be solved at the bottom of a cup. The tinkling gold bell brings forth a huge, familiar grin from my favorite barista when I walk into the café.

"Well hello, Miss Julia." She throws her towel down and lifts the end of the counter to greet me. Ella is my favorite person outside the manor and I become normal by association. It's a spectacular feat.

"Hey, Miss Ella-pants, I'm in desperate need of chai."

I point to number two on the menu and she whips up my favorite concoction as I slink into a nearby booth with a loud conspicuous sigh. A few heads turn my way so I smile even though I'm not feeling it. Ella brings my drink and sits, but before I open my mouth, her face twists into an odd expression.

54

"Holy smokes; did you just spend a week at the spa? Wow."

"Pfft—I wish. What makes you think I've been to a spa?"

"I don't know, you look like a super model; what the heck?" No one has seen me since we drank the elixir, and I better find a convincing explanation for the change.

A spa could work. Thank God, my eyes are still green. I shudder at the alternative.

"Well I have to admit, Lillian knows how to give exquisite facials, and Lyra's been experimenting with my hair. Healthier eating and all that. You know." I'm an insect under a magnifying glass, her gaze suspicious. "The autumn party is still on for tonight, right?" Ella's antsy excitement and youthful enthusiasm is intoxicating. She's been coming to our autumn party for years now.

"It surely is my little pecan." My chai is a slice of heaven, and the aroma is intoxicating. "We needed last minute supplies, but now... I better get my hind end to the manor. I better see you tonight."

"Bloody straight you will." Ella hops from her stool, hugs me around the neck, and slips behind the counter to wait on a customer. She dismisses me with a wave and a huge cheeky grin. I swallow the rest of my chai tea, not so eager for the stinky ride back.

Chapter Four—The Autumn Party

The guest list reads as it does every year except for a last name that catches my attention—Van Buren. It brings to mind Van Buren Library, and the journal. Now it all makes sense. The name of our benefactor glares back at me from the top of glossy white paper. You can bet I'll be in *double-O-seven* mode tonight, tailing him every chance I get. On second thought, I *am* a little ball of fire. Nic's always right.

After prepping a barrel of peach tea for the party, I rub spices into the beef tenderloin. Raw meat grosses me out more than any other food, and the bloody, lumpy mass stares back at me with an accusatory glare.

While slicing fruit, my mind wanders to the faraway land of New York. Lyra saunters into the kitchen with tangled hair and dark rings under her eyes. It's obvious she didn't get the memo we're having an autumn party.

"Listen, sloth girl we have guests coming so move your butt." There's a snip to my voice because she's an inconsiderate slob. Lazy and disinterested on the day of the party grinds my hiney.

"Unravel your panties, Jules. I stopped for a cup of coffee before my shower." She lets out a disgruntled huff and I stop chopping to glare.

"What?" She demands, pouring the coffee.

"Nothing." I chop without looking up and bite my lip to keep from lashing out. Holing up in my room sounds great right about now. I could read Lillian's journal from cover to cover until I know every single secret she's been hiding for fifteen years. Instead, I'm slaving away in the kitchen like a fool.

"Hey, Julia, you got the beef tenderloin ready?" Nic breezes into the kitchen and gives Lyra a playful shove. My insides clench and she catches my eye on purpose, raising her brow to torment me. I point to the pan and hack at the vegetables with a vengeance.

"Thanks." He whisks the pan away while Lyra utters something sarcastic under her breath and shuffles from the kitchen in bare feet and sloppy pajama bottoms. Everyone thinks she's gorgeous, but she isn't—not on the inside.

Ingrate. I chop with newfound ferociousness.

Lillian enters the kitchen with a cheerful grin as if she doesn't have a care in the world. "Go on with yourself.

Scoot. Get ready for the party."

My gaze darts to the shiny copper pots on the wall, hoping to stop angry tears from falling.

"Wash your hair good so I can fix it later," she reminds me, and I give her a curt nod before exiting the kitchen. I bound up the grand staircase two steps at a time, thinking that's the reason my calves are so muscular. *Go, grand staircase.*

Nic's voice rings out in my head. *"Need your help in the yard, Jules."*

I don't respond.

"Goose, what's wrong?"

"Not a bloody thing. I'll be out later."

It's effortless with Nic and I can't stand it. The girls in town drool over him and every guy I know is jealous of his easy personality and good looks. Lillian adores him and he *never* gets in trouble. By my calculations, he's perfect and I'm crazy in love with him. It's impossible to hide, but I try.

The crappy part is I don't know if he feels the same. What will become of us in New York? I want control over my own darn life, not thrust into the hands of a total stranger. The shower is steaming hot and I scrub my face raw. Who cares about stupid skin? Twenty minutes later, I emerge not sure why I started this downward spiral. I've been out of sorts since we drank the elixir.

Nic's telepathic irritation jolts me back to the present. *"You're out of the shower. Want me to drag you out here?"* His impatience makes me irritable.

I'm overloaded with pent-up energy and getting it out on paper eliminates negative emotion, dissipating through my fingers. Words flow from my head and become a permanent record of how I felt at that moment. Sometimes I write so much I can't bend my fingers in the morning.

It should calm my nerves to journal like a maniac tonight and you'd think Nic knew how I felt after fifteen stinking years. If not, then I'm a master at concealing myself, but darn improbable since my heart is attached to my sleeve.

But I have bigger bridges to burn at the moment. If I follow Lillian's advice and live in the present I wouldn't be such a neurotic wreck. It's hard searching for clues from my past without worrying about a future I can't predict.

"I'm coming. Give me ten." My telepathic response is calm even though I'm miserable, shaky, and lovesick.

"Move it, brainiac. I don't have all day." His last reference makes me laugh.

His pet names for me range from brainiac to goose. That's all it takes to change my mood from cranky to cheerful. Nic's a roller coaster but I'm a hopeless addict of the ride.

I slip into a flower-patterned sundress and smooth it over my hips. The yard is sunny and smells of fresh cut grass. Nic's at the edge of our manicured lawn pondering where to put the chairs. I keep to the shadows, watching his unique body language.

His shoulder muscles flex beneath a thin cotton t-shirt and my stomach clenches. I paint pictures in my mind of our future together including a multi-million dollar wedding, ten babies, and a huge manor of our own someday. It's a stupid fantasy, but one I hold dear.

Take a deep breath and try not to embarrass yourself, dimwit.

I sneak behind him. There's nothing I wouldn't do for Nic and he doesn't even know it; or maybe he does. It's impossible to tell anymore.

"Hey, Jules. I thought I'd lost you up there. I'll get Dutch and Sebastian to help but where should we arrange the extra chairs?" He bumps me in the hip to lighten the mood and it reminds me of his playfulness with Lyra in the kitchen. There's an acidic taste of bile in my mouth and I swallow hard, stuffing the hollow ache like I always do.

He weaves his fingers through mine and leads me toward the barbeque pit. Our closeness feels nice and the last of my tension melts as I lean into him, giving the yard extensive thought.

I scrunch my eyes and tap my chin as if putting serious mental effort into the do-or-die decision. He finds my exaggerated theatrics amusing and rewards me with a huge cheeky grin, displaying flawless rows of pearly white teeth. *God, why did you make him so beautiful? You're killing me here.*

"Okay, professor, any conclusions?" He breaks the trance.

There's a patch of yard where our guests will have the best view and I spread my arms out near the raspberry bushes. A rogue gust of wind blows my dress up around my waist and I'm mortified beyond belief. I squeal, wrestling the fabric back down over my thighs. Nic tries hiding his obnoxious hyena laugh with zero success.

"Nice panties ya got there, brainiac."

Guys are easy to amuse. I shoot him a wilting glare and stick my tongue out. There isn't a cloud in the sky and belladonna blossoms fill the air with their sweet, comforting fragrance.

"Do you smell it?" He takes a deep breath and pounds his chest with both fists. And he thinks *I'm* a dork?

"How about two semi-circles by the chiminea?" I gesture toward a mottled stone fireplace, with paving bricks arranged in an alternating, circular pattern. It's an excellent spot for entertaining.

Nic and I agree on two separate seating arrangements, and I waltz upstairs to prep for the party. We invited over forty guests, and the food is prepped for the chefs. Now I can un-wreck this mess and pretend to be proper. I'll get gorgeous with my bad self and make an interesting night of the whole affair.

"I'll see you later. Lillian has it in her head she's curling my hair. Don't ask."

Nic studies my face for clues. "She wants to talk you." He shoves both hands in his pockets and looks out over the lawn.

"Yeah. I need to get it out of the way." Nothing is ever straightforward with Lillian.

"We'll talk tonight." He pats me on the head as if I were his kid sister, and my stomach plummets to the ground, as he pays no mind to my obvious devastation.

In my room, I find a form-fitting black gown with a gossamer train hanging on the door of my closet. On the floor is a pair of strappy silver stilettos.

Nice.

Lillian raps at the door and enters with a heaping utility tray of makeup and funky-looking hair accessories.

"What do you think of the dress?" The sight of her pursed lips is a sign I better love it. She must have put effort into the elegant ensemble.

"It's stunning, but I didn't expect it to be so formal. And the shoes—they're awful small. Do you think they'll fit?" She offers an appreciative laugh, and then motions for me to sit at the dressing table.

My reflection in the oval mirror is a lie. The eyes are much too green and my hair is perfect. I inhale, square my shoulders, and let Lillian run a brush through my thick mane of auburn waves. Fifteen minutes later, she has me sporting an up-do worthy of the American Oscars.

"Where did you learn to style hair?" I can't keep from touching it and she swats at me for disrupting her masterpiece.

"Hands off the chignon! I wasn't always this old you know. In fact, men considered me a dandy little catch back in the day." She rolls her eyes as if it's common knowledge.

"It's just so perfect. Hard to believe it's me."

64

"Well it's *not* Mona Lisa." She plucks a bottle of foundation from the utility tray and orders me to close my eyes. It's relaxing and I slip into another world while she rubs, pats, and applies. My head slips toward my shoulder and I catch myself, snapping back to attention as Lillian continues her ministrations.

"You can open your eyes now." She turns me toward the oval mirror and waits for a response.

Holy shite.

"Watch your language, young lady. You'd think after fifteen years, I'd have cleaned up that mouth." She's in my head; I should have known.

"They say people who cuss are more honest; it's a cringe worthy character trait but a good one to have. Sorry, but I can't believe it's me. Good lord, Lillian, I'm not thirty." She places her hand on my lower back and peers over my shoulder in the mirror.

"You don't know how you affect those ridiculous boys, do you?" She questions as my cheeks heat.

"That's right beauty queen, you needed the extra color." With that, she pats me on the back and orders me to get dressed, then pauses. "You're on display tonight, and influential people will be here. Don't conjure up any bright ideas, little lady."

"You mean Mr. Van Buren?"

Her lips relax in a soft, demure smile. "You're much too clever for your own good. It's why I love you best."

The door closes with a soft hitch, and the sharp clicking of heels echoes in the hall. I study myself in the mirror, wondering what the night has in store for our merry band of misfits. Tonight's mission? Follow Mr. Van Buren like the psycho stalker I am.

My elaborate ensemble rests on the bed and I inspect it from every angle, figuring out how to slip into the tricky fabric without ripping the gossamer train. The act of getting into this damnable dress is like stuffing sausages into casing. By the time I halfway manage the feat, it becomes obvious Lillian underestimated my size. A knock at the door startles me from my steadfast determination to cram myself into the offending fabric.

"Just a minute." I yell. The zipper gives way and moves upward. I slip into the obnoxious, too-high stilettos and exhale.

"Okay, you may enter, peasant person." I sound breathy and it's not as if I need oxygen or anything.

Sebastian stops short.

"Oh, it's you. What the hell do *you* want?" My hand

slips off my hip and I stumble forward on unsteady heels and right into his arms.

"There *is* a God." Sebastian breathes into my ear as I steady myself. He's in a black tuxedo and his disobedient blond hair is slicked behind his ears in soft waves.

"God doesn't dress me, you idiot. What do you want?" His elegant appearance does funny things to my stomach, but I pretend not to notice.

"You're my date tonight. Didn't Lillian tell you? She paired me with you, and Nic is the lucky recipient of Lyra." His announcement is a dagger to the heart but I don't know why Sebastian seems fine unless he lives to torment me.

"Nic with Lyra? Why would she do that?" It's hard to tell whether I'm crushed, humiliated, or ready to have a meltdown of nuclear proportions. Collapsing on the floor in a defeated heap won't help the matter and might just ruin my smoking hot dress to boot. Sebastian's face softens, and he tries without success to comfort me. I turn toward the window to hide frustrated tears.

"She's hell-bent on proving we're a close knit team. There's no sinister master plan so don't take it to heart. Am I *that* awful?" He places a hand on my bare shoulder and tilts my chin to meet his gaze. "You look amazing, really."

His sweet words break my ironclad resolve and I crumble.

Anticipation of this week's events and my confusion over Nic gushes out in a flood of uncontrolled tears. Neither of us hears a second set of footsteps, and the scene becomes a frantic blur of chaos.

"What did you do to her, man?" Nic rushes forward and Sebastian steps back to foil his attack with a defensive block.

"What the hell are you doing?" I screech, throwing myself in the ring to break up the brawling brothers. Something strikes me in the face—hard. Horrified, they stop swinging and haul me to the bed.

"Oh my God, Julia, are you okay? Are you hurt?" Nic's face is the color of pale parchment, and I rub my throbbing cheek.

"I *was* okay until you guys threw fists for no reason." My irritation dissolves into horror when I glance at my train to find it ripped to shreds. "This is perfect, just bloody perfect."

"What's this cotton pickin' ruckus abou—" We turn to see Lillian's jaw hit the floor, her expression fifty shades of thunderstorm.

"Julia…Jean…Malone." She directs her wrath at me. "Get in my office now."

"But I had nothing to do with—"

She cuts me off and barks the order again. "I said *now*." Her whole body is shaking and I can't even describe the horrid color of her face because it's somewhere between tomato and eggplant.

She marches me across the hall by the scruff of my neck and thrusts me into her office. Her expression says *defy me and die* as she rips the remaining train from my dress with a brutal yank. I've never seen her out of control furious, and I flinch when the door slams with a bang.

"One night—you can't behave like a lady for one night? You mischievous and frustrating girl!"

"Nic is the one who started the fight. Sebastian told me he was my date for the night and then all hell broke loose after that."

"I don't want to hear it Miss Malone. You and those boys get me so hopping mad with that jealousy nonsense." Her lips are pressed together so tight she looks lipless.

"Will you let me explain?" I squeak out, unable to breathe in the suffocating dress.

She doesn't listen to a word I say, her rigid body language screaming *hostile*.

"There's no time because our guests will be here any minute. Let's get you back in order." She whips me around, forces the zipper down, and orders me out of the ruined dress. I obey, frustrated because she never listens. My teeth snap shut and her face pinches up like a pincushion.

"Well, now what?" I press my lips together in a razor thin line to mirror her agitated expression. She relaxes, because I'm a ridiculous sight standing here in panties and stilettos, with now cockeyed hair.

"You absurd and ridiculous girl. New York is known for its drama, theatrics, and such. It's right where you belong." Lillian huffs. I give her my best *whatever* expression and she marches from the room, returning with another gown. This one is much more revealing than the first and eight sizes too small—at least.

"No way. You've *got* to be kidding." I stare at the scrap of a gown and inch toward the wall. If I scale out the window, I can hide at Café Boroughgard until this mind numbing party is done for another year.

Lillian ruffles the gown in my face, demanding I take it. The flimsy fabric is much too unforgiving, and it's clear that every curve and bump will be on high display with no room for such luxuries as eating or breathing.

"March, young lady." She points toward the door and I stomp off in a hissy. She's acting like a nasty yard hen and on my last tattered nerve.

"Fine." I storm from her office with the offending loincloth and stomp across the hall not caring if I have spectators, which I always do.

Bugger off, Lyra. She's by her door with a self-satisfied smirk, but dips into her room when I come barreling down the hall.

I slam my door so hard it's a wonder the walls don't collapse. After re-pinning my hair, I force myself into what I'd describe as a saran wrap disaster. The fabric is fine black silk without a lick of embellishment and it's unforgiving as it clings to my body. Twenty minutes later, I re-emerge in a much calmer state of mind after several rounds of deep breathing.

Sebastian offers his arm and I take it. I'm not sure how this date business works and I have awkward mixed emotions where he's concerned. When we reach the bottom of the staircase, I notice familiar people milling around the foyer, and servers carrying trays of appetizers and flutes of champagne.

I waste no time in snatching a glass of bubbly, not caring one iota if we're allowed. My throbbing cheek is a painful reminder never to involve myself in the affairs of teenage boys and their ridiculous, testosterone driven insanity.

"You look good enough to eat." Sebastian notes, staring straight ahead toward Nic, Lyra, and Linc. I ignore his telepathic comment; it's not like I have time to devise a comeback.

Nic throws us an unappreciative glance and I shake my head, warning him to control his temper because my nerves are all but shot to hell. I guzzle the glass of champagne and grab another before the server disappears into a thicket of murmuring guests.

Rose Hall is filled with men and women decked out in elegant formal wear, most of whom I recognize from past parties except for two people who could to be together, but aren't. I elbow Sebastian and motion toward the silver haired gentleman.

"Who's that?" I ask.

He glances where I'm looking and shrugs his shoulders. "No idea; never seen the man before tonight." The only thing that interests Sebastian is besting Nic.

Lillian stuffed Lyra into a similar nightmare, but she's much more comfortable in her own skin, which makes me dislike her even more right now. She chooses tonight to shine? The notion rattles around my champagne fuzzy mind and spits it back out with a silent *phooey*.

When Lyra catches my eye, she crushes her body closer to Nic in a classic taunting move. As it stands, she's plastered all over him like cellophane. A dateless Dutch steps into our cozy little twosome and hugs me from the side.

"Don't worry about it, doll. She's trying to make you jealous. Two can play that game you know." He grips my waist and pulls me in for a second squeeze, crushing my ribcage.

"Who's your date?" I ask him.

He looks confident as always. "I asked Ella."

"You dirty little scoundrel. She never mentioned a thing this morning." My smile fades when I catch Lyra running her hand along Nic's back.

He doesn't mind or notice, and my hackles stand on end. Then the slinky little minx wraps herself under my future husband's arm and I'm three seconds away from a catfight of my own. My head spins with fuzzy little bubbles after I guzzle the second glass of much-needed champagne, which in my mind, is black eye protection for Lyra.

"Easy there, killer. A guy could take advantage of you in that state." Sebastian's remark should be funny, but something in his expression makes me re-think giving him the benefit of the doubt.

"Get real." I stare into his eyes looking for signs of humor and find none. He's not kidding.

With Dutch on one side and Sebastian on the other, I devise an escape route. The room is buzzing with several conversations at once, and our guests take on a hazy glow when the champagne hits. I spy on the aristocrat and his admirer while Dutch and Sebastian scan the room for hot chicks that don't exist unless they're into senior citizens.

Still focusing on the doubtful duo that captured my attention, I raise my mental blocks and everything becomes focused and concise in my head once again. The ability to read minds is great, but having telepathic housemates in my business all the time isn't wonderful. That's why the skill of blocking became necessary around here.

No, they're not together but she's following his every move. I swing my arm out and snag a third glass of champagne, then follow on the coattails of the server. Sebastian and Dutch might be right behind me, but I don't bother looking back. Linc watches me from across the room and I stick my tongue out.

"Bring it sweetheart, I've got all night." He licks his lips in a lewd gesture, and the liquid in my stomach curdles.

"Can we do normal in this house for once? Did

wolves raise you? Honestly."

"You look delicious. I'm sharpening my teeth for the kill."

Lillian catches the exchange and I curtsy. She'll wring my neck later, but why doesn't she ever catch these rotten boys in the act?

"In your dreams, reptile." Lincoln's chuckle registers in my head, but I ignore him and move toward the unknown girl and her target until I'm standing by her side.

"Nice party isn't it?" I tip the champagne flute to my lips and gaze out over the guests. She squirms, shifting from foot to foot, feigning a smile. "I don't think I've seen you at our autumn party before, have I?" I ask, already knowing the answer.

"Oh. Um, no. It's... uh... my first time. The party is spectacular." She stammers, and it's obvious she's over her head. I thrust my hand toward the petite blonde and blast her with a smile that could melt the polar ice caps.

"I'm Julia Malone, but everyone calls me Jules for short."

"Nice to meet you, I'm Rhenn. Rhenn McAdams."

"Do you have a date?" It's hard not to laugh at our comedic predicament and Rhenn knows she's busted.

"Oh dear; please don't blow my cover. I followed

Mr. Van Buren from New York. It sounds like I'm stalking him doesn't it? Well—to be honest, I *am* following him. You see—" I hold my hand up because this one requires a lengthy explanation.

"Follow me." I jerk my head toward the back yard and we weave through a thick group of chattering guests.

Nic's burning a hole in the back of my head. *"Tell you later."* I say.

"Whatever." He cops an attitude for no reason and yet Lyra is pawing him half to death. I'm the one who should be in a pissy mood; not him.

The back yard glows with colorful lanterns in shades of pumpkin, yellow, and rose, and so far, it's free of guests. Rhenn follows me to a nearby table glimmering with intimate candlelight, and we sit. At once, the dam bursts wide open.

"I'm a beat reporter from New York." She keeps her voice low. "Just graduated to be honest, and Claude Van Buren is my ticket to becoming a featured news writer. The paycheck is a royal suck, but there's prestige and glamour involved. If I can snag an interview with the elusive Mr. Van Buren, I'm in the elite crowd for sure." I think her head might explode and I laugh as she stares in confusion. The poor girl is too cute for her own good. Then

76

it hits me.

"Wait...you're from New York? And Mr. Van Buren, he's from New York as well?"

"Yes, Brooklyn, but I have Manhattan in my sights. Someday, I hope to live there." Her smile is captivating and I adore this girl. Someday, we're destined to be friends.

Welcome to my life, Rhenn McAdams.

***

Sultry instrumental music filters into the secluded section of yard, and Lillian walks toward our table with Claude Van Buren in tow. The painted on smile glues me to the chair even though my instincts shout run the other direction. I'm not ready to meet our mysterious benefactor, and I focus my attention on the colorful lanterns. They cast a magical glow across the backyard and make a great distraction from one's certain doom.

Candlelight flickers in the middle of each table and pulls it together in circles of pleasant intimacy while the rest of our yard is blotted out in blue-black darkness. The contrast is unsettling.

My stomach twists in knots but I hide behind the bravado of a grown-up dress, impeccable make-up, and half-witted Lillian inspired hair. I can do this. Mr. Van Buren stops by my feet and studies me as if examining a bug.

"Miss Malone, I presume?" He extends his hand with the grace of old money and I reciprocate by offering mine, not quite sure it won't burn.

"Yes—and you are?" Wow, I'm rock-solid inspiring at playing coy. If I could reach out and pat myself on the back, I'd do it.

"My name is Claude. I'm sure you recognize the last name on this manor's library." *Did he just trump me?*

"Mr. Van Buren, it's a pleasure to meet you. This is Rhenn. She flew in from New York." His reaction is less than impressed, but he remains impassive and unreadable. He'd be great at poker, and I'd lose the baby's shoes.

"Rhenn, how nice to meet a fellow New Yorker. We must exchange cards. Mind if I borrow Julia for a moment?" He disarms her with a disingenuous smile. Rhenn is struck dumb and nods, jumping up to dismiss herself and Lillian follows.

Holy mother of Troy, this man is intimidating.

"My apologies—I try not to intimidate anyone." If it weren't for the crickets, I might have heard my own heart lurch to a stop.

"Yes, I can read your mind. We're the same."

"Oh." I mumble over the thundering in my chest. I

78

realize at this point he had me outnumbered from the moment he walked through the door.

"You're young, Julia, but bright and beautiful. I have high hopes for you." The atmosphere between us is palpable. He pats my hand and I flinch but his next words come as a welcome relief.

"Enjoy this fine evening among your friends. We can discuss matters later." A line forms between his brows and he adds, "I look forward to knowing you better in New York," with that, my champagne buzz takes a nosedive.

Chapter Five—Ghosts From the Past

Nic breezes through the doorway and I'm slumped at a darkened table with the last bit of candlelight flickering out. I stare at party lanterns wondering about our new life in New York City, and the unimaginable lifestyle that waits.

"Penny for your thoughts. Oh wait, I get em' for free." Now is an excellent time for his humor; it helps. He stretches his legs, acting composed but I sense turbulent emotion beneath a quiet exterior. When will he learn I can read him like a haiku hot off the press?

"You don't have enough pennies in the world for my thoughts but your endowment might cover it. You realize we're moving to New York, right?"

"It's all I can think about these days. Not sure I want to move halfway across the world and live with strangers. It feels like a complete loss of control."

"It's obvious we don't have a say. Why did you ask to stay with me?" I hope in an absolute moment of clarity, he realizes it's because he loves me.

"From the first day we met you didn't have a clue. You're sensitive to everything, and I tried to protect you from the world."

"A protective big brother—how sweet." His words have a way of slicing me to the core and he doesn't even know it.

"I would never say big brother. Just protective." He corrects. "You're my goose, Jules."

"And here I thought I was your brainiac. How silly of me."

Lillian leads our guests to the outdoor tables and our intimate conversation is cut short.

Lyra, Sebastian, Dutch, and Lincoln settle into chairs beside Nic and me. At least we can present a united front at the party if not in real life. I spot Ella from Café Boroughgard and she's dressed in a pearlescent gown that clings to her body. Dutch's eyes bulge from his head, and I laugh at his reaction.

She waves back, excited as I've ever seen her, but she's ushered to another table. I realize how much I'll miss Ella when we move, and it's bittersweet watching her admire the enchantment of our last autumn party together.

"Need more liquor, Jules? You sure slammed em' back earlier." Lincoln tries embarrassing me for his own sport and smoothes his lapels with a cocky grin.

"Now that *you're* here, and I need booze just to cope." My amiable demeanor just left the building. "You'd drive a nun to drink." Lyra laughs and gives me a mental high five. That's a first.

The servers bring plates of food to the table and they present Nic's beef tenderloin as colorful kabob skewers, with grilled vegetables, and my mouth waters at the luscious scents. Then I look at my form-fitting gown and scowl.

"Lyra and I are the lucky recipients of a luxurious night of growling bellies. Thanks, Lillian." I tip my glass and she nods with disapproval at our obvious dilemma.

The party lanterns sway overhead and mild autumn air settles on our skin like a silk blanket. The weather is temperate and I'm surprised at how comfortable I am in this conspicuous scrap of a gown.

There will be no eating while I'm wearing this cling-on dress, and I hope Claude Van Buren leaves early so I can eat the food I spent all day prepping. One can dream. The dinner service goes off without a hitch and guests chatter in animated voices over coffee and elegant puff pastries. As if on cue, Nic reaches for my hand when an unseen force sets the dinner music in motion. The melody is familiar and we move in sync as if built for each other.

Midway into the second set, Lillian and Claude leave the party together and I relinquish the love of my life for the God-awful pull of curiosity.

"I need to check this out. Can we dance later?"

Nic nods and I weave my way inside the manor, stopping once to look back.

He's still watching me and I sigh but the delusional love spell goes up in flames when Lyra takes her place beside him on the dance floor. I'm aware of the painful ache in my heart and don't know why the despicable tart won't bugger off... or at least combust on the spot.

The tempo picks up and I triumph for once. *Ha!* There will be no slow dance for the nasty little opportunist and my heart can sit this one out. There's eavesdropping to be had.

Our hallway proves impossible as I tiptoe across the hardwood floors, so I slip my stilettos off with an impatient yank and strain to hear voices behind the library door.

Bingo.

I press my ear against the five-inch solid oak, trying to decipher tidbits of muffled conversation. Lillian calls my name and I freeze. Anyone with a lick of common sense would have bolted, but I lack that lick. The door swings open and they smile as if expecting me, which I find odd and disturbing.

"We've been waiting for you." Claude doesn't bother hiding his amusement and my scalp prickles. Darn near certain I'll break out in hives, I kick myself for getting caught. It always happens when I'm humiliated.

"Please, have a seat." He motions for me to enter with the sweep of an arm and Lillian steps aside to allow entrance to the scene of my crime from the other night. The leather-bound books in the library shout guilty, guilty, guilty, but I press onward.

"Have a seat Julia." I follow him to the table and dip into an end seat to avoid subordination. It's a psychological thing, but helps in uncertain situations.

Lillian and Claude eye each other and I wait for them to make the first move. The tension in the library is choking me and I struggle for breath.

"Let me start by saying you will love New York." He announces out of nowhere. My passive poker gaze rests on Claude's face, and he continues. "You'll never run out of things to do or learn and it's the perfect location for a curious girl."

"Everything is moving too fast. What do you want

from me?"

"I want you and Nic to be the first to start your internships with Van Buren Industries. Together, you have a sizable allowance for housing so finding a penthouse won't pose a problem." He ends with an ordinary smile, throwing off an innocuous vibe while every nerve ending in my body screams beware.

"That sounds great, but I wanted to go to college. Anyway, we're inexperienced and wouldn't be much use. What would I *do* at Van Buren Industries?"

"We have our fingers in several pots." He adjusts the handkerchief in his suit pocket.

"That's vague, Mr. Van Buren."

Claude holds his hands up in defeat. "You got me there, Julia. Van Buren Industries is an empire of sorts. We dabble in research and development, advertising, marketing, publishing, and prototype development. In fact, we've invested considerable time and money in several new projects." His entwined hands rest in his lap. "You'll fit right in with the launch of our new line of facial care."

"To be honest, I *am* interested in research and development. I'm naturally curious, but I'm sure Lillian filled you in on my troublesome nature."

Claude studies me, his brows furrowing as he

makes a gentle push at the edge of my mind. I block his attempt.

"Lillian taught you well." He's satisfied and glances to our mum.

He has the nerve to wink and I shift, feeling like a stuffed cabbage in this damnable dress.

"Why check to see if I can block your telepathic intrusion? I'm straightforward and you can ask me anything you want to know. Over the past few weeks, we've taken an unknown elixir and learned of a wealthy benefactor. Now you're putting us in strategic positions at Van Buren Industries. Why?"

Lillian blushes in furious shades of pink and clears her throat, grappling at her pearls. "Julia, you're being a tad bit forward, don't you think? Claude has nothing to hide and his only purpose was to ensure your care." Her gaze darts from me to Claude then back again. She grapples with her necklace again but this time it snaps. At least twenty pearls roll down the front of her gown and bounce to the floor, clinking and rolling in different directions.

"Oh dear lord, what have I done?" She bends to gather the fallen pearls, her cleavage almost spilling from the gown. It brings another furious blush to her cheeks as she tries to readjust the dress. The dresses, all of them, were a bad idea from the start.

"Leave them." Claude snaps and she leans back, heaving.

"Now back to our conversation. I'm not putting you in strategic positions in my company; I'm bringing you there to learn all aspects of our enterprise." He scowls at Lillian and I'm irritated he shows so little compassion for my caretaker.

"Sorry, I guess the clothes are making me smarter than I am. I'll dumb myself down if it helps." Claude raises his hand to deter Lillian's reprisal.

I know I have it coming but don't care. They can deal with my less than proper approach because I'm sick of the lies and secrets.

"I'm not an experiment *or* a puppet."

My mum and newfound benefactor keep quiet so I uncross and re-cross my legs because they're going numb in this dress.

"Yes—about that. We're well aware you've been digging through Lillian's personal effects." Claude's expression remains angry so I cross my arms to protect myself.

"What you think you've found, and reality, are two different stories. Trust me on that one. Lillian retrieved her notebook while you entertained that pesky beat reporter from LaraMax Publishing." His jaw stiffens and facial muscles grind behind tight flesh.

He's a little too well preserved. I can't help thinking.

"Information in the wrong hands causes more harm than good—this goes for uninformed girls who misinterpret what they're reading." His facial muscles relax and he attempts a cordial expression. I'm not buying it.

"Lillian hides everything from us. Did you know Sebastian, Lincoln, and Lyra's eyes changed color after they drank the elixir? And now they're weird." Weird is an understatement.

"Lillian informed me. They weren't uncommon reactions."

"According to what I read the reactions weren't normal." Something slithers down my back and I realize it's a bead of sweat. Panicked, I stand and prepare to leave but Claude has different plans.

"Ouch." I protest.

"Please sit." His vice grip digs into my flesh.

The library door swings open and Nic glides in holding two champagne flutes, and an enormous grin plastered on his face. He looks like a dopey, awkward puppy that's had his fair share of the bubbly.

"Way to go, you're just in time. Get me the hell out of here."

I wrench my arm from Claude's grip, wobble in my five-inch heels toward Nic's outstretched hand, and take the extra champagne glass.

"You, milady, owe me a dance—and I'm here to collect." Again, he gives me that adoring stare but completes it with a gentleman's bow.

"Well now," I declare and glance back at my slack-jawed benefactor and flustered guardian. "That's an offer a girl can't refuse. If you'll both excuse me?" My hips sashay in rhythm with the clicking of stilettos and I thank God I'm female.

Men can't get away with theatrical departures like that, and for the first time in my life, I feel powerful. The doors shut behind us with a sense of finality and we make a beeline toward the still buzzing party.

"Do you mind telling me what that was all about?" Nic spins on me.

"Not sure what you're asking—"

"Don't even try it. I heard everything."

"Nic, that's impossible. You can't hop heads."

"That's just it. I heard the entire conversation at the

same time." Nic whispers, his tone urgent.

"You pretended to be drunk?" I slap him on the shoulder. "Nice act."

"It was an act, you dingaling. Reading several minds at once was the weirdest experience I've ever had."

I grab Nic's hand and lead him back to the yard where our guests are chatting by the bonfire, laughing, and eating finger foods from small, rose-colored plates.

"Don't breathe a word of this to anyone. We need to get through the party unscathed." I sigh and pinch the bridge of my nose. "We'll figure this craziness out tomorrow."

Lyra's head rests against Lincoln's shoulder and their fictitious intimacy is nauseating. She's bored and tired, and Lincoln doesn't care enough to shrug her off him. Nic leaves me standing alone to throw a couple more chunks of wood on the bonfire, and appreciative guests gush over him while I watch from the sidelines.

Ella shines like the North Star and I can't help pining for my old life. Our move to New York City will be an interesting ride, and I look at the familiar faces as if already tucked away in my memories.

The night dies down with no major mishaps, and guests trickle out over the course of an hour. I'm relieved when the last person bids us adieu, and I lean against the door jamb with an exhausted sigh.

Lillian stares at me cross-armed in the doorway so I curtsy and trot up the grand staircase before she gets her hands on me again. Claude Van Buren is in one of the guest rooms but I don't bother looking. My first inclination is to burn this horrific dress and ditch the stilettos, but God help me tomorrow.

Chapter Six—Aftermath

The sun illuminates my bedroom with a radiant yellow glow and cracking my eyes open is a painful lesson in moderation. That champagne must have gone to my head because my skull feels as if it's ready to split.

"Bloody hell." The bathroom is too far away and I grimace while rubbing my temples.

My feet hit the chilly tiles, and there she is, ready to pounce. Judging by the deep lines forming around her eyes and mouth, this conversation won't be a pleasant one.

"Morning, Lillian. It's rather creepy to find you staring at me when I wake up." I grind sleep from the corners of my eyes and stretch both arms upward. She purses her lips so the innocent act isn't working. Her peach velour robe and matching slippers must have been a gift from Claude because they're new.

"Good morning, Julia. Have you recovered from your night of mischief?"

"Not sure what you mean. I just don't trust the man." I turn my neck to the left hoping for a crack, and then to the right in a slow stretch.

"Invading my privacy wasn't trouble enough? And those pearls have been in my family for generations." She takes a sip of coffee and I notice an extra cup steaming on the vanity. I shuffle over to wrap my icy hands around the mug and swallow a mouthful of *rouse the dead.*

"You're welcome." She huffs, examining a loose button on her nightgown.

"Thank you," I concede. "Listen Lillian, I invaded your privacy and I'm sorry, but I won't apologize for needing answers. My entire life is a mystery."

"The elixir and your benefactor *are* a mystery but that won't last forever. You have questions about your family?" Her eyes plumb the depths of mine.

"Is is even *possible* to slow the aging process?"

Lillian relaxes, fixing to answer my question. Her head lowers for a sip of coffee and she clears her throat. "There's information you wouldn't understand and secrets I doubt you could handle."

"Out of everyone in the manor, who gets the highest grades? Who does all the work around here? Don't even get me started on the others. What do you mean I won't understand or be able to handle it?"

She tucks a stray lock of silver hair behind her ear

and moves to a standing position. "You'll know these things in time, dear—when you're ready. Get dressed and find Nic. Meet us in the library in half an hour."

"Am I in trouble?"

"No. We need to prepare you for New York." She swallows the last of her coffee, pats me on the shoulder, and exits the room in her fluffy peach slippers. My head is pounding with my heartbeat, and I need more coffee.

After a hot shower, I knock on Nic's door to see if he's awake. He doesn't answer so I creep inside to find his bed empty. This is weird; he's never up this early.

He taps my shoulder and I yelp, whirling to see him showered and standing behind me. "I listened to the whole conversation from my bed." He says, looking irresistible. It takes all my concentration to focus on his face.

"Do you know something I don't?" His cinnamon body wash curls under my nose and tugs at my heart strings.

Kill me now.

"Never."

"What? Oh, never mind. Quit getting up in my head." Where Nic's concerned, I forget to put my blocks up and embarrass myself senseless.

"I enjoy it in there. It's sweet, and muddled. You

and I are going to New York with Claude. That's what I know."

"Just us?"

"We're the first to go, but everyone else is coming later." Nic grabs my hand, leading me downstairs. He raps on the library door and we hear a resounding "come in" and enter.

Claude is dressed in a tailored business suit and looks as if he spent an entire month at the spa. Lillian is pale-faced and wringing her hands. We're instructed to sit and look to each other for reassurance.

"I've booked tickets and we'll be leaving for New York tonight." Claude's voice takes on a smooth, silky quality.

"Tonight?" I balk, and Lillian forces a smile.

"Investors snap up real estate fast in New York so we have to move on it. You'll get a tour of Van Buren Industries where you'll be doing your internships."

I push at the edge of Claude's mind to tap into his thoughts. Either he's so arrogant he doesn't think to block us, or he lets me inside his head for sport. No one is *that* pliant to intrusion.

I'll put Julia in research and development, and Nic can lead sales. I can't put this off forever. She's not a little

95

girl anymore.

The cavernous library closes in, and I push back from the scene as if leaving my own body. There's always the chance he didn't sense me in his head. I eavesdrop on Claude's thoughts while he chats with Nic on the real estate market.

I wonder if it will be a problem for her. As long as she doesn't dig too deep it should be just fine. Both hands rest under his chin in a comfortable posture.

"Holy shite," the words slip out under my breath and Nic elbows me under the table.

"So what do you think; does that sound agreeable?" Still reeling from the thoughts in Claude's head, I glance at everyone's expressions for clues as to the current topic of conversation. Why does this always happen to me? Nic furrows his brow, and bails me out once again.

"I think a penthouse in Manhattan is perfect. Don't you agree, Julia?" He kicks me under the table.

I squeak out a diminutive, "Yes," from both shock and pain. He hit my dang ankle bone.

After our discussion ends, I find myself back in my room packing everything I own. Lillian rambles on about our wonderful opportunity and I can't comprehend most of what she's saying. I've been busy interpreting the meaning

96

behind Claude's thoughts.

"Do you mind if I help Nic pack? Seems I'm done here." My suitcase is overstuffed so I jump on the top and snap the latches.

"I'm sure he'd appreciate the help. Are you *sure* you're okay with the move?"

"It's not as if I have a choice. Have I ever had one?"

"Your new life will be absolutely perfect. Everything you've ever dreamed of and more." She tries to leave.

"Is there something you're not telling me?" My question makes her turn around and our eyes meet in a dance of wills.

"Whatever gives you that idea, my dear? Why must you find the negative in everything?" She grabs a stray shirt off the floor and tosses it by my suitcase. Unable to resist, I plunge inside her head without the slightest resistance.

She suspects something and lying isn't my strong suit. I better get my arse to scooting.

That's all I needed to pluck from Lillian's head to know she's not being honest. We're nothing but pawns in a great big game of something unknown. I offer her a weak smile and she dismisses herself, clucking like a hen about dinner. When the door shuts, I trip over my own two feet to get to Nic's room.

"Nic…" I breathe, slamming his door. My butt hits the floor with a thud.

"Julia, what the heck are you doing? A flair for the dramatic much? Seriously. What the hell has gotten into you these days?" He stops folding a pair of jeans and stares at the rumpled mass of arms and legs on his bedroom floor.

"That's me, *all theatrics and such*. But to be honest, don't you think it's happening way too fast? Why aren't you questioning it more?"

"And why are you looking a gift horse in the mouth? Relax your ruffled feathers, goose." He folds a shirt and drops it into an aged leather suitcase. It's well used and the kind you might find in a quaint, out of the way antique shop.

"Did you even *try* to get into Claude's head to see what he's hiding?" Nic's patience is spread thin and his sigh is long and exaggerated to make a point.

"The last time I checked, I wasn't stupid so lay off. His shields were impenetrable." He grabs a pair of jeans and tosses them in the suitcase. "Did *you* even try? You zoned out and embarrassed yourself again. Were you hung-over, or what?"

"Do I *look* hung-over to you?" My mood sours and

I can't believe he didn't crack Claude's barrier. I jump up and fold his clothes. *Should I tell him?*

"So let me fill you in on what you missed while vacationing in la-la land. First, he wants us there as soon as possible because real estate in Manhattan is difficult to find. Second, he's placing us in internships to learn the ropes. We have stakes in Van Buren Industries you know."

"Stakes? What stakes?" As usual, I'm lost, but then again I was busy getting the real scoop.

"We're shareholders—and from what Claude explained, the company will be ours someday." He grabs a bottle of cologne and spritzes his neck before tossing it on the suitcase.

"That's unheard of and you're not questioning it?" The urge to tell Nic what I found in Claude's head is overpowering, but I keep it to myself. "How hard did you try?" His suitcase is stuffed and I stop packing. "To get into his head, I mean. Did you try hard?"

"Let's just say it was like trying to hack through the Great Wall of China with a toothpick—impossible." He stops folding and looks at me with narrowed eyes. "Why?"

"I wondered if your newfound ability to read multiple minds might help."

"No such luck. Yeah, it was nuts. His mind was

tighter than Fort Knox."

We finish packing in silence, the unspoken tension causing an uncomfortable rift. I suggest calling a house meeting but he doesn't agree with my plan to demand answers before we leave.

"You're being ridiculous. We'll fly out, find a place to live, and everyone else will meet up later. You act as if we're off to the firing squad."

"As always, you're right." Tired of arguing, I shuffle back to my room, throw myself on the bed, and cry.

Tomorrow we'll be in New York and I'm powerless to stop it.

***

Our plane taxies across the runway and with my nose plastered to the thick fiberglass window, I search for a reason to stay. Nic elbows me when I don't respond to the stewardess, declining refreshments and dismissing them both.

Claude sits one seat forward and to the right, reading *The New York Times* and my beloved England will soon be a distant memory. My instincts scream I'll never see it again, and for once in my life, my heart agrees.

"Hey, you okay?" Nic touches my cheek and studies me for clues as to the cause of my apprehension. I have flashbacks of saying goodbye to the only family I've ever known and wonder what will become of us in New York.

"Yeah." I shrug. "No... I'm not fine. And I'm not okay with any of it."

"It's a new adventure so you're bound to get overwhelmed, but these changes? Who gets an insane opportunity like this?" He's animated and I nod, not so sure of his logic. I hit the call button and ask for a can of Pepsi but maybe I should drink cool-aid like everyone else.

The stagnant air in our first-class cabin is dry. We pitch to a stop on the runway and I hold my breath. This is it. We're taking off, and my chest constricts, making it difficult to get air in my lungs. Nic tells me to breathe and squeezes my hand. His touch sends a jolt of energy through me and I overhear his thoughts.

I've got you, love.

I turn toward the window and close my eyes. Tears rest on my cheeks and the engines roar to life. The salt of despair leaks from my eyes and settles in the corners of my mouth. Lift off should have been exhilarating. Instead, I curl into my safe spot, hoping Nic leaves me alone for the rest of the trip.

At one point I had fallen asleep and when I rouse,

101

the dim cabin contrasts with the darkness outside my window. Nic is slumped in his seat with a pool of saliva collecting at the corners of his mouth. The sight of him is pathetic and amusing and I laugh. Claude turns around to catch my eye, gesturing for me to join him in first class.

Our flight attendant offers a weary smile, and dark under-eye circles tell stories of sleepless nights. She asks if I need refreshments, but I couldn't eat or drink anything if I tried.

"No thank you, I'm fine." She nods and continues her rounds.

When she passes, I squeeze past a sleeping Nic to join Claude. He removes his glasses and studies me for a moment, his scrutiny uncomfortable. He says nothing, but hands me a three-ring binder with *Van Buren Industries* inscribed in gold lettering on the front.

"What's this?" Our gazes meet.

"Go on, read it." His expression gives nothing away but I sense something deep and calculating below the surface.

I'm startled by the first page because my name is at the top with a title—Vice President of Research and Product Development. The words jump out as I flip pages and read about a line of skincare called *Immortality*: 'The new fountain of youth for the twenty first century.'

Claude shifts in his seat waiting for my reaction and I'm clenching my jaw tight enough to crack a few teeth.

"You know I can get inside your head whenever I wish. But I'd like you to share those thoughts of your own accord." His self-assuredness is daunting.

"Shock pretty much covers it." I rub my temples and sigh.

"Which part shocks you?" He asks.

"You're putting small traces of the elixir in a face cream. Then you're marketing it worldwide?" Pain throbs at the side of my head. "It wasn't long ago we thought the elixir had killed Lyra. And it changes people—not just eye color either."

"You're special Julia. The dose you took enhanced abilities the rest of the world does not have." Claude smiles and I'm bothered by the familiarity. He's an elusive memory struggling to reach the surface.

"There were adverse reactions when we took it. Lyra, Sebastian, and Lincoln's eye color changed to black. Claude, they *had* blue eyes. The public wouldn't overlook something like that."

"It's a minor detail that our chemists have fixed. I can assure you it won't happen again."

"We were guinea pigs? None of us have been the same since we drank the elixir." I lock my mind because he can't know of my newfound abilities—ever.

"This is true. It can heighten inborn traits." His face is so familiar I'm sidetracked for a moment, but continue the interrogation.

"What does that *mean*?"

"It personifies their character, say intellectual, physical, or emotional. Even abilities are heightened." He reaches into the lapel of his suit to retrieve a stick of gum. He gestures toward the pack and I decline.

"Yes, but now those traits are spooky." I slap the binder shut and hand it back to him. He holds up a hand.

"You'll need that."

"For what? I'm not getting involved with something that might endanger the public." It's claustrophobic next to Claude, and this first-class seat turns coach because I feel trapped and feral.

"That's why we need you as acting vice president as soon as possible. You'll be in charge of product development, and with your scientific mind we'll have *Immortality* perfected by the launch date."

I glance back to find Nic staring at me and he prods at the back of my mind, insistent.

"What's your deal with Claude?"

"We'll talk later. I'm headed back to my seat." I stand to leave but he touches my hand and I receive his thoughts.

Julia's a stubborn and impetuous girl. She has the world at her fingertips and doesn't even know it yet. I inspect his face for signs of recognition but he's unaware I heard his thoughts without detection.

"Nic's awake. Are you finished with me?" Claude tilts his head to acknowledge the end of our conversation. I jump up, ramming into the flight attendant.

"Er, excuse me, I'm so sorry." After apologizing, I slide into my own seat and Claude faces forward, his attention on a stack of documents.

"So? Your mind was racing a mile a minute." A line forms between Nic's brows. "I couldn't make any headway on your thoughts. What gives?"

Claude pays us no mind, engrossed in his work so I keep my mental guards on full alert in case it's an act.

"He plans to put the elixir in a line of skin cream and launch it under the trademark *Immortality*. According to Claude, I'm spearheading the project." I have a strange habit of smoothing my eyebrows when I deliver frustrating news.

"Are you bloody kidding me? That's insane. Look what happened when we took it!"

Our benefactor issued one-way tickets to chaos, but at least we're of the same mindset. My scalp and nose itch, and stress hives erupt everywhere.

"We need to be careful because this launch is bigger than our small-town minds can comprehend." Not that I have to spell out the obvious.

He wraps an arm around my shoulder and shakes his head. Claude watches our exchange so I close my eyes, pretending not to see him. The rest of the flight is uneventful and I fall asleep in Nic's arms until we land.

We're in a different world when we step off the plane and Claude escorts us to a black stretch limo. The driver is wearing dark sunglasses and I wonder why anyone wears sunglasses at night if not to obscure their identity.

This can't be good.

Chapter Seven—New York

Cool night air chills my cheeks and a rush of adrenaline surges when I step onto the tarmac. The sky is lit up as if someone painted a million diamonds on a wet, black canvas. It's surreal set against the New York City skyline.

A tall man with dark skin ushers us into the limo and I scoot to the farthest corner to avoid further conversation. To my dismay, Claude positions himself across from me. The interior of the limo has a new leather scent without the disgusting stench of cigarette smoke, vomit, food, or other signs of a thoroughly used limo.

It must be new.

"It is new, and it's for your own personal use. Your driver's name is Leopold, and he's at your service twenty-four seven." I didn't expect Claude to read my thoughts without permission.

"I hate our stupid abilities." My terse response is harsh so I shoot for courtesy instead of exasperation.

"Thank you, Mr. Van Buren. I'm sure it will come in handy

as opposed to the expense and irritation of having to take a taxi everywhere." I strike a nerve with my reserved formality because his lips tighten into a thin disapproving line and he turns his head toward the window.

"How long will we stay with you?" Nic asks to break the thick, suffocating tension in the limo.

"Depending on you, it could be days or weeks."

I roll my window down to escape an awkward and unwelcome interaction.

Leopold maneuvers through crowded New York streets with a deft eye, vying for space among yellow, checkered taxicabs, and drunken pedestrians weaving in and out of traffic.

It's impossible not to smirk when I spot a woman in a skin-tight leopard dress teetering on six-inch stilettos; she looks like a hooker. The sights, sounds, and scents of New York City are interesting—a city I've only dreamed about before now.

"Hey, goose, you're not in England anymore." Nic jabs me in the ribs and I go in for a sideways kidney punch.

Claude launched us into a world we can't fathom, but we're still just kids about to grow up in the fast lane. Our brave faces are nothing but a facade, and our benefactor knows it. Odd-looking pedestrians are the least of our worries.

The limo slows in front of a gated high-rise and I crane my neck out the window to see an entire building of smoked glass. The lit windows catch my eye as much as the ones shrouded in darkness.

Leopold punches numbers into a silver-plated box at the gate, and it swings open in a slow, methodical fashion. A modern carport greets us with rows of vehicles that appear expensive, most of them in black and silver.

Don't New Yorkers believe in red, white, and blue?

"You're witty, Julia. It's a pleasure getting to know your intimate thoughts." Claude's eyes crinkle at the corners and he gets more familiar every time I study him.

Getting to know my intimate thoughts? Buddy, it would take a lifetime to understand me, so don't flatter yourself. I chastise myself for lowering my mental guards—yet again.

Leopold parks the limo near the elevator and opens our doors to help with luggage. Claude instructs him to bring our bags later.

"I need my bag," I object, not wanting my suitcase misplaced right there along with the rest of my life.

"Everything you might need is already waiting for you. Your things will be safe for now." Claude exits the vehicle, followed by Nic. I trail with reluctance.

We follow him into a wide, silver elevator, and when the doors close, I notice the building has forty floors. He hits the *P* button and enters a twelve-digit code. The abrupt upward motion startles me and I teeter into Nic.

"Okay, wow." He laughs. "This elevator doesn't mess around does it?"

I try to relax by taking several deep breaths, and my anxiety subsides. Doors open and the grandeur of Claude's penthouse leaves me speechless.

"Is this the *entire* top floor?"

"Yes." He assures me, his voice soft and amused. The penthouse is immaculate, with not a single object out of place.

He gestures our entrance with the sweep of a hand and my shoes squeak on the black marble flooring. I imagine it's a nightmare to keep polished and look around for his poor house-keeper standing in the wings with a cloth. The sunken living room has a grouping of leather sofas and wing backed chairs in various shades of charcoal. A gray and white tiled fireplace lines the back wall and I've never seen anything so elegant. The room is stunning, but doesn't feel like home; this world is much too sterile for comfort.

"Your home is amazing, but…" I grapple for a suitable response. My telepathic blocks are in place because Claude has a nasty habit of eavesdropping on my inner contemplations.

"There's not much color." He sets a briefcase beside a black marble desk resting beside the elevator.

"You could use color for sure. Everything's black and white." I wander around studying his art and photographs in chic black frames.

"I love it. It's manly. A man lives here." Nic's humor has a way of warming up uncomfortable situations and I loosen the rein on my nerves.

"Shall I show you to your rooms?" Claude points toward a long hallway lined with black frames that must number in the hundreds, containing pictures of him all over the world. He's feeding stingrays and parasailing, horseback riding, hang gliding, and cutting a ribbon in front of a brand new building. One of him posing with a group of men and women catches my attention because Lillian is in the picture.

I examine their faces, recognizing two. They appear to be at an archaeological dig with a man who resembles our host. His arm is draped across Claude's shoulder.

"Is that your father?" I point to the man in question,

studying his face for clues. I'm missing something.

"That's my father, John Van Buren. We have plenty of time for exploration so let me show you your quarters." He walks toward a winding staircase and pauses at the bottom.

When we catch up, he's standing in a rounded hallway with two doors. Between the doors is a polished wood balcony that overlooks the great-room.

"You, my dearest Julia, shall take the suite on the left, and Nic, you get the leftovers. Go ahead and explore. My butler will bring trays of food and I'm sure you'll want to shower and rest. See you both in the morning." He nods and bows, then turns on his heel. We stand there dazed and watch him disappear.

"Will you stay with me? I don't want to be alone tonight." I wring my hands and he turns the door handle to reveal a luxurious suite. The opulence is unbelievable and I spot an enormous freestanding Jacuzzi. To my delight, there's color everywhere. My colors—shades of pink and rose, orange, and gold. It's every girl's dream come true and I couldn't have imagined a room more perfect if I had envisioned it beforehand. Nic looks over the top of my head and gasps.

"I dunno, Julia. It looks a girl exploded in here. I

might go into sensory overload." I jab him with my elbow and he follows me into the room.

Without thinking, I toss my jacket on the floor and leap onto the four-poster bed, skidding up to the headboard like a ten-year-old girl. Nic jumps in excited and out of breath, and for the moment we are blissful and content.

Claude's butler brings trays of food and we polish off cucumber sandwiches, romaine salad with raspberry vinaigrette, and scones for dessert.

"That was amazing." I note as if Nic didn't have his own taste buds. We lie back on the bed and nestle in together. It feels good being crooked under Nic's arm even if it doesn't mean as much to him as it docs me. At this moment, I'm suspended in the perfection of circumstance and it won't matter in the morning.

***

Nic's body rises and falls with shallow, soft breaths and I lift his arm, trying not to disturb him. We fell asleep spooning with my arm tucked around his waist and I bend to sniff his hair one last time as I close my eyes. He has no clue how much I love him.

The bathroom is next to the bed and I close the door, making sure not to wake Sleeping Beauty. He looks as innocent as a Disney character when he sleeps. A variety of toiletries lines the countertop, but the wall-to-wall glass is excessive, and I double-check the lock. Nic doesn't need a shock if he wanders into the bathroom.

I shed my travel-worn clothes, kicking them into a haphazard pile in the corner.

What's with all the jets and nozzles? Talk about overboard.

"Ahh. Now I see why Claude likes these fancy little contraptions." I catch myself talking aloud, thankful Nic's asleep. He'd be shocked if he ever found out I'm a bona fide dork. So far, he thinks I'm ultra cool and in control, but he'll soon figure out I'm a *doofus* in disguise.

I just about jump from my skin when there's a rap at the door but I have the wherewithal to grab the wall handle to steady myself.

"Julia, is that you in there?" He asks, the question ludicrous because who else would sneak in here while he's asleep. Nic is such a rocket scientist sometimes.

"Yup. If you need to use the bathroom, run next door." I smear strange exotic soap over my skin and scrub my scalp. It doesn't matter there's a bath product for every body part known to man. Simplicity is my calling card.

"Ten-four, I'll be back in a few." He says.

I've scrubbed every square inch of my skin with

dazzling fruit and sunshine and now I'm a new woman. There's an assortment of combs, brushes, and hair care products in the drawers. I wrap my hair in a towel, and another one around my chest.

Nic is nowhere in sight when I emerge from the bathroom with steam pouring out behind me. He's either showering next door, or found something noteworthy and scandalous. Knowing him, I'll take a mad stab at scandalous.

As I ponder the love of my life, he kicks the door open, dragging both our suitcases behind him. He has a towel wrapped around his waist, and his hair is dripping wet. As I suspected, he took a shower.

"Let me help you with that before you pull a back muscle." I walk toward the suitcases but his stubbornness is legendary.

In the mix of things, he fails to notice that his towel caught on a buckle. Nic's face turns bright red and it must have happened in slow motion because it takes a minute to register. I'm positive he thinks the hand over my mouth is stifling a scream but I'm trying not to laugh.

"Bloody hell." Nic snatches his towel from the floor and covers his privates, backing out of the room without his suitcase.

He stops without turning around, his eyes wide as saucers. There is a young woman standing in the hall and she's staring at his naked butt.

"Jules... is there someone behind me?" He's frozen in place and I'm laughing so hard tears roll down my face. This nonsense always happens to me so I better mark my calendar as the most humiliating day of Nic's life.

"Sir Nicholas, I have your breakfast." The female says, and he turns to read her nametag. Now he's mooning me. So far so good. I've seen the front and now the back.

"Uh, yeah, Lorraine, you must be Claude's housekeeper?" He grips the towel like a lifeline and mutters, "Someone kill me please."

"Yes sir, we can have that arranged. Where would you like your tray?" Her mild reaction must be from years of training because I'd be snorting and falling all over myself.

"My room is fine. Do you mind if I…" his voice cracks and he can't finish.

"No, sir, by all means tend to your business." She grins at her use of the word *business*.

He re-wraps the towel, holding it tight enough to cut off circulation and prevent future children, but a man has to do what a man has to do. He opens the door for Lorraine

116

and I'm rolling on my bed in hysterics.

"I'll get your bag from next door." She says after setting his tray on the nightstand. I'm watching from the hallway now.

"That would kinda, sorta... be great. Do you mind if I hide in the bathroom for the rest of my life?" He asks, humiliation scorching his cheeks.

"No sir." Lorraine leaves his room giggling, and I guess her to be around twenty, not much older than us.

"That's not something you see every day is it?" I ask as she brushes by me.

"Oh heck no. That made my whole month." She laughs and makes her way toward the main entrance.

I run back to my room and throw on a cream sweater with dark jeans in a matter of seconds. When I return, Nic's hiding in the bathroom to avoid further national incidents of the flashing variety.

"Look at the man cave. Nice score."

"I guess." He tugs at his ear, avoiding eye contact.

"Sir Nicholas, you sure impressed Miss Pine with your backside." I offer a demure smile and a curtsy, hoping like hell he doesn't tackle me to the floor. I'd deserve it though.

"Your smart assery is getting dangerous, Jules."

"It is indeed." I tease, flopping onto his bed and luxuriating in thick folds of jade damask. "Don't you think this penthouse belongs in a magazine?"

Nic dances over to the suitcase holding his towel with one hand while dragging his luggage with the other.

"Be out in a sec." He says, slamming the door. A few minutes later he emerges wearing faded jeans and a tight black, turtleneck sweater. It's still temperate in England and adjusting to the harsh winters of New York might prove difficult.

"Voila." He says, his grand exit from the bathroom eliciting oohs and ahhs to make up for the humiliation.

"Did you eat yet? I'd kill for more of these pastries." My gaze rests on his food and I pluck a chocolate croissant off the plate. "And the coffee? To die for. If you don't want it..." I nibble on the end of his croissant and set it back on the dish. It turns out that torturing Nic is an awesome pastime.

"What's mine is yours."

"I have a major FYI for you. When we're done here, Claude wants us in the study. Better eat now because I don't know how often they feed the prisoners around here." He's so fun to tease. "And we shouldn't keep your *admirer* waiting."

118

"I'll never live this down, will I?"

"Not in this lifetime, but you can try the next one."

He eats eggs, toast, ham, and pastries while I chatter about exploring the stores and restaurants near Claude's high-rise. He stuffs his face and watches my mouth move, but I doubt he's listening.

"Ready?" He asks, swallowing the last bite of croissant.

"As I'll ever be." I jump off the bed and grab his hand. Off to the guillotine.

Chapter Eight—Unusual Meetings

Nic lags in the hallway so I slow my pace, snaking my arm through his. When the great room comes into view, I can't help thinking of *Lifestyles of the Rich and Famous.*

Claude is on a charcoal couch sipping coffee and immersed in his newspaper. Lorraine appears to be waiting for orders. Her olive skin and dark eyes contrast mine like yin and yang. When she spots us, a deep blush erupts that even dark skin can't hide. She must remember Nic and his oh-so-adorable butt. The front view isn't any less spectacular but I can't even go there right now. I blink my eyes, shaking my head at the vision.

"There you are. I was ready to send out the dogs." He laughs at his own dry humor and we glance at each other, trying not to roll our eyes.

Old people are easily amused. Maybe they don't take themselves that serious after decades of experience. Nic joins Claude on the couch and I slide into a tall, wing-backed chair.

"I Googled the neighborhood and found several

nice shops and restaurants nearby. I'm dying to explore. And thank you for the laptop; it's much too generous." I gaze at my jeans but sneak a sideways glance when his head is turned. It's unnerving how he can read me with such ease.

"Nonsense, it's my pleasure. Besides, you'll need it for business." He turns to Lorraine, and she hands over a manila envelope she's been guarding with her life. He lifts the flap and lays the contents on the coffee table, handing Nic and I platinum cards with our names on the front.

"The limit is a hundred thousand dollars on each. In this town, you'll need it." His expression is composed and I'm staggered into silence. Nic doesn't flinch.

"Is this how we access our endowment?"

"No, we pay for things around here with cards. You don't want to be carrying a checkbook or wads of cash in New York City. These are insured." His facial muscles tic and I wonder what he's thinking. "And here are your bank accounts, and online access information." Claude hands me a thick stack of paperwork but my hand remains poised mid-air. I'm reluctant to accept thinking there must be a catch but Nic snatches it from his hand, wasting no time on suspicion.

"Oh, and Lorraine, can you fetch the kids their cell

121

phones? I believe I left them on my desk in the study. You can't miss them." He waves her off and concentrates on me; his gaze intense enough to bore a hole through my forehead.

"As you wish, Mr. Van Buren." She acknowledges with a slight nod and disappears down another long corridor. It makes me wonder at the size of his penthouse, and I glance around to calculate the approximate square footage.

"I don't have plans for either of you this week. You have Leopold, Helt, and Lorraine at your disposal and they can help with whatever you need. I'll be flying out this evening and won't be back until late Friday night. My casa is your casa, so make yourselves at home." We're startled by the announcement since we just got here. Why would he turn around and leave?

"Are you going right now? We have so many unanswered questions." I lean forward as if the action could stop him from leaving.

"Yes, I have meetings all day and I leave for the airport after work. Not to worry, dearest Julia, you're in fine hands. I've instructed Lorraine to get you settled." Both Nic and I stand at the same time and he shakes my hand first, then Nic's. "You have my direct number programmed in your cells. We've addressed everything you need to know for now, so relax and enjoy yourselves. Consider it a vacation."

"Thank you Claude—for everything." My body tenses when I utter words I don't mean. This arrangement bothers me; it's too easy, the transition to our new life too smooth. It's as if someone decided our fates at birth.

I drift off for a second and his words bring me back.

"No, Julia, thank *you* for placing your trust in me. See you both soon?"

"See you next Friday, then." Nic remains impassive, and I'm ready to launch into nervous, inappropriate laughter. In what fairytale do these things happen? *That's* what bothers me. Claude disappears down the same corridor where Lorraine went, and she reappears with two phones in her hand. It's strange how she's moves without sound as if gliding on air.

"For you, Mr. Maye, and you, Miss Malone." We accept the phones and she stares at Nic. "And if you need me, I'm programmed in the phones as Miss Pine, or you can hit seven on the internal phone line. Please enjoy your day." She disappears down yet another corridor and I admire the way Lorraine moves, her shoes darn near soundless. Her facial expressions are unreadable, but the eyes hold secrets of Claude Van Buren behind gated walls of mystery.

"What the heck are we going to do all week?" Nic scratches his chin, rubbing two-day-old stubble. "Ooh. We might find ourselves entangled in an international spy-jacking incident. Yeah... that would be cool." His eyes glaze over with crazy fantasies of world domination and zombie apocalypses.

"I want to go shopping, sit in a trendy coffee shop and find a nice eclectic eatery." There's a hitch. "But we don't dress like native New Yorkers. We'll stick out." He's impressed with my use of the word *eclectic* but won't give me kudos. Ahh, guys make me crazy; this one in particular.

"I want to hang around and check out the materials Claude gave us. You mind?" He looks around the penthouse and I know he's dying to explore the rest of it.

"Not at all. I saw shops lit up when we got here and they looked fascinating. I shouldn't be gone too long."

"Do you know how hard it snowed last night?" He asks. It never occurred to me to look out the window this morning.

"Are you kidding me?" This isn't good. "I have nothing warm to wear." My sweater is heavy but not warm enough to act as a coat, and I need boots.

"Check your closet. Claude thought of everything."
His ironic smile tells me I'm in for one heck of a surprise.

He hangs behind in the great room knowing my
curiosity will get the better of me and I jog to my suite.
When I open the closet doors, there's a cavernous space
with built-in closets and floor to ceiling clothes in every
imaginable color and style.

Shoes, purses, jeans, slacks, sweaters, t-shirts,
blouses, jackets, coats, built-in jewelry racks, and nooks for
every accessory—it's breath taking. Two rows of clothing
stretch out, as far back as the eye can see, and holds
suitable fashions for every possible occasion. Imagine that,
everything is my size. How convenient. The number of
shoes is obscene. I remember the new phone in my hand
and check if Nic's in my contact list. *And there he is.* I tap
his name and wait.

"Julia?"

"The one and only. Am I programmed into yours?"

"Why, yes…yes you are. Imagine that, Miss snoopy
pants."

"I have a good idea because I'm standing in *my*
indecent closet right now."

"Indecent is a gross understatement. I think he
bought us." For once, we're in agreement and I giggle at

the absurdity. This can't be real. I slide my fingers across a variety of fabrics while passing through the closet, gawking at the clothes, scarves, boots and various female accessories. "Well, look at this, I found a winter coat and boots. Sure you don't want to venture into the concrete jungle with me?"

"Yeah, I got this. No, I want to check out my laptop and this stack of business papers, and you know, roam around the penthouse to see what I can find. Don't go too far, okay?"

"Me? No way." Tailored business jackets slide through my fingertips, their fabrics a new sensation. A pant suit in black catches my attention along with a three thousand dollar price tag. *Oh my God.* I drop the cuff as if burned.

"Yeah, you. Just be careful." His protective tone is that of a father figure—or maybe even a husband. My heart lurches.

"Bye." The call on my pink iPhone ends. I squeal and throw myself into a massive collection of brand new dresses on the other side and inhale the new fabrics.

This closet is insanity.

Then I slip into a pair of brown suede boots, zipping them to my knees, and throw on a cream-colored swing

126

coat. It's my style and I give Claude props for doing his research.

The black speckled flooring seems impervious to the soles of my boots so I jog down the hall toward the elevator. I have my trusty iPhone, wallet, and shiny new platinum card. What more could a New York transplant need? The card gives me a thrilling sense of power. It's like driving a car for the first time, or the anticipation of your first kiss. At least, that's what I imagine.

When free of the building I burst onto the street in a whirlwind, looking left, then right, and back again. Right is a decent enough direction and with no particular destination in mind I follow my instincts.

Where she ends up, folks, nobody knows.

***

I stomp snow from my boots and step inside a classy establishment called Sigmund's because my toes are frozen. Once inside, I recognize the scent of cigars and liquor, and realize I'm in a gentleman's lounge. The only thing on my mind is wrapping my hands around a hot cup of cocoa.

The bar seems innocuous enough, and wealth hangs heavy in the air with a thick fog of stale smoke. I'm surprised at the number of people here midday, but it's

127

loaded with much older men who come from obvious affluence.

I master the maze of obstacles and reach the bar, averting my gaze to avoid eye contact with men, at tables overflowing with ashtrays and empty cognac glasses. One of the patrons catches my eye and sends a creepy sensation skittering down my spine.

Not in this lifetime, buddy. Holy hell, I hate that. I increase my pace before someone grabs my arm. A striking bartender with a squared jaw and piercing green eyes gives me an appreciative once-over before wiping his hands and walking to my perch at the end of the old polished bar.

"What can I get you ma'am?"

"Ma'am?" I raise an eyebrow. "You've *got* to be kidding me. I'm eighteen." When the words leave my mouth, I realize it might not be a good idea to broadcast my age around this crowd. They might not be as refined as their exteriors suggest.

"I guess my momma taught me well." The bartender grins, his eyes sparkling with a playful glint. "It's just an innocent pleasantry, I swear." He's older, but not by much—I'd guess mid-twenties.

"Well, in that case, sir...emphasis on the *sir*...I'll take hot cocoa with chunks of peppermint and chocolate on

128

top. If you don't have that, I can't be held accountable for what happens next. I don't want to have to hurt you."

He slaps the countertop. "For you? Anything. In fact, I'll race across the road in bare feet to get you the goods."

"Someone is a very bright boy." I love it when I get to tease someone new. His smile reaches his eyes and I relax.

He drifts away busying himself with the hot cocoa maker, then dips behind the counter, produces an unopened box of candy canes, and slits the plastic coating while keeping his gaze locked with mine. It's impossible not to laugh at his antics. He shakes a can of whipped cream, throws it in the air for a few aerial acrobatics, but fails when the can hits the floor with a heavy thud. We watch it roll away in mock horror and I laugh at the botched attempt. Cute, real cute.

"Oops," he says from the other end of the bar and scoops up the can.

After a couple minutes of putting together the world's best cup of hot cocoa with peppermint, my diligent bartender presents me with his masterpiece.

"The best you'll ever have. Enjoy while it's hot." He pulls a silver mechanism from behind his back and grinds fresh chocolate on the whipped cream and chunks of peppermint.

"Now *that's* what I call service. I might leave you an outrageous tip. So outrageous as to be tad ridiculous." I lick the tall peak of whipped cream.

"Looks like you got it on your face. Let me help." He leans over the counter and licks whipped cream off my nose.

"Bloody hell?" I push him back. "That's as gross as it gets."

"My ex-girlfriend used to get food everywhere. I'd kiss it from the corners of her mouth. Sorry if I grossed you out."

"You just took me off guard. I mean, you *are* a virtual stranger. Nose licking shouldn't happen until at least the third date. Cripe."

"We'll... you reminded me of her and my brain malfunctioned."

"Thanks. You'd think my name is Grace, but it's not." He hands me a napkin and I finish the job.

The bartender seems crushed I didn't respond to his flirting, crossing his arms in defense. I take a slow sip of hot cocoa, peering over the edge of my cup at him. His facial expression is intense as if studying a foreign reaction.

He relaxes and takes a less defensive stance by uncrossing his arms before posing the inevitable question. "So what's your name, stranger?"

I eye him, contemplating whether to lie or tell the truth.

"It's Julia. But you can call me *precious*."

"Cute. Lord of the Rings, right? Do you have anyone who calls you that?" He checks out my naked ring finger and smirks. No *precious* and no engagement ring.

"You're not entitled to ask all the questions here, pal. What's *your* name?" I tap the bar with my index finger.

"It's Rowan, but everyone calls me sugar loops." He leans forward on his elbows waiting for my reaction.

It's my misfortune to have a mouthful of hot chocolate when he tells me his ridiculous nickname and I choke. Rowan reaches over the bar. After a couple swift whacks between my shoulder blades, he steps away and gives me room to breathe

"Uh, thanks I guess, but I had the lung clearing thing covered." Is embarrassment a fitting reaction, or should I be thankful he didn't have to resuscitate me?

While I stare at Rowan, trying to figure out if all New Yorkers are this weird, a hand snakes down my back and rests near my bottom. I turn and discover a drunken old

131

chap leering in my face.

"Yes?" *The nerve.* His eyes are bloodshot and he reeks of hard liquor and cigar smoke.

"Can I buy you a drink, Miss?" The man's crooked teeth are stained dark yellow, obvious signs of indulgent cigar smoking and lack of hygiene. His left ring finger has a telling gold band.

"Why don't we call your wife and see if she would like to buy me a drink."

"Listen here—"

"You heard the lady, Bart. Now get back to the gang; they're waiting on you. She's not even old enough to drink." Rowan tosses a hand-towel over his shoulder and the man steps back.

"Maybe next time," he mutters, stumbling toward a group of drunken men with his tail tucked between his legs.

"*Gack.* Really?"

"Pretty much," Rowan's flat expression tells me he deals with it all the time. "I'm outta work in twenty minutes. If you want to grab lunch it's my treat. What do you say?" He leans against the bar, and I notice his muscular build. Rowan is *not* a boy. Nope. Not at all, and my mind goes a little fuzzy.

"I'm headed to my benefactor's…I mean…wow; I

132

don't know how to explain this. Closing my big yap." I grapple for the right words and he examines me, much more interested than a second ago.

"A benefactor huh... interesting. That means you're rich and I should ask for your number."

"That's how it's done here? Very interesting approach." There's no way to explain my unusual circumstances without sounding like a player.

"Rowan, it's been shockingly wonderful to meet you, but my life is too complicated for normal people. And please don't be offended that I lumped you in with normal people. If it's any consolation, you're the first friend I made in New York, so that's saying something isn't it?" I trace my name on the highly polished bar and see *Julia* in the curly streaks.

"There *is* a man in your life. I knew it." I can't tell whether he's genuinely crushed or teasing me for sport.

"Well, yes. No, I mean, not really. Not like that. At least…oh, never mind." I'm grasping at words so he puts his hand over mine when I reach for my wallet.

"Listen, hot chocolate's on the house, and it's great to meet you, precious." Our gazes linger for a second longer than is comfortable and I resist the urge to dip inside his thoughts. He seems like a good guy and doesn't deserve

133

my mistrust, or the headache my prodding might cause.

"I know where you work, and trust me, I've got my eye on you." I grab my purse trying not to giggle, which I often do when I'm nervous "Thank you…for everything." My quiet departure captures everyone's attention as I slip between crowded tables of men, who gawk like love crazed teenagers. To label it disturbing is an understatement.

Rowan waves and I push my way onto the snowy sidewalk, smacking right into Nic. He's as still as a statue and dead silent, never a good sign. He watched me in the bar and based on his appearance he's not thrilled. There must be somewhere else to avert my gaze. Oh yes, traffic will do.

"New York winters are proving to be hell's miserable mistress aren't they?" His voice is edgy. He's not even wearing any outer gear.

"Why are you out here dressed as if it's summer?" I wrap my arms around myself for protection.

"You disappeared for a long time. I thought something might have happened to you, but as it stands, you're *just* fine."

"Are you talking about the bartender in there?" I dismiss Nic's obvious accusation. "His name is Rowan, and he's actually a nice guy."

"He sure had you fooled. In fact I'd say he had you wrapped around his little finger." He storms off ahead of me.

We walk toward the penthouse and my mind whirls with mixed emotions. It's never a good idea to talk when I don't know what to say. It always comes out wrong, and when I say that, I mean world-class screw up, wrong. Nic sounds more like a jealous boyfriend than my best friend.

A fluffy white coating drapes the city of New York in winter's shawl, and it's an urban fairytale come to life. Snowflakes drift to the ground from heights far above the skyscrapers and the sight of it is extraordinarily surreal.

I struggle for sentences scrambling around in my mind and choose silence instead. Nic turns and grabs my gloved hand, dragging me back to Claude's, none too happy about it. Onlookers don't even blink an eye at the scene he's causing and New York City is another world altogether.

Chapter Nine—Brotherly Love

The elevator doors swish open, and Nic is still distant and fuming. I've never seen him this angry and I'm not sure what to expect—the silent treatment, a lecture, or decapitation? I did nothing wrong, but he capitalizes on the guilt trip with a vengeance. Nic isn't my boyfriend and I can make new friends if I want.

On the way to our rooms he pins me against the wall, his heart racing near mine. The action happens so fast I have no time to counter the move.

"You put yourself in danger." He growls in my ear, his arms pressed against my shoulders. The physical contact has me both furious and confused. I can't move, speak, or react. Something primal stirs and I hold my breath not knowing whether to kiss him or use self defense.

He refuses to let go until the sound of distant footsteps echoes through the hall. Then Nic releases me, smoothing back my hair, and kissing my forehead. He pats me on the head like a disobedient puppy and I'm flabbergasted.

"Dang it Julia, you make it hard to keep you safe. Don't be foolish enough to wander too far in a city like New York. *Anything* could have happened."

"I, I, okay." My bottom lip stings because I've darn near chewed it raw on the way back. This side of Nic is new and I've never seen it before—not once.

"Lorraine made pasta primavera and garlic toast. Get cleaned up and meet me in the dining room." He stalks off, leaving me midway between the elevator and our rooms. In an absolute daze, I walk to my suite on autopilot and change into slippers.

Chaotic emotions make it impossible to form rational thought. Nic has never acted that way no matter what I did or said. *Guess I shouldn't have wandered out alone.*

"You got that part right. You coming?" He finds my thoughts with little effort.

"Yeah."

Since our arrival in New York, we haven't communicated with telepathy as much as we did at the manor. We're out of our element in the city and haven't yet adjusted to the dramatic changes.

The dining room is a quiet departure from Claude's usual black and white theme. Walls glow in a soft rose hue,

137

accented by horizontal shades of taupe. High backed chairs in a paisley black fabric add elegance to the design. His table reminds me of rosewood and is so glossy I see my reflection on the surface.

An area rug with a geometric pattern pulls the room together and I take special note of the colorful flower arrangement sitting on an antique server. It has peonies, Asiatic lilies and ferns prettily arranged in a rose colored pitcher. The white, stressed wood of the server adds a touch of casual charm to the room.

Nic waits behind a chair, and it takes a second to realize he's holding it out for me. Look up *daft* in the dictionary and you might find my headshot.

"Ever hear of a cloaker?" He sits and meets my gaze from across the table.

"Can't say I have." The pale rose walls lend to a much homier atmosphere and Claude should carry that theme into the penthouse. It takes my attention away from Nic and I'm happy for the distraction. His anger makes me uncomfortable.

"It's a person who feels no empathy and doesn't have a conscience. Mainstream society calls them sociopaths or psychopaths." He grabs a gray, cloth napkin and lays it in his lap. I follow suit, wondering where he's going with this conversation.

"Well, I've researched sociopaths before, but *why* are we talking about this?"

Lorraine places a heaping plate of pasta in front of me, setting the bowl of bread between us on the table.

"That bartender is a cloaker," he explains, trying not to look at Lorraine. His cheeks turn pink every time she enters the room.

A forkful of saucy noodles rests on my plate untouched. "I've never heard of a cloaker and your motivation for inventing your own terminology is transparent. No one here needs your over-protectiveness and if you think I can't take care of myself you're wrong." I shove noodles in my mouth.

"That's just it. You think you can take care of yourself and you can't." He ignores my glare and ferocious chewing. "I'm serious though. I've watched these people for years and can't crack their calculating codes. Even their body language is planned, and if you ask me, they're freaks of nature." When Nic gets excited his eyes change color, and now they're a fierce shade of sapphire.

His expression doesn't waver, so I slurp a few bites of pasta, and grab a garlic roll from beneath the linen covered basket. Our gazes lock across the table in a battle of wills.

"I can't eat and talk, so let's do this old school, shall we?"

He snatches the parmesan, shaking it over his plate until I can't see a speck of sauce or noodles. His parmesan fetish is well known at the manor. Nic alone keeps the industry in business, which makes me laugh and eases tension between us.

"Thought that might make you smile." He takes a sloppy bite, leaving a trail of sauce on his chin; it's the same old Nic no matter where we live. His consistency is comforting even though Claude slammed us with changes from every direction. *"Why don't we eat and talk in your room afterward? Apparently, you need to get a few things off your chest."*

I drag the garlic roll through sauce and shove it in my mouth. *"Sorry for stuffing my face like this but I'm starved."*

"Good grief. Why don't you just tuck the tablecloth under your chin? Oh and stay away from that guy."

"Fine. I don't even know him well enough to care."

We finish the rest of our meal with saucy smiles and continued shakes of the infamous parmesan container.

***

We take a running dive onto Nic's bed and I chuck a pillow at him before he has a chance to tackle me. After a few good whacks, we collapse, out of breath and laughing. I roll onto one elbow and study him for a second.

"Okay theory master, let's talk about life. But first, explain your behavior in the hallway."

"I wanted to knock sense into that fluffy little head of yours." His expression turns serious. "I'm sure you've heard of kidnapping and murder."

"That's it?"

"Yes."

"I was in public... in the middle of the day. Who would have hurt me?"

"Who knows; let's just drop it." His emotional barriers make me want to grab a sledgehammer and crack them wide open. "Nic, you pinned me to a wall, and if I'm not mistaken you were in a rage."

"You misinterpreted my actions *and* my emotional state."

"My perceptions are just fine thank you very much."

"You aren't even close."

Frustrated with our deadlocked conversation, I throw my hands in the air and let them crash to my sides. I don't want to be the drama queen here, but communicating with the opposite sex is exasperating.

"Okay, then. What emotion *did* I sense from you?"

"Fear."

"I was never in danger!"

"This conversation is done." The muscles in his jaws flex.

"The hell it is."

"You just don't get it, do you?" Nic puts his hands behind his head on the pillow.

"Get what? You pull the big brother routine and practically throw me up against a wall. Then you tell me I didn't feel what I felt. Did I miss anything?"

"I'm not your big brother, so stop saying that." Red blotches flush his cheeks in what appear to be agitated brush strokes.

Flustered and confused by his reaction, I snap my mouth shut. In all the years I've known Nic, he's never behaved this way. I'm not sure if it's stress, hormones, or a fear of the unknown causing his erratic behavior. For all I know, it's the elixir.

"Hey, goose, I'm sorry." He reaches for my hand and holds it to his chest. "Let's talk about something else; this conversation is going nowhere fast."

"I'm stressed out of my mind too. Don't act like you have a patent on it." His selfishness is getting old real fast.

"Can we talk about the bartender again? He's not someone you want as a friend."

"Fine, let's talk. You think he's a cloaker."

Nic flinches at my use of the word. I want nothing more than to slip inside his head, but he's already in an uproar so I ditch the idea.

"Julia, come on. Are you telling me there's not a single person you can't read? You're good but nobody's *that* good." He's propped up on an elbow, and the urge to kiss him is irresistible.

"I've never encountered a person I couldn't read... except you. So nope, I *am* that good."

He touches the back of his hand to my cheek, caressing the delicate skin and I turn into his hand, closing my eyes for a second.

"Well, I know one thing. I couldn't get a read on him and I don't trust the guy." He frowns, and adds, "What do you mean you can't read *me*?" His expression switches from tender to stormy. And here I thought I was the one with the mercurial disposition.

"You were standing outside, and I was up close and

personal. It was impossible for you to get an exact read. I've always had a hard time reading your emotions. Does that make *you* a cloaker too?"

"Wait, what? Up close and personal?"

"You know what I mean."

"No, I don't. What happened before I got there?" He sits up, and this conversation is heading south fast.

"Are you *jealous* of the cloaker?"

"What if I am?"

At that moment, something inside me snaps. Maybe it's my frustrating inability with impulse control but I press my lips to his and wait. The whole darn world could come crashing down around us and I wouldn't care.

Nic responds by winding his fingers through my hair, and somehow we lose control together. His other hand anchors the small of my back, and he molds me to his chest, deepening our kiss.

My heart thunders with uncontrolled emotion and without warning, tears leak from the corners of my eyes. Nic senses something wrong and stops. He grasps my face between his hands.

"What's wrong?"

"Nothing. Everything is finally right."

"Don't say anything." His mouth probes mine, eyes

144

open as if gauging my every reaction. Just as quick, he stops and rolls to his stomach. Propped on both elbows he stares at the headboard.

"What are you feeling?" He asks. I sense his emotion this time, raw and tight, like a dam ready to burst.

"You have to ask?" I swipe at the traitorous tears and cough, feeling somewhat idiotic for my inability to maintain control.

Nic slumps to his side and growls, exasperated by my vague response. He rakes a hand through his hair, taking several deep breaths I interpret as frustration.

"What did I do?" His reaction makes no sense. But then again, I can't even interpret my own darn emotions right now.

"It's not what you did. It's what I *want* to do—and can't."

"Oh." And why can't guys speak plain English?

"Not *oh.* You don't *know* what you think you do."

"Then why don't you enlighten me. I can take it." Tears threaten what's left of my thin composure, but I hold it back. *He's too embarrassed to admit he made a mistake.*

"Are you insane? Obviously, you're insane." He tilts my chin so I'm forced to look in his eyes.

"Stay out of my head." It seems I forgot to put my

145

mental guards up because he's quick to respond. He exits as if tiptoeing from a forbidden room and I exhale the pitiful breath I've been holding.

"You're the most beautiful girl in the world."

"Then why do you keep pulling away?" I swallow a sob refusing to show vulnerability.

"I *never* pull away." He chucks a pillow across the room and grunts between gritted teeth.

"Then what's stopping you now?"

"You." He shakes his head, dumbfounded I don't understand what's happening here.

His confusing signals are impossible to interpret and I'm positive I have rivers of black mascara running down my face.

"I have no clue how to make you understand, but you're not ready." He plants his back against the headboard and crosses his arms, refusing to look at me.

"I've been in love with you for fifteen years but *I'm* not ready?" I want to crawl in a hole and flip dirt over myself as the words leave my mouth.

"Wait, you love me?" His eyes glisten, and he chews his lower lip.

I sit on my hands, rocking forward and backward. Now it's out there like a huge, gaping wound—all because of my mouth.

"Look at me, Julia."

"No."

"Please?" His voice cracks.

"Why?"

"Because I want to explain something." His watery eyes make me want to run and hide. "You think you're the only who has to pretend? My God, it eats me alive having to hide my feelings." He crawls in front of me on the bed. "It wasn't so much that Rowan is a cloaker and I couldn't read him. He threatened what I love most."

"Which is?"

"Your love for me."

Something inside me snaps. It's not what I expected him to say, and fury boils to the surface for reasons I can't figure out. The indentation on his bed returns to normal when I hop to the floor, squaring my shoulders for a standoff.

"My love for *you*? It's a threat when someone you have no control over shows me attention?" My heart is beating so hard it makes me dizzy.

"Julia, wait, that's not what I meant." He reaches out and I take two steps back.

"Is that so? Do you realize it's *always* about you?"

147

My vision blurs.

"Wai—"

"Hell no. I'm not listening to your pathetic explanations. Want to know what you are?"

"No, but you'll tell me anyway." His expression tightens, and I want to hit him so hard it knocks him into the fourth dimension.

"You're an emotional cripple. You love it when everyone fawns over you, but did you ever stop to consider that other people have emotions too? That maybe, my heart feels everything you don't even notice?" The thundering in my chest might be anger, shame, or humiliation, but to be honest, I can't tell anymore. Nic jumps up and grabs my shoulders, shaking me until my teeth rattle.

"Bloody hell. You're freaking out as if I murdered your best friend. What did I say that was so wrong?"

"Nothing. We're just different!" I wrench myself from his grip and storm from the room, making the walls shake when I slam his door.

Tears blur my vision and I can't find the doorknob to my room, my shoulders sagging against the door in defeat. Nic wraps his arms around my waist, pulling me close.

"Can't we just talk?" He turns the doorknob, which

148

a moment before I couldn't even see through my blinding tears. Nic leads me to the bed and we face each other as he brushes a stray lock of hair from my eyes.

"I want to *show* you how much I love you." He whispers, gazing at me.

I'm confused and overwhelmed and shake my head. "What?"

"For hours…days…years." His expression is hopeful which confuses me even more. We lay on the bed facing each other, but forever on different pages.

"I love you, but that's not happening. Do you enjoy messing with me?" I'm so exhausted I could collapse.

"It was never my intent to mess with your head." A baffled expression twists his beautiful mouth, and I regret the kiss along with the words that couldn't stay locked away in my head.

"Now you're mad?" I brace for his answer.

"I can't cope with this confusing tug of war. It's darn near impossible knowing what you want."

"I'm sorry." And no one says another word as we roll in opposite directions and face our own walls.

Silence gives way to yawns, and we fall asleep on my bed. Dreams turn into nightmares and I toss and turn until daylight breaks the horizon. How did we go so wrong?

Chapter Ten—Van Buren Industries

Our week without Claude passes with no further incidents and it's different between Nic and me now, but I don't know whether the change is better or worse. After the night of our fight, we friend zoned each other—again.

A commotion at the elevator captures my attention and I recognize Claude's mental signature after scanning everyone's thoughts. I'm sick to my stomach about what transpired in his absence. We're starting our internships at Van Buren Industries, but the week without Claude was a much needed break from reality.

Ironically, I'm to become Van Buren's newest and youngest vice president of product development. I'm in charge of launching a new line of skincare that promises to revolutionize the world.

My pajamas are unsuitable to greet Claude, so I rush back to my room and slip into jeans and a sweater. When I return he's already standing with Nic, the big suck up, and his admirer, Lorraine.

"How was your trip?" I extend my hand, noticing his skin is darker than when he left. His destination must have been tropical but who knows with him.

"Julia, my dear girl." He pulls my hand and brings me in for an unexpected hug. Lorraine is taken aback so hugs must be out of character for her boss.

"Nic, my boy." He pulls Nic into a side hug and gives him a hearty clap on the back. Claude is oddly cheerful, and his normal controlled demeanor is nowhere to be found.

Not that I know anything about these things, but he acts like a man who just dallied with a woman. He asks Lorraine to bring coffee and pastries to his study, and motions for us to follow. Although hesitant, we do as instructed, and my mental guards are on high alert.

We sit in black leather wing-backs, noticing the formality of Claude's study; his color scheme deviates from the rest of the penthouse and is bathed in shades of blue and green hound's-tooth. His level of organization borders on obsessive compulsive because when I take in the details, even his books are in alphabetical order. There's not a single paper out of place or a speck of dust anywhere. I can't shake the eerie feeling of abnormal cleanliness so I'm the first to speak.

"So how was your business trip?"

"It was wonderful, thank you for asking. As you're both aware, you start your internships on Monday." He glances at his answering machine, somewhat distracted by its incessant blinking. Truth be told, it's driving me crazy as well.

"I still have doubts about your expectations and don't know why you want us in such important positions. We have zero experience."

"I expect nothing to make sense my dear, but it will someday, I promise."

He directs his attention toward the window for a moment and I enter Nic's mind to field his thoughts. Either his guard has slipped, or I dove in without detection. I surmise the latter.

I hope to God he never finds out what happened between Julia and me.

"So Nic, did you have a nice relaxing week in the penthouse, or exploring, whichever the case?" Claude has a way of unnerving people with his direct, unblinking gaze. Nic shifts with obvious discomfort.

"I did, Mr. Van Buren, thank you for your hospitality. When can Julia and I look for our own place?" His abrupt response is unusual for Nic.

"Someone is in a rush to branch out." Claude's expression is curious as he steeples his hands beneath his chin. "In fact, I've arranged for showings this week. You'll love what my real estate agent has in mind."

"We must be a burden though." I insist. "You know, having teenagers under foot and all." His reaction is impassive, and he shuffles through paperwork on his desk.

"Nonsense, you're not a bother. But you will fall in love with the penthouse Dita has in mind. In fact, I'd lay millions on it." He swivels in his chair, elated. This new side to Claude is more than just unusual.

"She'll be here tomorrow morning at ten-thirty," he says, stapling an envelope to the front of a paper, "and I hope it's a done deal."

Done deal? Claude doesn't talk like that.

"And we start at Van Buren Industries on Monday? Can we get a tour beforehand?" Either I'm exhilarated or loaded with dread but it's hard to tell at this point. Our futures are unraveling whether we're on board or not.

"Nic, I don't know how to feel."

"I can't tell either."

"Well what good are you then? You're supposed to be my emotion decoder. Let's get out of here."

"You don't have to ask twice."

"Okay, kids, enough business for tonight. See you tomorrow morning." Claude claps his hands to dismiss us and we walk back to our suites in silence.

"Do you mind if we talk later? I'm overwhelmed with everything and need alone time."

"No, I was thinking the same thing. Good night," he says, adding at the last second, "and sweet dreams." Nic kisses my cheek and leaves me in the hallway.

Claude has a way of turning worlds' upside down, but there's no way to predict the future. Sebastian might though. My cell is vibrating on the bed when I get inside my room and it's a familiar number.

"Hello?" I wonder which deviant is at the other end.

"Hey, it's me." Sebastian sounds panicked.

"What's wrong?"

"Nothing's wrong, but you guys haven't called since you left. I just wanted to check up on you." His voice is thick with tension.

"Is everything okay because you sound weird? Are you coming to New York?"

"Lillian said we're flying there in a few weeks."

"How *is* Lillian?" I try making small talk, somewhat disadvantaged because of the distance.

"Fine."

"What about Dutch and Lyra?"

"Dutch misses you something fierce."

"Really? I thought he and Ella had started a torrid love affair before we left." I lie back on my bed and adjust the phone against my ear to get better reception.

"Come on, Julia. Don't act like you don't know."

"Know what?"

"You're the glue. Everything's wrong since you left." There's a chance he's telling the truth, but knowing Sebastian, I doubt it.

"I'm sure Lyra's stoked out of her knickers to have the whole house to herself without me on her case."

"Yeah, about that." He hesitates.

"I knew it, something's wrong. And one question—"

"What?"

"Why didn't you call Nic instead of me?" He waffles at the other end, and I hear muffled voices in the background.

"Who's that? Are you alone, or is someone with you?"

"It was Lincoln, but I got rid of him."

"Sebastian, you need to spit it out. I'm not a mind reader you know." That's an ironic statement if I've ever heard one, but none of us can read from a distance—not yet.

"Lyra has us worried. She's been acting—somewhat insane."

"What do you mean by *insane?* She's always been a nutcase."

"Well, you know Lyra."

"Unfortunately, but what's changed?"

"I don't know; it's weird. She's, *umm*, how to say this…"

"Okay, wait, is she homicidal weird or bitchy weird? Let's narrow this down." I'm getting impatient with him dancing around the issue. Sebastian has no problem with drop-dead honesty under normal circumstances.

"Both. I lock my bedroom door every night and it's not as if anything scares me."

"Shocker. So she's after *you* now that Nic's gone? That's hilarious, and I should be concerned because?" Having a sincere conversation with Sebastian is strange because he's always obnoxious or tormenting me. I'm in uncharted territory where our relationship is concerned.

"It's not funny, Jules. She scares the hell out of me."

"Did you guys—you know?"

"Have sex? Not in this lifetime. Anyway, it's not like you're virtuous or anything." It's as if he's needling me for information because he really doesn't know.

Silence on my end. I can't believe we're having this conversation half a continent away. I'm interrupted by a light rapping.

"Hang on; someone's at the door." I tell him and then call out, "Yeah?" Nic steps inside my room. He's been privy to our not-so-private conversation, so I signal for him to give me a second and return to Sebastian.

"Nic's here. Can we talk tomorrow?"

"No problem." He whispers, "Julia?"

"Yes?"

"I miss you."

"I miss you, too. Talk tomorrow, okay?"

"Night."

"Night." I hang up the phone and wait for Nic's response.

He sits beside me on the bed and I don't have the strength to talk after such a weird conversation with Sebastian. Every imaginable scenario runs through my mind in a whirlwind of crazy, convoluted thoughts.

"I assume you heard everything."

Nic narrows his eyes to slits. "Pretty much."

"What's with the attitude?" I walk to the window because Nic's lukewarm response doesn't cut it. For once, I want him to say what he means and mean what he says—in plain English.

"Why did he call you? I'm his brother." His expression is both confused and hurt, but something deeper flits across his face.

"Well, how the heck should I know? I don't have control over other people's actions."

"I just find it strange is all." His gaze rests just below my chin.

"That makes two of us. Can we go to bed now?" I snap, turning to face him.

"Are you going to call Sebastian back when I leave?"

"Read my mind." Animosity isn't my strong suit but when I'm tired and scared, I can push that stupid thing called love to the background. My sensitivity goes right out the window. He nods and walks out without saying good night.

Well, that's just perfect.

I cry until I fall asleep but billions of stars still twinkle outside my window. Stupid stars.

***

Morning arrives with a shock of blinding sunshine, and an hour later, I find myself in the back of a Cadillac Escalade with Claude, Nic, and Dita Sinclair. His real estate agent has processed blonde hair and several inches of red lipstick caked to her lips.

Her appearance is grotesque in a clownish way, but she seems friendly enough. I peek inside her head and discover her mind is calculating the big fat royalty check she'll make from this sale; no big surprise there. At the tender age of eighteen, I know people well enough to predict their thoughts and motivations. I'm never surprised.

The ride takes less than ten minutes and we pull to the curb of a brick building with giant orb-shaped windows. Upon closer inspection they resemble the inner workings of a clock and I'm at once, fascinated.

"Who is the architect?" I crane my neck upward to inspect the workmanship. There's no way we can afford this. Dita smiles back at me, and there's a dab of red lipstick on her front teeth. I cringe and rub my front teeth until she takes the hint and fixes it.

"Oh thanks, honey. I've been meaning to buy lip stain to avoid this problem. You're a doll, just like Claude said you were." She inspects herself in the mirror one last time.

He shoots us a furtive smile as we open our doors and step onto the sidewalk. Once inside the building, there's a strange sense of déjà vu in the elevator when Dita hits the penthouse button and the tiny box roars to life.

The doors open to an expanse of stone and glass, unique whimsical architecture, and those amazing windows I admired from the street. There are several open levels with an elevator that runs alongside a stone fireplace and cathedral ceilings. The sheer expanse of space is awe-inspiring and every inch a designer's dream.

"It's breath taking. Yes." I meet her gaze but move no further into the penthouse.

"I know, right?" Dita's smile deepens, and she makes her way to the other side of an enormous, open great room. Her heels echo on the hardwood floors, the sound more solid than hollow.

"No, I mean yes…as in we'll take it."

"But I haven't even shown you around yet." Her expression is one of disbelief and she points to the fireplace, bringing my attention to the detail.

"I want to live here. No doubt in my mind. I'll take it."

Nic steps in, prepared to lecture me on impulsivity, and I hold my hand up to stop him.

161

"Sometimes you just know."

"But you haven't even seen everything yet. How can you possibly know?"

"We're talking about me, here."

"Right. I forget how you are."

"I think the lady has her mind set on this one, and I'm in agreement, but let's look around to make it worth your time." Nic gestures to the gaudy real estate agent. She claps her hands, and dollar signs line up in her eyes like a casino slot machine.

Claude and Dita walk with us through an open space filled with windows, light, arches and angles along with the richness of deep stained woods. The window clocks are remarkable and we gaze at the complexity, which must have arisen from an artist's dream.

"Are they clocks?" I study what appear to be the internal mechanisms of a timepiece; the hands, roman numerals, and other mechanisms indicative of a clock.

Dita busies herself with a calculator, adding up her commission, but peers up through mascara caked lashes to respond. "Yes, you're looking at the internal mechanisms of a clock, but the structures are more open, allowing light to pass. Aren't they spectacular?"

"That's the understatement of the century. Claude,

do Nic and I have enough money for this? It looks well beyond our price range. I imagine all six of our housing allowances wouldn't cover it." When the words leave my mouth, a light bulb goes off in my head. "How many bedrooms does this penthouse have?" I narrow my eyes.

Dita looks to Claude, and then my direction to answer. "There are six bedrooms. Two are en suites, and you have an additional four bedrooms that share Jack and Jill bathrooms."

We walked right into this one, and the pipe dream, which doesn't include Lyra or Lincoln as housemates, crashes around my ankles.

"No. No way. I'm not living with them again. I'd rather gouge my eyes out with a screwdriver. Okay, that was harsh, but you know what I mean." Remnants of last night's conversation with Sebastian rattle around my head with the dust bunnies. I'll walk away from everything—the manor, Claude's money, and the internship.

"Hold up, Julia. No one has ulterior motives on this end. Lincoln and Lyra have their own money. And to be honest, I don't believe you're their cup of tea, either." Claude is quick to reassure.

"Dita, we'll take it. Can we go back now?" I walk to the elevator, my movements rigid, and everyone has the

163

good sense to follow for once.

On the drive back to Claude's, weariness takes a toll. I take a mental break from reality, knowing I'll wake up any moment now. It's all a dream.

"You okay in there, Jules?"

"What? Yeah, I'm fine. What happened?"

"Nothing, you fell asleep in three seconds flat on the way home."

I wipe my bleary eyes and take in the surroundings as Dita pulls into the parking garage of Claude's penthouse.

"Are you ready for lunch? I'm famished." Once again, my benefactor's cheerful voice has me puzzled by his mercurial nature.

***

I re-dial the last number in my cell and wait for a familiar voice on the other end.

"Thank God. What took you so long?" Sebastian sounds desperate.

"I told you I'd call back. What's got you so upset?" I can't imagine anything drastic happened in less than twenty-four hours.

"I had a weird dream."

Sebastian used to dream of me by raspberry bushes long before Lillian and I planted them in the backyard. We

164

didn't connect the dots concerning his ability until years later.

"Go on." It's best not to lead him.

"There was a wolf attack. I pulled out an arrow and shot him just as he landed on the back of a deer. The whole thing happened in slow motion."

"Then what happened?"

"I saved the deer's life. It stared at me for a second, as if to say thank you, and ran off into the woods."

"Am I in danger?" Something in the way he recants the dream makes me think archetypes are involved.

"I think you were the deer. That was my impression, and you always ask how I felt afterward."

"Are you positive I'm the deer in your dream?"

"Yes. That was my impression. The wolf archetype could be several things so be careful."

"It's okay; I'll keep my eyes open. You realize I always *know*, right?"

"Yeah, you're good that way." His voice is sullen and hesitant, and it's obvious he's trying to prolong the conversation.

"There's no need to worry because we've never been able to prevent anything from happening," I remind him. "We can't prove they're premonitions and there's no scientific proof that precognition even exists."

"You can believe what you want but I trust my instincts."

"I know you do Sebastian and thank you. When are you coming to New York?" I hope a shift in topic will lighten his somber mood.

"We're coming in four weeks. Lillian told us this morning. So you and Nic start at Van Buren Industries on Monday, huh?"

"That's the plan. I already know too much so I'm not looking forward to it."

"Care to share? Sharing is caring, you know."

"I can't, Sebastian. I wish I could, but I can't."

"Thanks for calling with the low down. Tell Nic I said hey." His mood turns sour when I don't reciprocate the flirtation.

"You should call him yourself, but I will see you soon." We both hang up and I'm left wondering why he called *me* and not his brother.

The rest of the weekend is uneventful except for planning the ultimate outfit for my first day on the job. I'll knock everyone off their chairs with a cream-colored skirt, tailored mango jacket, and a matching necklace that hangs in the shape of teardrops. I wonder what Nic is doing and locate his mind.

"You in bed yet?" I stare out my window and count the endless stars.

"No, just lying here."

"Nervous?"

"I'm nervous as hell, but mostly excited." A complex mix of his emotions washes over me and I sense fear, excitement, anticipation, and insecurity all at once. That's a first. His emotions are always on lock down.

"I suppose you've picked out a killer outfit for tomorrow." He mocks.

"Of course, I'm a girl."

"Yes you are."

"Will you sleep with me tonight?" I walked right into that one.

"Not in this lifetime. No way. Nope. Not gonna do it."

"You know what I mean so quit being a dork. I'm in my pajamas so come over." He slips into my room and I choke because he's wearing footed Spiderman pajamas. We can now assume Claude has a twisted sense of humor. Good lord, at least they fit. I throw my comforter back and pat the mattress. It doesn't take long before we're both sleeping.

The annoying buzz of an alarm clock rattles me awake, and I focus on the glaring neon numbers that read six a. m. This party is now starting at Van Buren Industries for one Julia Malone, and one Nicholas Maye.

Chapter Eleven—First Day

The front of Van Buren Industries is unique among the skyscrapers I've seen in New York City. A black, glass tower shoots upward into the sky for hundreds of feet and there's no end in sight. The bottom third of the building is wide and takes up the entire block. A graduated second level is narrower and continues upward. It's the last level that takes my breath away. The glass appears made of gold and sun ricochets off an almost seamless surface and disappears into the sky. A black and gold sign reading Van Buren Industries clearly marks the building.

"It's so elegant," I breathe more to myself than anyone else.

"Come along." Claude instructs as Leopold opens the door.

We step onto the street single file and are quickly gobbled up in pedestrian traffic. After weaving our way to the front of the building, a footman holds the door. Claude stops at security, nodding at the familiar officer and continues walking. On the fourth level, Claude introduces us to his personal assistant and I hate her on the spot.

"Julia, Nic, I'd like you to meet Catherine Saunders, my executive assistant." He steps back and an elegant blonde extends her hand. Her gaze lingers on Nic as if sizing up her next meal.

"Nic, I can't stand her."

"You're being judgmental, she seems nice."

"No. She isn't. She's a bitch."

"Give her a chance."

"Oh, hell no—not happening."

"Catherine will oversee your training until you know the company well enough to branch out on your own. If you have questions, she can handle them." He looks at her as though a pet, but nothing more—an object of devotion.

When Claude leaves, Catherine rewards us with a winning smile. "Are you ready to see your offices? I had full design leeway so I hope you appreciate my vision for each of you." Her satisfied tone burns me and I don't even know why—yet.

"We sure are. Let's get to it." Nic's enthusiasm further adds to my nausea because he's blinded by her mile high legs and exaggerated curves.

Much to my dismay, she doesn't hide her natural

endowments, but flaunts them to the best of her ability. Catherine takes the lead and we fall in line like minions, passing glass-encased cubicles by the dozens on our way to the unknown. We reach Nic's office first, as shown by the gold plate on the wall that reads, *Nicholas Maye*.

She opens the door with a grand gesture to allow entrance, and I have to admit, the sheer opulence is awe-inspiring. The entire back wall affords Nic a spectacular view of New York City's skyline with floor to ceiling windows.

The furnishings are deep cherry and black leather, and she paired the décor with early 1920's art. Scantily clad women with long cigars dangling from pouty mouths add an aura of absurdity to the office.

Nic is enthralled, but I find her taste disturbing for a young man breaking into the business world. Something isn't wound tight in Catherine's head, and I take this opportunity to enter her mind and see if there's intelligent life rattling around in there.

I think he likes it. Good job, Catherine, you never fail to impress. He's a sexy little thing, but his bitchy sidekick needs to go.

My mental departure is abrupt, and she grabs the sides of her head in pain. My housemates describe it as an

171

ice pick to the skull. I shouldn't have left her head that fast but her thoughts pissed me off. The pain passes and I give her a few seconds to recover while Nic shoots me a knowing glare.

"You okay, Catherine?" My words are laced with false concern.

"Yeah, that was the weirdest thing. I never get headaches. I'm fine. Let's keep moving."

We follow her from Nic's office past a long stretch of hallway and I'm impressed by the choice of royal blue carpet in the building. Catherine leads us around a corner and opens the door to my office and is met by silence.

A mismatch of hideous hues threatens to overtake my senses so I close my eyes for a moment and refocus. I enjoy color, but not obvious decorating nightmares of bright red and green, mustard, and fuchsia. Catherine even had the audacity to top the ensemble with a lime green border and garage sale art. She had malicious intent, and it's an embarrassing eyesore. There isn't a single window, and it's no bigger than a storage closet.

"Who picked out our offices?" I blink and refocus again while her brazen response confirms it.

"Claude gave me authority for the designs. Isn't it fabulous?" She appraises Nic, her stare moving up and down his body.

"Fabulous isn't exactly a word I'd use to describe this office." I bite the inside of my cheek to avoid cussing. Catherine acts offended, and to my absolute horror it garners Nic's sympathy.

"I'm sure Ms. Saunders put thought into our offices. We should be more grateful for the trouble she must have gone through." His rebuttal is ridiculous. Is the fool blind? It looks as if she vomited in here.

I bite my tongue because they both have it coming, but I'm accustomed to catty and conniving women. I've lived with one for fifteen years, and their antics are as transparent as glass.

"It's nothing major, Catherine. I'll just tone it down a bit, but the actual space is fine. Thank you." Diplomacy in light of obvious passive aggression taxes my last nerve and I want nothing more than to punch Nic for taking her side.

"Glad you love it." Her snippy tone drips insincerity but Nic doesn't notice since he's focused on her legs.

"Do you mind if I get settled in, read, and get an idea what's expected of me?" My doe eyes meet her snake orbs.

"Not...at...all. I'll show Nic the ropes while you

get acclimated. I'll come back later, Patricia."

"Julia."

"Julia…right. I'll be back around lunchtime and we can discuss questions you might have. Are you ready, Nic?" He follows as if in a trance and I'm stunned.

"Really, Nic?"

"She's nice, I like her."

"I hate her guts."

"You're being dramatic and acting ridiculous."

Barracuda lady leads Nic from my office, and I fume. A thick blue binder rests on my desk and I cram my body into a tight corner, exasperated. I collapse into a stiff and uncomfortable executive chair, wincing at the absolute garishness of the walls. Catherine came in here and puked up a color wheel straight from Hell.

There are five hundred and seventy-five pages of directives, and my eyes cross. It will be a long existence here at Van Buren Industries.

"Julia?" I'm staggered when I recognize the familiar face grinning at me.

"Rowan?" His black business suit is a sharp contrast to the laid back bartender I met last week.

"What are you doing here?" My smile must be enormous, but the memory of Nic's severe disliking of him cools my enthusiasm.

"Yeah, crazy isn't it? They hired me right after I met you." His gaze drifts to the hideous walls and he shakes off a confused expression.

"What made you think to apply at Van Buren Industries?"

"I saw an ad in the paper looking for entry level ad executives. When I called and asked for details, that lady—" He taps his forehead, trying to remember the name. "Catherine Saunders. Yeah, Catherine told me the training is in-house, and doesn't require previous experience." Rowan smiles, but it's forced. He's dying to ask me what the hell is wrong with my office.

"You've been here a week?" I notice the contrast between his suit and Claude's. There's a distinct difference between real money and the pretense of it.

"Yep as of today." He glances at the walls again.

"Well, come in and sit." I gesture to a drab, worn chair next to my pressed wood desk. I'm thinking the whole ensemble came from a back alley dumpster.

"Nice, um—is this considered an office?" We burst out laughing and I find myself at ease, regardless of Nic's warning.

"That would be barracuda lady, but her real name is

175

Catherine. You know, the lady who hired you?" I can't hide a crooked smirk.

"Yeah, she's something. Ten miles of legs and a body that refuses to—"

"Got it. Yep, I got it." My impatient interruption has Rowan scrambling to recover.

"Those types of women?" He throws a hand in the air. "Empty shells, no effect on me." Rowan raises a brow to see if I'm buying it. I'm not, but the gesture is sweet. "You don't believe me?"

"Oh, *hell* no. Give me credit for owning a brain cell."

"Well, then. I'll just have to prove it. Lunch?"

"I wish I could, but barracu—*Catherine* has plans for us. She's showing Nic the ropes while I rot in this color spew. Nice, huh?" I scan the walls in disbelief and envision myself as an intelligent version of Cinderella.

Rowan's grin disarms me and I hope my swooning isn't noticeable because the memory of his thick corded arms, sculpted chest, and sleeve tattoo makes me blush.

"I have to get back to my glass cubicle and make it appear as if I'm learning something, but you're in my sights, Miss Julia Malone. Tomorrow might work better for lunch then." He winks and excuses himself, waving on the way out.

"Well, that was an unexpected surprise."

"What was an unexpected surprise?" Nic asks,
cutting into my thoughts.

*"Not meant for you, so butt out. How's it going with
what's-her-name?"*

"She's great and I wish you'd give her a chance."

*"Yeah. Not happening. Unlike you, I can connect
neurons when it comes to the female gender. Come get me
at lunchtime. I have a load of reading to tackle."*

"Sure thing, boss."

Someone else shows him a slight bit of interest and
he's off and running with the other testosterone junkies—it
figures. It's a true love fairy tale written in the stars. Wake
up, Snow White, men are all the same.

My attention diverts back to the binder and I choose
the chemical and technical sections that explain the active
component of *Immortality*. I better settle in for the long
haul because all this information isn't going anywhere but
in my head—Lord help me.

* * *

The alarm rattles me out of my skin and I can't
believe it's our second day on the job. After lunch with Nic
and *legs-a-hoy* yesterday, I spent the rest of the afternoon

reading, and taking special note of my job duties before and after the launch of *Immortality*. I never saw Rowan again.

After a rushed breakfast of toast and cheese, we meet Leopold in the parking garage ready to take on the business world like the hot little novices we are.

"How'd you sleep last night?" Nic starts in on the small talk and I cross my arms. He doesn't know what an absolute wanker he is.

"Just fine. And you?" I'm curt and he seems confused.

He never bothered putting his guards up last night, so I heard every last uninhibited fantasy he had about one long-legged, Ms. Catherine Saunders. I'm not sure if it's possible, but I fell out of love with him while watching every lurid scene unfold in his head. I thought Nic was my forever, but that dream went up in smoke.

"Is something wrong?"

"Not a thing. Why do you ask?" The muscles in my jaw tighten.

"I don't know. You're offish this morning." He settles back into the plush leather of the limo.

"It'll pass. We're just getting used to everything at Van Buren. Did Claude say when we can move into our own place?" I refuse to look at him and stare out the window. The buildings are as gray and colorless as my mood.

"As a matter of fact he said we could move in this week. Dita is furnishing it with pictures I sent of your decorating style. No one knows you better than me. I've got a PhD on the infamous goose, otherwise known as Julia Malone."

"You might want to get your money back. The goose species rendered your hot-shot degree null and void." I glance at him from the corner of my eye.

He grins as if I'm kidding, so I dish out my stoniest expression. It's one that comes with an invisible ice pick in my hand. There's a fine line between love and hate, and he's teetering on the edge.

"Wow, you need to lighten up." He gathers me in a side hug and rests his chin on my head. I'm rigid and unmoved by his affections. His Catherine fantasies were disgusting. They went well beyond sex education, thank you very much, but *drop dead soon*. The one time I wish he was reading my mind, he doesn't bother. Figures.

The rest of our ride to Van Buren Industries is nothing more than silent moments of continuous awkwardness, so I keep my mental guards in place. My thoughts aren't particularly nice this morning and he'd be

179

shocked. Once we're inside Van Buren, I greet the guard and walk toward my office without looking back at Nic. There's a gentle tug at the edge of my mind.

"Have a good day, goose. I lo—"

"You too." My terse response cuts him off, and his unfinished thought aches in my heart. I'm not going there again. Friends it is then.

Rowan follows from his cubicle and surprises me on the way back to that monstrosity Catherine calls my new office.

"Well, good morning, gorgeous. Is *this* a better day yet?" His attire hugs him in all the right places and I imagine the tattoo under his pale lavender dress shirt. Normally, I don't give such things much thought, but today? Yeah, I'm going there.

"Not at all, but it's nice seeing you." I fake a smile. It would be nice to see him if not for my current state of mind.

"Hold up, not so fast." He blocks my office by spreading his arm across the doorframe. I'm on the verge of tears.

"It's not a good time. I'm sorry, maybe another—"

He swings open my office door and I'm taken off guard by re-painted walls in normal beige along with tasteful pieces of art. I burst into tears.

"You hate it? Oh wow, I'm so sorry. I just figured after yesterday that—" I put my hand up to stop his needless apologies and the tears fall harder.

"No, it's perfect. In fact, it's the single nicest thing anyone has ever done for me." Then, I fall apart in his arms, trying to shield my face. He backs us farther into my office and closes the door, hugging me close. Before I wipe my tears and apologize, the door flies open. Nic stands there looking as though flames were rolling off his back.

"What the hell is going on here?" His glare locks with Rowan's in a battle for alpha position.

"Nothing, dude. Who are you to barge in like a raging bull on steroids?" He doesn't back down to Nic's intimidation, and I admire his courage.

"In case you missed it, I'm Julia's boyfriend. That's who I am. Get the hell out before I rearrange your face." Nic's smaller than Rowan, but you'd never know it by the fierceness of his stance. He's a formidable opponent but a ridiculous looking one and I step in to de-escalate the fight.

"First off, you aren't my boyfriend." I'm in his face. "Second, I'm crying because Rowan did something downright nice. Look around, Einstein—not that you'd notice anything but Catherine's feminine assets." I turn my

181

back on them both, staring at a piece of artwork behind my desk, thinking how perfect it suits me.

When I return my attention to the boys, Nic's face burns a deep shade of pink and Rowan is satisfied I set him straight.

"We'll talk later. As for you," he warns, poking a finger at Rowan's chest, "Watch yourself." Nic sneers. Then he storms from my office in a dramatic huff worthy of accolades.

"Listen, I'm sorry about that. He's not my boyfriend, but we grew up together and he's over protective where I'm concerned. Nic's harmless, so please don't hold it against him." *Wow, am I defending that wanker right now?*

"No explanation necessary. I have a sister, so I get it. I'm glad you're happy with the new office though. What Catherine did was rotten, and she's well known around the water cooler as a real piece of work." He thrusts both hands in his pockets, and then winks.

"What you did was kind and thoughtful. Thank you." I hug him and he leaves me to my new space. The door clicks shut and my sigh of relief rushes out with pent-up frustration.

"Is the creep gone?" Nic's voice disrupts my train

of thought.

"Don't talk to me you bloody wanker. Sod off."

"I heard you crying and didn't know what was wrong. I still don't like that guy anywhere near you. What's he doing here?"

"He works here. I can't have friends of the opposite sex, but for you, it's a different story?"

"You're being ridiculous. I'm not even attracted to Catherine, just grateful for her help."

"Please. Your fantasies were pretty darn clear. Tell it to someone who believes you," I snap, and add, *"You were stupid enough to let your guards down last night."*

"We need to talk. I'm coming to your office."

"Don't even think about it."

"You're being unreasonable, Jules."

"I'm a girl. Get used to it." And with that, I shut him out with the drop of my mental guillotine.

Chapter Twelve—The Trouble with Nic

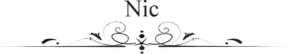

He doesn't understand why I can't see through Rowan's so called facade. 'You read everyone else like a hawk, but not the bartender? He's a total blind spot, and I'll prove it.' Nic had blasted me. *Hogwash.*

Guys make no sense with their deep, confusing, buried emotions. Then wham, they hit you with an emotional geyser. It's as if they save up every perceived violation until it shoots out in a steaming pile of cow manure.

Nic strides toward Rowan's cubicle, and I follow, sneaking up on them inch by inch until I hear both sides of the conversation, hiding behind a divider.

"Well, well, well. It's the infamous Nicholas Maye staking his claim on the fair maiden. Save it, buddy." Rowan turns in his chair and I have to admit, the guy has brass.

"I'm not your buddy, so stay the hell away from

her. I see what you are."

"You see what I am?" Rowan's disdain is clear by the tone of his voice.

"You're a sociopath. No conscience or empathy, and you use people to get what you want." Nic leans up against his cubicle, his body language menacing.

"You believe in God, Rowan?"

"Nope, not a lick of it."

"I see." Nic clenches his fists and I should intervene but stay put.

"Only sheep believe in God."

"You'd be correct. Wolves don't answer to anyone but themselves."

"Listen douche bag if I wanted to debate religion I know where your shiny gold nameplate is located. Trust me; I'll knock on your door if that day ever comes. If you'll excuse me I'm getting paid to do a job here, rich boy." Rowan's response drips with acid.

"I wish Julia could see what a creep you are, but as it stands, you've got her pretty snowed."

"Hey; I've got a brilliant idea. You do you. And Julia can do Julia. Last time I checked the two of you were nothing but friends."

"We'll see about that, freak." Nic takes a step

forward and rethinks starting a physical fight so he stands down.

"You should move up in the world, Nic. Take Catherine for example—sizzling. She'd rock your world." Rowan laughs and slaps a hand on his thigh.

"I'll take that under advisement, and thanks for the inappropriate tip. Now here's one for you. Find another target." He taps the glass of Rowan's cubicle and I duck as he marches back to his office with angry strides. I'm stunned by what Rowan said to him about Catherine.

"Hey Julia, you there?" Nic's telepathic inquiry has me racing back to my office from the other direction so Rowan doesn't catch me.

"Barely." I huff, out of breath and close my office door.

"How's it going in product development, learning much?" I can still hear the anger in his voice but it's controlled.

"No. You finished with me now? I'm buried under mountains of paperwork." I don't even try keeping the edge from my voice.

"Yeah, I'm done, so see you after work. And stay away from the creep."

"That creep redecorated my whole office on his

186

own time. Not much of a creep by Webster's definition is he?" Their discussion on God and Catherine didn't impress me. Those two shouldn't even be in the same sentence much less a full length conversation.

"Don't be fooled. He's not who you think he is."

"Is that so? You wouldn't have surprised me. In fact, you thought I should have kissed Catherine's butt for this hole of an office. Did you do a comparison, or did that slide right by you? This little chat is done."

"If he puts your name in lights would that do it for you? Apparently, love means nothing."

"Words mean nothing but actions say it all. Then again, some thoughts scream loud and clear in the middle of the night. Who's to say, Nic?"

A rap at the door disrupts our telepathic argument, and I glance up and see Catherine's counterfeit smile. I'm not sure why Nic likes her so much, but she's nothing but a nightmare if you ask me.

"I see you're acclimating to your new office. Do you understand your role in product development?" She points to the blue binder on the corner of my desk.

"I've been studying. It's complex. Can I ask you something?"

"You can ask whatever you wish." She runs slender

187

fingers through her long blonde hair and then places her hand on her hip.

"Well, it's two things. My office is underwhelming compared to Nic's." I take a breath and add. "Are you dating Rowan?" My hand tightens on the arm of my chair and I'm not backing down.

"No. I'm not dating Rowan, he's all yours. You'll be working with him on projects. Anyway, your office is fine for research and development. You need a quiet space while Nic needs an elaborate office to entertain potential clients." She readjusts the hand on her hip, annoyed by my line of questioning.

"It's claustrophobic in here and I don't think Claude had this in mind."

"I'm afraid it's all we have." She sneers, leaning in to see what's on my computer screen.

Nic knocks and Catherine snaps back to a standing position, moving to the other side of my desk.

"Can I help you?" I'm disgusted how his gaze rakes her body and he doesn't even try to hide it.

"Ooh Nic, we should grab lunch together." She squeals, grabbing his arm and turning her back as if I no longer existed. Catherine moves close to Nic who seems mesmerized. *Do offices come equipped with vomit bags?*

"I need to get back to work. Claude wants a full report when we get home, so not to be abrupt but—"

"Don't say another word. We can have lunch whenever you want." She runs a manicured hand along her hip, tilting her head in a seductive manner.

"I can't, but another time?" Nic glances at me, his expression mortified.

"We have nothing *but* time. No worries." She walks out with a sexy sashay and adds, "See you later, Janelle."

"You were saying?" I mouth to Nic and roll my eyes.

"Hey Jules, I... uh. Never mind." He walks out without finishing.

I'd slap my own forehead, but the effort would be wasted. I'll never understand that guy and reach for my binder, settling in to read. A moment later, I catch movement from the corner of my eye.

"Claude, I didn't see you in the shadows. Please come in."

"Lost in thought?" He moves in to sit.

"Something like that. Not that it does me any good."

"Do you need help?"

"If you can help me understand guys, I'd be forever

189

in your debt."

"Is the yin/yang equation giving you trouble?"

"Precisely! You crazy *yangs* are exasperating. Any advice?"

"Sorry, each relationship is a snowflake. You'll figure it out with time." His hand fists under his chin as he watches my reaction. "Catherine. She's nice is she not?"

"Well…she puts the '*ow*' in *kapow* if that's what you're asking. To be honest, I can't stand her and I hate this office."

"The office is a temporary roadblock. Yours will take some extra doing as far as design and we're not quite ready" An amused expression breaks through his serious facade. "Listen, I have wonderful news; are you ready?" Claude claps his hands together and I startle. I hate when he does that. He's like a bloody defibrillator.

I swivel and face Claude, hoping it's news I want to hear. His cheer is contradictory, almost as if I'm looking at another man altogether. I can't get over his weirdness, but shake my head, waiting for the news.

"Dita put the finishing touches on your penthouse. You can move in tonight." He rocks back and forth on his heels in a childlike gesture. "At any rate, I'll leave you to study product development—or men, whichever you prefer."

"That's the best news I've heard all day." I notice his teeth are so white it's abnormal.

"Leopold will take you to the penthouse at five. I'm leaving town this afternoon, but I had the florist deliver a nice surprise." He studies me for a moment, stands, and then leaves. Does anyone believe in the old-fashioned concept of common courtesy anymore?

"Bye!" I yell after him, dumbfounded as usual.

***

Nic attempts contact several times throughout the day, but I'm silent and have Rowan with me every chance I get. It's hard to blame me after watching Catherine drape herself over Nic like a fur pelt. I stumble across something phenomenal and end our silent war.

"Get your butt to my office. You need to see this."

"Thought you weren't talking to me." He pouts.

"No time for your little boy games. This is important."

"Be there in a second. Little boy games?"

"Never mind."

Nic rushes through my door a minute later.

"What do you have?" He's out of breath and closes the door, trying to enter my mind.

191

"Really, Julia, you're blocking me now?"

"My thoughts don't concern you."

"Okay, fine, I understand you're mad. What do you want to show me?"

I rifle through the binder and find the page in question. He slides into the chair by my desk and I turn it around for him to read.

"There, page two hundred and seventy-eight. What's your gut say?" I place my finger where I want him to read and he does.

[Substance X enhances inborn psychological traits that may have otherwise remained latent. For instance, subject 10 (Rowan) showed instability with the introduction of Substance X. In a blind study, the ingestion occurred in an alcohol-based beverage. Recruit Saunders studied the subject for eight weeks to determine how fast the changes manifested. At week twenty, he stabilized.]

"Red alert. Someone misfiled *that* paper." Nic's raises a brow.

"What's your educated guess?"

"I'm not that educated." His smart assery gets him nowhere.

"You have *that* right." I snap.

"So I'm right about Rowan? Is this an apology?" He glances to the art deco on my walls. I'm sure he wonders where Rowan got the money to pay for it.

"If it's the same guy, you have your apology."

We're silent as we ponder the ramifications of the paper.

"Not to downplay our discovery, but Leopold's coming at five. Dita finished the penthouse this afternoon." My announcement gets his attention, but in a negative way.

"She picked out our bloody furniture?" His mouth pulls down at the sides.

"It's one less thing to do. We can change whatever we hate, but at least it's a start. Claude said he had a surprise delivered."

"Let me grab my things and I'll meet you out front. I have to take care of something first." His blank expression gives nothing away.

I didn't think I'd miss being in a guy's head so much, what with their confusing and contradictory thoughts, but I do—so much it hurts.

***

Leopold pulls in front of our brand new penthouse and I'm eager to see what she's done with the place. I hope it's not God awful, but something tells me it's not.

"Okay, we're here. You ready, Nic?"

He stares out the window, sullen and lost in his own world. I'm positive his rude behavior is because I blocked him from my thoughts, but if he had any decency, he'd block me from his. Hearing someone I love fantasize about someone else is the last thing on earth I ever wanted to experience. The memory haunts me, making me sick to my stomach as I try to push it from my mind. I step from the limo and wait for him to follow.

"Yeah, I guess so." His voice is hollow, and he doesn't move. "You know what; I'm going back to Claude's. You need a break from me." If slumped shoulders are a sign of defeat, he hangs his head between his knees to prove it. Nic's never unhappy. My instinct is to end our cold war and start again. Instead, my pangs of empathy go unanswered.

"Okay. It's obvious you need time alone. I'm a phone call away." Before I shut the door, Leopold calls my name and rolls down his passenger window.

"Miss Julia, your keys and the elevator code."

"Oh, good lord, where did I stash my brain this morning?" I lean in and take the packet from his hand, offering him a crooked smile. "Take good care of him." I gesture to the limp body in the back seat and he nods.

This week turned into a knowledge seeker's worst nightmare and I could have done without stumbling onto a few things. Is ignorance bliss? I open the double glass doors and walk to the elevator. It feels as if I'm doing everything in slow motion, or I've done this before and can't get the strange sense of familiarity out of my head.

"Nic, are you there?"

"Depends on what you mean."

"I didn't think you could hear me. Something feels weird. It might be because you're not here with me."

"You don't need my dark and disturbing thoughts messing up the surprise. It should be the best day of your life."

"What do you mean by dark and disturbing thoughts? What's going on?"

"You don't want to know."

"I don't?"

After letting myself in the front doors, I walk to the elevator and punch in the code. The trip up is exhilarating and I hold my breath. When the doors open, I sense my

195

shock register in Nic's head.

"Julia, what's wrong?"

My mind goes blank.

"Hey there, gorgeous, it's good to see you." Rowan is standing in our insanely appointed penthouse holding dozens of multi-colored roses. His smile alone could light the city of Manhattan, and my jaw moves to form words, but nothing comes out. The elevator doors close, leaving me trapped and stupefied.

"What's happening? Do I need to get back there?"

"Yes. Get back here right now. You didn't see this coming?" At least telepathy still works.

"I take it you're surprised?" Rowan lifts a brow. I recall with increasing discomfort the words from the misplaced report.

"You just took me off guard." I shrug as if unconcerned. "How did you get in here?"

His predatory gaze follows me as I set my purse and keys on a table near the elevator.

"Claude arranged it. Surprised?"

"Very. I didn't realize you talk to Claude. He's not into the human resources aspect of the business."

"Since we're working together on the *Immortality* project, he figured we should get acquainted with one another. Claude sent the bouquet. I'm just the delivery boy." His words ring false.

"You realize Nic lives with me, right?" I look past him at the lush decor, wishing he'd disappear.

"Claude figured he'd change his mind. He was right, huh?" He shifts the flowers in his arm. "Nic and I don't get along, but you already knew that." Rowan gestures to the roses. "You have a vase for these?"

I'm at a loss because I haven't even seen the furnished penthouse yet.

"I guess...well, I'm not sure."

We scout for something resembling a vase. Despite Rowan's awkward presence, I'm in awe of my new home. Dita worships her wallet, but she spared no expense in decorating. Everything is formal and gorgeous. Then I spot a crystal vase in the kitchen and point to the flowers in his hand.

Rowan relinquishes the roses, and my hand brushes his. From the entryway, I hear Nic's voice through the intercom and jog out front to buzz him to our floor.

Rowan is on my heels and I turn with an uncomfortable smile. I've never been good at deception.

"Nic's on his way. He changed his mind." I glance around the penthouse, noticing every detail.

"That's my cue to leave then. At least I helped you christen your new pad." He winks and my eyes narrow at the suggestion. Nic rushes in, and Rowan slips past him, waving goodbye as the doors slide shut.

"Few things in life floor me, but this?" His face is blood red, with vessels ready to burst.

"How did Rowan know you wouldn't be here?" I ask Nic.

"Claude mentioned a surprise and judging by the size of that flower arrangement—" His eyes are unblinking. "He accosted the delivery boy?"

"Yep, that's what he did. Claude doesn't mingle with the natives at Van Buren."

I lean into Nic and he encircles my waist. In spite of everything, we still make sense in this crazy world.

Chapter Thirteen—Just a Dream

Nic and I fall asleep in each other's arms, and brilliant yellow sunlight rips me from the grasp of hazy dreams. Light passing through the clockwork windows is blinding and I have nothing but foggy memories of his lips on mine.

"Hey, sleeping beauty, wake up; we have work in an hour."

The back of his hand brushes my cheek and I rouse to full consciousness with a contented smile.

"About last night," he whispers, "I'm not sorry for it."

"I'd be devastated if you were." I have no idea what he's talking about and move to a sitting position. The covers snake around my legs, and I work to untangle myself.

His shoulders shake and it's because he's laughing. I must look a bloody wreck and run fingers through my tangled hair, holding up a hand to block the sunlight.

"Holy hell, it's burning my retinas."

"We christened the place last night." He inspects his

fingernails and my stomach twitches.

"I'm afraid to ask. We didn't—" The breath catches in my throat. "I mean you and me?"

"Relax. We had too much wine, and I hope it wouldn't be *that* forgettable. Last night you were," he pauses and smiles, "amazing."

"*Amazing?* What do you mean?" It bothers me I can't remember last night, having had too much wine. Flashes of memory pop here and there, but nothing I can piece together for a coherent picture.

"It means you finally let your hair down." He hands me an unfamiliar robe and I snatch it from his hand since I'm suspiciously underdressed in a t-shirt and panties. He even has the decency to blush.

"It's obvious I said too much last night." I tie the robe and smooth my hair back.

"Your soul absolutely takes my breath away. It felt good discovering everything you hide from me."

"What makes you think I hide things from you?" The suggestion makes me mad since I'm the open book in this relationship.

"Last night we danced." His implication is veiled, but he leaves the room so I shout after him.

"Put your dance shoes away buddy because I'm

jumping in the shower—shouldn't take long."

An hour later I meet him by the elevator. Wine bottles and candles are strewn everywhere. It's an absolute disaster area. There are Doritos, and Sun Chip bags crumpled on the floor with trails of chips near the couch.

"What did we do last night?" I squint, imagining the horrors of every possible indiscretion.

"Nothing *wrong* if that's what you think. It was awesome. I wouldn't trade a second of it for all the money in the world." He covers his mouth, but he's grinning through parted fingers. "Your sense of humor knows no limits."

"That statement makes me think I dangled from the chandelier naked." I insert my key into the elevator and we step through the doors. "We need to get you a key."

"If I stick tight with you I don't need a key, now do I?"

"Is that how it goes?" The elevator opens at the bottom, and as sure as summer leads to autumn, there sits Leopold waiting by the curb.

I don't say much on the short ride to the office, or once we're inside the building, because I'm busy trying to remember last night. When we reach his office he touches my cheek. It's a tender gesture. Something unsaid remains

201

between us. I walk away with my heart thumping in my hand once again and maybe there's hope for us after all.

Rowan isn't in his cubicle when I walk by, which makes me wonder if he developed a conscience about his hack job yesterday. There's an itinerary taped to my door and I grab it while slipping inside to unload everything by the wall.

I'm too young for this insanity. The itinerary displays my day from beginning to end without a single detail left to chance. It smacks of Catherine's delicious control.

9:00: Tour of the lab
10:00: Van Buren Industries presentation
11:00: Meet the scientists
12:00: Lunch
1:00: Chemistry lesson
4:00: Wrap up meeting

The clock reads fifteen minutes after eight and I haven't eaten a thing. If I don't get a cup of coffee, I'll need an attitude adjustment by noon. My head is pounding and I feel nauseous.

Thankful for the elaborate amenities of Van Buren

Industries, I make my way toward the cafeteria on level two. The dizzying array of cubicles and executive offices morphs into long hallways and doors without windows until I arrive at a wall plaque that reads *cafeteria*.

Once inside, I find small, round café tables, an empty buffet stand, and a middle-aged woman tending the front counter.

"What can I get for you this morning?" A pleasant face greets me from behind a long steel counter surrounded by plexiglass.

I read her nametag and say, "Ah, Lauren, I'm in dire straits. If I don't get a caffeine drip I might kill someone. Not really, but you know what I mean."

"It means you need coffee, stat." She pours me a grande. "Would you like cream and sugar?"

"I usually do, but not today. I'll take a sweet roll as well."

"No sweet rolls for you."

"Are you the sweet roll Nazi or something?" I pray she catches my reference to the famous episode of Seinfeld and she laughs.

"You can have all the sweet rolls in Heaven my dear, but I don't recommend it after a night of indulgence. You'll get sick. Let me whip you up a breakfast sandwich."

"You're right. Just the thought of sugar makes me nauseous." I scrunch my brows and add, "Thanks for looking out for me."

Lauren has a coy smile I find intriguing. She busies herself preparing my sandwich and I examine her like a kid with a new toy. I'm fascinated by something I can't figure out just yet. The laugh lines beside her eyes have me focusing on her dangling silver earrings. A few gray hairs peek out around her ears and I wonder if she's wearing a wig.

"Celebration last night?" she asks. "You don't look old enough to drink yet." Her manicured hands pull drawers, open lids, and shuffle foodstuffs on the countertop.

"You're observant. I indulged last night, but it was a special occasion. I'm from England and the standards are different in Europe than in The States." I pause, and then add, "Hey Lauren, you don't know a new employee by the name of Rowan, do you?"

"Rowan? He comes here all the time. I think he gets low blood sugar or something. He's a super nice guy."

"Really?"

"Yep. He's a doll." Something in the way she moves suggests affluence as if she doesn't belong here.

"Okay, well...thanks. I appreciate you saving me from myself this morning."

I turn to leave, and she queries, "Should I put this on your tab?"

With my coffee deprived brain, I grab for a purse that isn't hanging from my shoulder.

"It's Julia Malone, right?" She writes something on an index card and glances back at me.

"How did you?" She points to my nametag and I palm my forehead. Not everyone is a mind reader and I have to get used to the real world like Lillian warned.

"Thanks, Lauren, you're a gem." She fills the last salt container and turns to spray disinfectant on the counter.

"No problem, sweets. You have a nice day."

Back in the safety of my office, I inhale my sandwich, and wash it down with hot coffee. Rowan knocks, but walks in before I extend an invitation.

Why knock then? Is that a ten second lead, or just enough warning to hide the bodies? People are silly.

"Hey, beauty, you ready?" I notice him inspecting my outfit and wonder if I spilled something on my suit. A quick glance reveals nothing.

"Give me a second here." Cups and plates go in the trash as I gather my briefcase and itinerary.

205

"Did I get you in trouble with Nic last night?"

"Get me in trouble?" I cram the blue binder into my bookcase and notice his grin from the corner of my eye. Smoothing my skirt, I keep my face expressionless.

"Nic doesn't like me. Male jealousy, you know."

"I can get in trouble on my own thank you very much. And Nic isn't jealous, but he *is* protective." I study his expression, wondering if Lauren is right.

"Here, let me take this." Rowan grabs the strap of my briefcase and hefts it over his shoulder. "Holy smokes; this damn bag is heavy! Are you harboring illegal bricks in here?" His question is legit because I've wondered the same thing, the ache in my back a dull reminder.

"Probably—but they're legal. They got their green card last month." He laughs at my idiocy and we leave under less uncomfortable circumstances than last night.

Rowan leads me to an elevator and through several long corridors. The farther we get from the executive offices, the more sanitary our environment becomes. Even the smell of bleach hangs heavy in the air, the pungent scent reminding me of a hospital.

"I take it you've been to the lab?" My inquiry is innocent enough.

"Catherine gave me the full tour before you started

at Van Buren. She had more time before you and Nic arrived."

I broach the next question. "How common is the name *Rowan?*" I stop in the middle of the hallway so he can answer. His expression is puzzled and I see the wheels turning in his head.

"Okay, complete change of topic, but I'll roll with it. I'm of Irish descent if that's what you're asking."

"Are there many Irish laddies in New York?"

"Yes. We Irishmen are plentiful. Why the sudden interest in my name? It's common enough around these parts." He shakes his head and we push through metal doors that remind me of a surgical room. "And here we are. Keep your head down and your nose clean." He rests his hand on my back.

"What?"

"Never mind; we're here."

The lab is an ultra-modern version of a futuristic movie. Men in white lab coats scurry from test tube to table and back to their computers again. The walls are blindingly white and free of any adornment. Even the tables and cushioned stools are white. It's obvious someone went to a lot of trouble to make the lab appear sterile. A scientist whips by us and I notice that even his shoes are white.

Fresh out of a nightmare, Catherine sidles up beside us.

"Fabulous, you're here." She grabs Rowan by the elbow and leads him toward a table lined with Petri dishes, test tubes, and microscopes. I follow only because my curiosity forces me to comply.

"This is where Van Buren Industries makes magic," she declares with charismatic flair, smiling as if I should be impressed with her revelation.

I'm unimpressed and the phony smile fades from her face just as quick as she summoned it. Rowan seems interested though, but who can blame a man for his stupidity? If her skirt got any shorter, someone would offer her money. Catherine distracts Rowan with small talk so I sneak off to explore the lab.

I stand behind an engrossed scientist, tapping him on the shoulder. "Holy mother on the mountain, you scared me out of my skin." A thin man wearing dark framed glasses steps back and studies me. How very interesting since I *am* in a lab.

"Sorry. Here's your skin back if you want it." I hold his imaginary skin in front of me and he relaxes, thrusting his hand into mine.

"The name's Dexter and the jokes are forthcoming, just wait." His smile meets his eyes and I'm relieved to find someone I can trust. His mousy brown hair sticks to his forehead and I notice the hem of his pants riding several inches above his shoes. He's an epitome of the stereotypical science geek.

"Me? Make fun of someone's name. It's bad Karma." A taller scientist glances our direction in passing and I offer a genuine smile. He scowls and proceeds to his station. "Who's the stiff?"

"I don't know you, but I like you already. That's Dr. Anderson. He's a super spectacular guy." His sarcasm isn't lost on me and he pushes his glasses up the bridge of his nose to study me further.

"I'm Julia Malone, the new vice president of product development." I'm positive my smile shines in actual megawatts, and Dexter's casual demeanor vanishes.

"No disrespect, Ma'am. I'm sorry if I was forward." He recoils as if burned and I'm somewhat taken aback.

"Disrespect? Ma'am? You can loosen the noose, Dexter. I'm just a simple girl from England who's here to learn the ropes."

"It's unexpected, I guess. We've heard...I mean. I should stop while I'm ahead here." Dexter's cheeks brighten behind his olive skin and he shifts from foot to foot.

"You've heard what? Be honest; I can take it." He piqued my curiosity.

"It's nothing negative Miss Malone, quite the contrary. We've heard you have a discerning eye and not to trifle with you. And if you don't mind me saying, you're so personable you could disarm a sniper." He dips his head, somewhat embarrassed by the remark.

"I'm guessing that's a compliment. You have an amusing way with words." And just as we break ground, the barracuda and her minion show up to kill a budding new friendship. Her snotty perusal of Dexter makes me want to smear that fuchsia lipstick across her face with my thumb.

"This is my new friend, Dexter." I gesture to the dynamic duo to my left. "Dexter, meet Catherine and Rowan." They exchange polite nods and he goes back to examining something in a Petri dish and dismisses us.

Catherine moves our tour of the lab along, and I glance back to find Dexter following me with his eyes. We exchange a knowing smile.

"And this central location is our learning center. It's where our chemistry and biology interns learn the dynamics of our product line and study the chemical components of *Immortality*." Several of the male scientists stop what they're doing to stare at Catherine's... assets.

I ignore them, shifting my attention to a flat screen television suspended from the ceiling. "What *are* the chemical components of *Immortality?* What *is* substance x?"

She lights up like a Christmas tree. "That's just it, Janelle. Nobody knows. Claude wanted more intuitive and curious types on the project. It's why he wanted *you.*" Her expression contains both pride and jealousy and it's a curious combination that makes no sense.

"Um, Catherine? Her name is Julia." Rowan corrects, almost embarrassed by her purposeful discourtesy.

"Oh yes, Julia. I keep getting that mixed up. I'm so sorry." She fawns and I roll my eyes. This one is much more than a piece of work; I'll give her that much.

The rest of the day becomes a blur of information on Van Buren Industries and its various subsidiaries, along with technical information on *Immortality* and other endeavors.

I make a mental note to contact Dexter to teach me about the chemistry of our product. Perhaps he'll become an ally. Catherine dismisses us at four, and I'm relieved. It's been a long, boring day, cramming in too much information at once. I'm not even sure I retained much of it since I'm a hands-on, visual learner.

"Wanna grab a bite after work? It feels like my brain might explode." Rowan rests a hand on my shoulder as we walk back to our offices.

"I can't. It's our first real night in the new place and Nic is cooking." I suck at being put on the spot. It looks like Nic is cooking tonight.

"Tell him we have a work project and invite me to dinner." We both stop.

"You know this can never work, right?" I think I'm conveying a serious expression, but he smiles and tucks a stray lock of hair behind my ear. His touch is gentle, and I can't imagine he's as crooked as Nic says.

He puts both arms on my shoulders and leans in to rest his forehead against mine.

"You, Julia Malone, are a challenge." He walks away, leaving me staring after him, confused.

The obnoxious shoulder bag waits inside my office and I gather the too-heavy tote and glance up when Nic taps.

"Ready, Freddy?"

"Yup, let me power down my computer, and I'll be just…one…second."

"I met your boyfriend in the hall. Pleasant guy.

Can't say I don't want to knock him flat though."

I pop my head up to see if he's serious because I can't tell by the tone of his voice. "Well, you weren't very nice to him. I doubt the two of you will ever shoot hoops or grab a brewski together."

"You'll only see that day if the apocalypse hits. Do you want to eat out tonight? We have no food back home."

I push him out in the hall and then lock my office door. "Guess what? We're cooking tonight. Rowan asked me out to dinner, and I had to come up with something."

"We can't go out to dinner because you lied to Rowan? *Rowan?* I don't give a flying London Tower about Rowan." His expression turns foul and we walk out together.

"I didn't do it on purpose."

"You didn't lie on purpose?"

"I'm not a good liar. Do I *look* perfect to you?" I twirl so he can get a better look.

"As a matter of fact…" He starts. His sarcastic response is enough to call for a punch in the shoulder. "I wish you'd open your eyes but if you want to learn the hard way... be my guest. Stubborn..."

"You think I'm stubborn?" Cool night air hits my cheeks when we exit the building.

"That's putting it mildly. I love your stubborn streak though."

"Yeah, I'll bet. When asked what you love about me, your first response is how much you adore my stubbornness. You're such a ding dong, Nic."

"And you're my goose." The conversation ends with both of us socking each other in the arm.

Leopold is at the curb and we ask him to take us to the nearest market, which ends up being Reggie's Organics. We buy porterhouse steaks and fixings for salad and my thoughts stray to the phone conversation with Sebastian. Lillian hasn't checked up on us even once and I wonder if *out of sight* means *out of mind*. The elevator arrives at the twentieth floor.

"Should we test the patio grill or play it safe and use the broiler?" Nic crunches the paper bag in his arms when he shifts the weight.

The crackling sound takes me back home because our grocer always bitched about those *newfangled* plastic bags that don't decompose. I wonder if we can be a real team despite our problems in the love department. Sometimes, I want nothing more than to throw myself in his arms and declare my undying love, but there's this nasty little thing called the fear of rejection.

"Julia?" His brows are furrowed in thought.

"Oh yeah, sorry, thinking too much. I say we test the grill and see if our new patio is functional."

Dita designed our outdoor living space with cold weather in mind, and the gas fireplace does a fine job of warding off chilly winter air while we eat our steaks and sip wine. We can see our breath and I shiver.

"More wine?" Nic tips the bottle and I hand him my glass.

"Thanks for getting Moscato." The sweet, intoxicating scent of peaches is pleasant.

"Don't thank me. Thank Dita—or Claude. He's the mastermind behind everything. Have you heard a word from Lillian?" He sets the wine bottle on a side table and leans against the railing. Under normal circumstances he's relaxed, but the stiffness in his posture is a dead giveaway.

"No, and it's as if we dropped off the face of the earth. If Sebastian hadn't told me Lyra's crazier than the mad hatter, we wouldn't know things are changing back home. I guess the street goes both ways though. Is the manor even our home anymore?"

Nic empties his glass and sets it on the table, sitting in the wicker chair beside me. His extended silence speaks volumes.

"I don't know." He peers through the glass balcony overlooking the city. "We'll see them soon enough, right?"

I reach over to take his hand, and our arms swing together between the wicker chairs.

"Yeah, I guess so." Nic's demeanor darkens.

He lifts my hand and kisses it and I kick at the light dusting of snow on the concrete. There's much less snow on the ground than when I met Rowan last week, but at least we have the outdoor fireplace.

"Ask what I learned today." Shifting the topic works wonders when Nic's moody.

"Tell me about your day, Jules. What did you learn?"

"Well, I met a scientist named Dexter, and he's interesting; looks like the stereotypical science geek, but the guy has a lot going on upstairs." I point to my head, and add, "I'll try to learn as much about Substance X as I can, but as far as I can tell it *enhances*." I'm babbling, and pause for air.

"What else?" He urges, emptying his glass.

"It enhances beauty, but does it on a cellular level that's more than skin deep." His curiosity pleases me because I don't even know if I trust my own intuition anymore.

"Come on, it's me. I know you're not crazy—crazy sensitive and accurate, but never crazy." He kneels between my legs and rests his head in my lap. I stroke his hair and continue.

"This discovery from the archaeological dig or wherever the heck they found it does much more than slow aging. It changes people on a genetic level."

"And the world is ready for something this big?"

"Not even close. You saw how it changed the six of us."

"And you wonder about people who are *already* evil? Or at the very least, have a few nasty traits?"

"What if *Immortality* causes the same reaction, but more gradual over time? No one could trace the cause." My implication is far-reaching.

"When the rest of the group gets here we have a good chance to observe. I haven't noticed negative effects, but the public wouldn't overlook a change in eye color." Nic admits.

"I'm not sure why Claude thinks no one will notice." I hope he didn't lie when he said his chemists had fixed the problem. "Did your thoughts and emotions change?"

"Not that I can tell, but I haven't paid much

217

attention." He stands and brushes the snow from his knees.

Next week the rest of our clan arrives and I'm not looking forward to the chaos. We haven't even acclimated to our bloody internships yet. Life should come with instructions.

Chapter Fourteen—Arrival

I pace the airport floors near the baggage claim while Claude and Nic converse with Leopold and Lorraine. Their arriving flight from England is long overdue but the guest bedrooms are prepped and ready even if we're not.

Nic and I are guilty of never calling home, but they didn't call us either. It's sad how fast family falls away with time and distance. Lyra's shock of black hair bobs around the corner followed by Dutch, Sebastian, Lincoln, and Lillian pulling up the rear.

Dutch bypasses everyone and rushes in to greet me.

"I missed you so much!" He grunts, lifting me from my feet.

Then he grabs Nic in a bear hug. Sebastian is next in line to hug me, lingering a little too long, and then Lillian scoops me up in a maternal squeeze. Lyra and Lincoln nod, devoid of any of any warm emotion.

"Let's get this show on the road." Claude interrupts our awkward reunion and motions for Leopold and Lorraine to take the luggage. Nic hangs back with his brothers chatting up a storm while Lyra and Lincoln seem uninvolved. I catch Lillian up to speed about our stay in New York, but as usual, I have more questions than answers.

"How are you faring with the new penthouse and your internship? I assume all is well since I've heard nothing from the lot of you." She sounds hurt and disappointed.

"As far as I know it's going good. Everything is so foreign. The penthouse will leave you breathless—just wait." I loop my arm through hers.

Passersby in the airport stare at our group with puzzled expressions. I wonder what they see in our perfect crowd of chemically altered atrocities. Enormous glass doors separate and we walk through to find an awaiting limo in the *reserved* section. Leopold and Lorraine dispatch with the luggage and my pseudo family piles into the back seat with excitement—everyone except Lyra and Lincoln that is.

A quick scan of their thoughts returns a solid block. This is new. I push harder and they push back with sly smiles before turning their attention toward the windows and the city. Seeking Nic's familiar mental path, I question the strange occurrence.

220

"Lincoln and Lyra blocked me."

"What do you think it means?" Nic's thoughts are a gentle buzz, low on the Richter scale for our communication.

"They're acting really creepy and I don't want them to stay with us."

"We'll get through it, we always do."

Claude breaks our uncomfortable silence with an announcement. "I think Lillian, Lyra, and Lincoln should stay with me until Dita finds them suitable accommodations." He gauges my reaction from his vantage point in the limo, lifting an enormous weight from my shoulders.

"That's a great idea. Nic can catch up with his brothers, and I'll just focus on my duties at Van Buren. Someone has to claim the title of intellectual nerd around here." My shoulders relax. When I glance at Lillian, her expression is composed and unreadable. "Lillian, it's your choice either way. Do you want to hang out with the girls?"

"Oh no, don't be silly, my dear. We'll spend lots of time together, but it doesn't have to be every waking moment. I'm fine with the arrangement, I just wasn't expecting it." She looks to Claude for a reaction and he's poker faced.

"You've been separated for a couple months. This will give you time to ease back into your normal routines." Again, he studies my reaction. What's with this guy?

Our ride is uneventful but everyone is curious about living in New York. To be honest, we don't have the answers because after seven weeks here, we've done nothing but acclimate to Van Buren Industries and our penthouse. Everyone files out with polite indifference when we arrive.

"Lyra, you'll love my old room." I try my hand at graciousness but she glares at me with those inky black eyes. Her response is weird, even for her.

"It was never *your* room." She stalks after Claude, who looks back with an odd expression and shrugs.

Lorraine shows Lyra and Lincoln to their rooms. Claude escorts Lillian down the corridor leading to his bedroom suite, and the rest of us make ourselves comfortable in the great room.

I expected Dutch to study the architectural details of Claude's penthouse, but didn't count on Sebastian staring at me the entire time. Nic's body language is rigid, not one to miss much, and I try easing the tension in the room.

"Are you guys looking forward to chatting all night? You've never been apart this long." The brothers nod, but Sebastian's steady gaze has me unnerved. I seek his thoughts, blocking the others.

"Stop staring at me. Nic's pissed."

"Nic doesn't own you. And you know why I'm staring." His gaze remains steady. Even though his eyes turned dark after we drank the elixir, he doesn't throw off the same vibe as Lincoln and Lyra—more intense, but nothing sinister.

"I don't know what you mean." I shift on the couch, making sure my blocks are in place. Nic seems oblivious, so that's good.

"Love's just a game to you, isn't it?"

"What? Where are you getting this?" My expression darkens because Nic tries deciphering it. He doesn't know I'm talking to his aggravating brother.

"Nothing, don't mind me." I quickly say to throw Nic off the trail and notice Sebastian's focus shift to Claude's penthouse. I'm not done with him yet.

"You're the one who brought this up so finish it."

"There's nothing more to say. It is what it is." And as an afterthought, he adds, *"Like I said, Nic doesn't own you."*

It's a pleasure to leave Sebastian's head because I'm incensed by his passive aggressive games. I tuck my

223

hands under my butt and cross my legs, a gesture meant to prevent me from jumping up and slapping him senseless.

Claude and Lillian return, followed by the others.

"Are you ready to go home?" He motions toward the elevator. "I ordered Chinese and had it delivered. Tomorrow, I'll have Dita take you on the grand tour. She has penthouses lined up, but there's no rush for anyone to decide." His smile is too optimistic, too fake, and I'm ready to end the day.

Back in the limo, Dutch speaks first.

"Claude has incredible taste. Thought and money went into that architectural masterpiece." His expression lights up while he babbles colors and design schemes, and how he wants his new place to resemble Claude's penthouse. Dutch is the most aesthetic of the group, sensitive and observant to the environment, but he has a tendency to talk too much about his favorite topics.

Sebastian cuts in and stops his incessant chatter. "I don't want to live by myself. Why can't I share a penthouse with Nic and Julia?" His question takes Nic off guard.

"It's not *my* decision to make. The penthouse is in Julia's name." All three brothers stare at me, each with different expressions. Talk about putting someone on the spot.

When the elevator reaches our level, Dutch sucks in his breath, eyes wide. Sebastian studies the architecture and Nic watches him, sensing something isn't right with his brother. It's a case of good old-fashioned sibling rivalry, but I refuse to get in the middle. The last time I broke up one of their fights someone socked me in the cheek.

True to Claude's word we're met with an array of Chinese food in the kitchen and our tiered marble countertop is buried beneath a sea of white boxes. It's enough to feed fifty people rather than four lanky teenagers. Why is everything overkill with rich people? It's as if they've never wanted for a single thing—ever.

"I don't know about you guys but I'm digging into this fine Asian par-tay. That's what *I'm* talking about." Dutch's enthusiastic excitement is enviable and Nic passes out paper plates and plastic dinnerware.

"Hey, guys, save me some food. I'll be right back." I point to the noodles. Nic and Dutch nod, promising.

"Yeah, this food can wait a few minutes. I'll go with you, Jules." Sebastian is at my heel but I keep walking.

We stop at a set of adjoining suites across from Nic's bedroom, and I turn the doorknob. He gives it a cursory glance but doesn't have a noticeable reaction.

225

That's fine by me as long as he's satisfied.

"You can have this suite or the other one; it's your choice." We walk through a conjoined bathroom to a bedroom designed in burgundy and gold, whereas the other one was royal blue and white. "They have the same basic layout." I say, leaning back against the wall as he inspects the artwork.

"This one works." Sebastian walks over and places both hands on either side of my head, trapping me between his muscular forearms. "It's perfect, thank you." His gaze moves over my body and I sense something dark and erotic. It's impossible not to blush.

"We need to get back to the others." I duck beneath his arm, rushing from the room before I embarrass myself.

"You felt that, didn't you?" He calls after me, trying to match my stride.

"Not sure what you mean." The moisture on my upper lip gives me away.

"I knew it was possible." He laces his hands behind his head and a slow smile spreads.

"You're talking in riddles again, Sebastian. English, please." We make it to the kitchen before he has a chance to respond.

Dutch engages Nic and Sebastian in design theory,

226

the finer points of living in New York and Van Buren Industries while I eat in silence. It's obvious he watches too much Home and Garden television. Everyone makes excited small talk, and Sebastian watches my every move. For a moment I'm lost in his black, cable knit sweater, noticing how it sculpts muscles that weren't there a few weeks ago. It's better if I dismiss myself.

"I'm pooped." My soggy plate flops into the garbage.

"Yeah, I'm exhausted. I hope you guys don't mind if I crash. Julia already showed me to my room." Nic's expression clouds over at Sebastian's mention of my name.

"No problem, bro. Did she show you my room while she was at it?" Dutch asks.

"Yep, we're in a connecting room. Yours is blue and white, and mine is burgundy and gold—can't miss it." Sebastian slaps his brothers on the back and I turn to leave.

"Good night you guys." I wave and exit the kitchen unaware I have a visitor behind me.

"See ya, Malone." Sebastian passes me in the hall just as I reach my bedroom door.

"Uhm... yeah. Get some rest and let me know if you need anything."

"Will do." He disappears around the corner.

I turn both faucets on my tub, melting into the enormous retreat with a sigh. Whoever designed it sure had an eye for opulence, showerheads the size of dinner plates.

Floor-to-ceiling windows on the exterior wall would make this space obscene if not for the fact I'm on the twentieth floor. Steam fills the bathroom and I check the temperature.

"Shite. Ouch!" I turn off the hot faucet and swirl my hand through the water to cool it down.

There are new towels hanging next to the showers, and I wonder how much Claude pays Lorraine to sneak in here. His control freakery is just plain weird, and the extent to which he manages the people in his world seems downright excessive.

My thoughts drift back to the boys while I steam my face in a glass basin, the hot water clearing my mind. The bizarre encounter with Sebastian replays on auto-loop and I can't shake the memory. My reflection in the mirror stares back with silent accusations of neglect. I'm thin—much too thin.

I distract myself by counting rows of periwinkle candles, each reflecting in the mirror to create an illusion of endless blue pillars. I light them one by one and slide into the hot, clear water to think about the strangeness of this day.

Images of Sebastian flip through my head, and I watch him close his eyes, settling into the lounge chair in his room. It's as if something forces the scene into my mind. He touches my body, running his mouth along my neck until our lips meet. Each time I push the disturbing thoughts from my head, they push back even harder against my will.

He slides his fingers through my hair and deepens our kiss without closing his eyes. I moan into his mouth, my lids lowering.

"Keep your eyes open. I need you to know how much I want you." His words echo in my head.

Steam from the tub whirls around me and I turn the hot water faucet. Sensual thoughts of Sebastian keep intruding no matter how many times I force it from my head. Exasperated, I sit up, splashing water all over the bathroom floor.

Sensations course through my body with pulses of unfamiliar electricity. I'm in love with Nic and *this* is all wrong. I've loved him since we were three and loving Sebastian at the same time isn't an option because life is complicated enough. I'm startled by a sharp knock at the door and grab several towels from a basket beside the tub.

"Just a second." I yell, wrapping one around my waist, another over my shoulders, and yet another one on my head. Cocooned in blue terry cloth, I open the door and Nic's standing there with a concerned expression. His lips curve down at the corners.

"Is everything okay?"

"What? Yeah, don't be silly I'm fine."

"What's going on?" He towers over me and I cower.

There's no way in hell I can't tell him about Sebastian so I scramble for an explanation, ducking under his arm to fetch my robe.

"I—I don't know. Do you think it was a panic attack?" My words come out thick, like peanut butter and I swallow the explanation, trying not to choke.

"Is there something you're not telling me?" His eyes narrow as I rush around my room tidying up, a nervous habit when I'm uncomfortable.

"There's not much I can hide from you so don't be ridiculous." I flip my head forward and re-tighten the towel as he rubs the back of his neck, a nervous habit Nic's had for years.

"Okay then, have it your way. I'm going to bed. You sure nothing's wrong?"

I push him from my bedroom, assuring him that

230

everything is fine. My breath rushes out and I'm thankful I didn't vomit. Please not his brother. It can be anyone in the world—just not Sebastian.

Chapter Fifteen—The Coming Days

My dreams are fitful and erratic, finding no logical explanation for Sebastian's strange new hold over me. I'm the first one up, sitting by myself in the kitchen, hunched over a cereal bowl when Dutch catches me by surprise.

"You're awake? Julia... it's only five-thirty." He rubs his eyes and I point to the cupboard where the bowls are and fetch him a spoon from the drawer. He pours a huge bowl of cocoa pebbles and it's good to have Mr. Sunshine as a distraction. Otherwise, I'd sit here ruminating for another hour.

I crunch my pebbles like a ravenous bear, peeping over at him ornery and bleary eyed. His spoon rattles against the bowl and he swivels to face me on the barstool.

"What the hell is wrong with you?" He snaps.

"Sore subject; I don't want to talk about it."

"Okay." He turns, staring straight ahead.

"Is it because we're crowding you?" His dejected expression tugs at my heart.

"What? No, heck no. I'm so stinkin' glad you guys

are here I can't stand myself. I miss you. But let's not include Lyra in that statement." I tip my bowl, drinking the rest of my milk.

"Can I ask you something Jules?" He rubs his hands on his pajama bottoms.

"For a dollar you can."

"What?"

"Never mind, I'm just being a smart ass."

"Is something going on between you and Sebastian?" He's dead serious and I choke on the milk. Dutch slaps my back until I push him away.

"I'm fine," I squeak between coughs, but he's unconvinced.

"Everyone is different now, and it's so much worse since you and Nic left." His expression clouds over and he stuffs a spoonful of cereal in his mouth.

"I got the same impression when Sebastian called," I admit "Anything else you're not telling me?"

"There's so much more. And Sebastian…" He hesitates not wanting to finish but changes his mind and lets it fly. "He's crazy in love with you."

"Please tell me you said *Nic's* in love with me." My breath hitches on the intake and I hold it.

"Well, yeah, Nic's in love with you. You're blind if

233

you can't see *that*. It's just different with Sebastian." The muscles in his jaw tighten and he stops himself from saying more.

"What aren't you telling me?" We face each other on the stools, and he traces lazy circles on my left kneecap, his eyes downcast.

"We're all different. It's hard to explain, but the hidden things are visible now." His fingers stop moving.

"Can you elaborate? I'm not a mind reader." My sense of humor isn't lost on him and he grins. His smile fades and his tone becomes more serious.

"Sebastian's always been intense. Now he's amplified. Lyra is bitchy and weird so imagine that times ten—and then there's Lincoln." His expression becomes dark.

"Yeah, he gives me the creeps too. Is he even *more* calculating now?"

"Much more." Dutch grips his cereal spoon and doesn't realize he's doing it.

"I guess that answers my question." I peer over with the intention of bringing my sweetheart back. "What about you?" It's impossible to keep my smirk under wraps.

"What *about* me?" He coughs into the crook of his elbow.

"Are you a sentimental poet on overdrive?" I sock him in the arm and he fakes insult.

"Yeah, I still write poetry like a lovesick little girl…dreaming…picking daisies, and dabbing stars in the sky with an imaginary paintbrush. It could have been worse you know." We bust out giggling just as Nic and Sebastian enter the kitchen wiping grit from their eyes.

"Gotta go, but thanks for making me feel like a normal eighteen-year-old again." I rest my head on his shoulder and give him a quick peck.

"Did we miss the morning love fest?" Sebastian leans against the doorframe.

"Something like that." I stalk past them to my bedroom.

There's a good probability I need a psychiatrist at this point. All I have to do is read their mind to see if I'm certifiable or not. They can't hide their perceptions, and it's more than possible I'm one hair shy of a wig.

This is downright dreadful. Where the hell is the holy grail of navigating love and relationships? It seems everyone read the manual but me. It's early so I might as well sleep until Dita Sinclair gets here.

***

I'm disoriented by a sharp rap at the door and crack

an eye as I recover from a crazy dream. I don't know how long I've been out of it.

"Yeah?" I yell through a sticky mouth, my eyes gritty and unfocused.

"It's ten-thirty. Are you ready?" It's Sebastian and my eyelids feel like lead.

"Why did you guys let me sleep so late?" I jump from bed, ripping through my closet like a hurricane and he enters without permission.

"Tried to wake you earlier, but you were dreaming and looked so peaceful. I didn't want to disturb the universe." His low, throaty laughter makes me shiver.

"You watched me sleep? That's creepy even for you. Where are Nic and Dutch?"

"They're waiting by the elevator and everyone else is on the way." He's amused by my sleepy disorientation and I have zero time to get ready. Guys slide from bed, throw on a ball cap, and they're out the door. It aggravates the hell out of me.

"Get out of my bedroom, but don't leave without me." I grab jeans and a turtle neck, and five minutes later, emerge with un-brushed teeth and a sloppy ponytail.

The prospect of Dita dragging us around New York is about as appealing as having bamboo shoots rammed up my fingernails. Lyra's moodiness will ping on my last nerve and Lincoln's sulky silence will have me unnerved by the end of the day. I can't stand to be near him for more than five minutes.

The boys are chatting by the elevator and I rush out looking like the hot mess I am. They poke each other.

"Now that's a train wreck if I ever saw one." Lincoln's lips peel back.

"Funny; you can all stop gawking now." They get my best *whatever* expression.

"You're the cutest wreck I've ever seen." Nic grins at Dutch, and Sebastian's expression tightens. He focuses his intensity on the walls and I'm dying to read his thoughts but can't.

Over the next eight hours, Dita parades us around penthouses of every persuasion while Lyra, Dutch, and Lincoln narrow their choices. Sebastian doesn't budge. Although Dita is an expert, it's been impossible to please him.

Towering sky rises, city streets buzzing with people, and dozens of cabs zip in and out of traffic, obscuring our view of the city. Neon billboards scream, *buy me, check me out, it's the next best thing since sliced bread... trust me.* Well, I don't.

I can only absorb small doses of New York before I combust. Men in power suits weave their way through crowds, speaking into their Blue-tooth, as if they're talking to themselves. Women rifle through purses, trip on cracks in the sidewalk, and sip from tall Styrofoam cups while chatting on their cell phones. Everyone is manic and stressed. I squirm in my seat, the city's frenetic energy draining me.

"We can try another time." Dita's remark is affable and Sebastian nods, his gaze directed out the window.

"Dita, that's the best idea I've heard all day," I yawn, rubbing my eyes. "I'm exhausted, and Sebastian is fine living with us until he decides." Our group reaction is tangible. Nic fumes, Sebastian lights up like Times Square, and Dutch raises his eyebrows. Lincoln and Lyra couldn't care less.

It seems I can't please anyone and bite my tongue to avoid snipping. I want to enjoy the rest of my Saturday without Dita dragging us around New York City a second longer than necessary. I'm frazzled. Leopold drives Lincoln and Lyra back to Claude's, and the brothers and I head to the penthouse. Once the elevator deposits us at the landing, I stomp off to hide in my room. Some days I don't want to be around anyone and save myself the aggravation of

238

having to pretend.

Lyra had draped herself all over Sebastian like a fur coat, which made me want to punch her in the head; I'm not sure why her obnoxiousness struck such a nerve because it's not as if the warning didn't come long before they arrived. Lincoln appeared murderous, and if looks could kill, none of us would have heartbeats.

Maybe I'm jealous, who knows—but Sebastian? My feelings for Nic enter muddy territory. Emotions are messy. That's what they are—nasty, messy, confusing, and irrational.

Nic barrels into my room without knocking, and if his upturned lip is any sign, he's furious. His beautiful mouth mesmerizes me even when he's mad.

"I can't *believe* you did that!" He waits for an explanation.

"Did what?"

"You told Sebastian he can stay with us as long as he wants?" He's pacing the floor and throws his hands in the air.

"He's your brother. I would have done the same for Dutch."

"Dutch isn't trying to get in your pants."

"Get in my pants?" I bite back the urge to jump up

and smash something, humiliation heating my cheeks.

"Well, yeah. You don't think he's actually in love with you?" That's the lowest Nic has ever sunk.

His cocky tone makes me want to throw him out of my room but I bite the inside of my cheek, drawing the horrid taste of iron into my mouth. The room is quiet and with my back turned on him, I wait for retreating footsteps. Instead, the bed sinks in beside me.

"Go away, Nic. I mean it." My muscles are rigid and ready to snap.

"I'm not going anywhere, goose. Look, I'm sorry, that was an asinine thing to say."

My words spill out before I can rein them back. "You and I just don't work." Tears sting my eyes and I'm all out of dignity. I don't know why I wait for him to disagree or take a stand. When he doesn't, a sob catches in my throat and I almost choke on it in a breathless, heart stopping moment. Emotional pain hurts so much worse than physical.

"Maybe you're right." The mattress springs back, and heavy footsteps echo in the hall after he shuts my door.

My heart just shattered into a million pieces, and something has to give. I can't force myself to fall out of love, but I *can* bury myself in an internship and emotionally withdraw. There's an elephant sitting on my chest and for the first time in my life, illusions of Nic disappear. The reality is that he doesn't love me as much as I love him.

Sunday is a blur of foul moods and sulky silence, but Monday morning couldn't be worse if it had a master plan. My alarm forces me from bed with its incessant blare. It takes sheer willpower not to rip it from the wall.

Claude gave everyone a grand tour of Van Buren Industries, and without me as the usual conversation catalyst, the ride is awkward. Everyone senses my mood. I part ways with the rest of our crew inside the entrance and Rowan is waiting for me by his cubicle when I reach the fourth floor. He jogs to catch up with me. My key jams in the lock and I wrestle with it.

"Easy there, killer. It's Monday but you're gonna need a tow truck if you don't settle down." He's wearing business casual today; khaki's and a light blue shirt rolled to the elbows.

"Sorry—bloody horrible weekend." Why the hell is he so chipper for a Monday morning? I swear to God; cheery Monday morning people should be shot on sight.

"Mine was a total bust too." Rowan becomes visibly impatient with my incompetence and grabs the keys

241

from my hand. He gets my uncooperative door open and I fall inside with a bag of illegal bricks otherwise known as my study material.

I turn on my computer, managing not to burst into tears. Rowan's reluctance to leave becomes uncomfortable. There's one way to avoid a long, drawn out conversation about my seemingly irrational mood.

"I'm going to bury my nose in work for a few weeks. Everything else doesn't matter." I toss my purse on the floor and kick my shoes off under the desk.

"Do tell." He narrows his eyes and leans against the wall, fingering his jaw line.

"No circus here. You can move along now." My pathetic attempt at stoicism proves ridiculous and I slam my binder on the desk. "I'm fine, but I need to keep my mind on business. If I'm moody, just ignore it." His gaze darts from my legs.

Good grief, are all guys this predictable?

"Love wound, huh? No worries, I've got a few battle scars of my own."

His empathy is unsellable, and I change the topic. "Do you remember Dexter from the lab?"

"Are you talking about the geeky guy with thick-rimmed glasses?" Rowan crosses his arms and returns to

242

staring at my legs.

"That's the one. He's not geeky—just brilliant."

"What about the guy?" He steps forward, placing his hands on my desk. I think he's trying to get a peek down my blouse so I lean back.

"I want to shadow him this week and learn the chemistry behind our products."

"You're the big, bad, vice president of product development. It's a good idea."

"You think I'm big and bad, huh? I wouldn't go that far. I can't even manage a personal life, thank you very much."

"Definitely a love wound." Rowan smirks and shakes his head as if I'm naive. "Let's do lunch today."

"Fine. Check with me later."

"Try not to let it get you down."

"That's easier said than done, my friend." I wave him off and direct my attention to a stack of junk mail sitting on my in-box.

Claude agrees to let me shadow Dexter, and after coffee with Lauren's famous breakfast sandwich, I make my way to the lab. He's more reserved this time, and I assume it's because he knows I'm the big, bad, vice president of product development. The sobering thought

243

makes me wish I could ditch the stupid title and be plain old Julia.

"And this right here," he does an *abracadabra*, gesturing like a magician, "is the key element."

"The ingredient no one can figure out?" I remember the day we drank the elixir at the manor and the breath holding nightmare that came next.

"That's the one." He stares at it like a lover, forgetting my presence for a moment.

The familiar color and luminosity pulls me in, and I cringe at the thought of us ingesting an entire vial of an unknown substance. The elixir brings back memories of watching science fiction on the telly. I recall witches brew bubbling over cauldrons, and mad science experiments conducted in obscure underground laboratories. An insane cackle echoes in my mind's eye, and I chase away the memories because unlike my overactive imagination, this is real life.

"How did they discover the elixir?" I tread with caution because loyalty is a funny thing. Assumptions often backfire.

"Henry Van Buren discovered it on an archaeological expedition. It was near Chichen Itza but somewhere off the beaten path. Are you familiar with

Mexico?"

"I've never heard of it. Henry is Claude's grandfather, correct?" The location strikes me as inaccurate but it's just a hunch.

"Yes." He says. No one can accuse Dexter of verbosity and he narrows his eyes. "How much has Claude revealed?"

"Most of it, but shouldn't I have access to all the information since I'm in charge of the launch? It's the only logical decision but what would I know?"

"It's hard to believe Claude put this responsibility on the shoulders of children. Pardon my forwardness, but don't you find it strange and unheard of?" He clucks his tongue, peering at me through bifocals. It takes a moment to find words, not wanting him to doubt my motives. *Immortality* and substance X are his life's work.

"I guess Claude trusts my instincts."

Dr. Anderson walks by real slow and gives us the stink eye. Dexter shrugs his shoulders and ignores the rude distraction. He's good like that, not allowing much to throw him off track.

"Then tell me why we can't stabilize this exasperating substance in a common base." He points to a jar of white goo. It's the color and consistency of ordinary face cream.

I flip through my existing knowledge of biology, physics, chemistry, and art. My mind whirls like a high-speed rolodex, with information coming and going until I land on the right page.

"What's the number one ingredient in your base?"

"It's a water-based facial cream. We didn't include anything fancy or add unnecessary preservatives. Those ingredients destabilize the compound at a much faster rate." He studies the cream as if it might spill its guts, or chat over tea.

"That's your problem right there." I remember learning about bacteria, viruses, and fungi from Lillian's science lectures and how they multiply in water.

"What's my problem?" He's fixated on the container.

"The cream is water based." We stare at the white goo together.

"You lost me." He pushes his glasses up the bridge of his nose, the same quirk I noticed when we first met. It makes him real and vulnerable, unlike the plastic caricatures I'm accustomed to in sci-fi movies.

"Skin can't absorb water. Water is the perfect host for growing bacteria. Try using an aloe-based cream."

"Who are you and what planet did you come from?" He steps back.

I shrug, not as impressed with myself as he is because I know my science and beauty products. Our way of life in Europe is natural and Americans have everything upside down and backwards in the states.

Dexter opens a drawer and grabs his notebook full of facts and figures, calculations and formulas, flipping pages and making the occasional grunt to show he's deep in concentration. He slaps the notebook shut and grins so hard his teeth might crack if his glasses don't shatter from the excitement.

"Dex, you're freaking me out. What did I say?"

"You are *brilliant* in your innocence. Claude is a mad freaking genius for putting you in product development!" He dances around clapping like a kid, and grabs both my hands in his, whirling me around the lab. "Tomorrow, I'll have the first batch of aloe-based *Immortality* formulated. But for now, you little genius, I have to get back to work." He lets out a girlish squeal and brings me in for a hug. Then he trots through a set of metal double doors and is gone.

Dexter is one interesting cat and his passion makes me grin like an idiot. Those scientific types are odd but

247

great distractions from real life. He pulled me from the emotional slump Rowan described as a *love wound*. Love wound, my ass. It's more of an amputation, but at least I'm not bleeding out—yet.

I'm still reeling from a discovery high as I reach my office, and who but Catherine is waiting to pounce. Great— she needs a word with me. Isn't Cruella missing a sister somewhere? If I don't plaster a phony smile on my face I'll be contrary. She's *not* stealing my Dexter high.

"Catherine, I wasn't expecting anyone to be in my office." She smirks and I notice her faded spray tan when she crosses her legs. Oh the irony.

"You've been gone a long time. Claude said you were shadowing Dexter today." Her pinched smile is so forced it's hard to believe she's so good at fooling the opposite gender.

"Yes. He gave me permission this morning." I admit. Her eyes narrow to slits despite the smile.

Guess what you wretched hag? Contradictory body language is my specialty.

"And you enjoy each other's company?" She keeps her tone innocuous but I sense jealousy. *Let's play the vague game, then.*

"He's okay I guess. Why do you ask?" I avoid her

gaze and check my email.

"No reason. Claude is accustomed to receiving progress reports. Do you have any?" If phoniness were a commodity, this witch would collapse the stock market.

"I don't believe so. Maybe you should ask Dexter." I take a deep breath and close my eyes for a moment, wishing she'd spontaneously combust.

"That's a good idea. Do you have plans for lunch?" She stands, smoothing her skirt, all the while glancing at my redecorated office.

"Sorry, but Rowan already asked."

Catherine gives me a crooked smile—one that says *beware my claws are sharpened.* "That's fine. Call if you need anything." Her back stiffens, and she holds our gaze a little too long for my liking. It's almost a silent challenge.

"Will do Catherine; thanks." I credit myself for control, and would have given her a piece of my mind if I could spare a few brain cells these days.

My email sounds an alert, and it's a message from Rowan. I respond and we go back and forth.

Rowan: Are you ready to hit the pavement? I'm starved.

Me: Give me five minutes and I'll stop by to pick

249

you up.

Rowan: Sure thing. Wear a jacket; it's cold out.

Me: Thanks for the reminder. See you in a second.

After a couple more exchanges, we decide on the Indian restaurant across the street and once he has me trapped in a booth, the grilling begins.

"What did Catherine want? I saw her waiting in your office."

"How did you know she was in my office?"

"Haven't you heard? I'm astute." He pulls a tin of mints from his coat and flips the lid. "Want some?"

"No thanks. She was curious about what Dexter and I came up with today. And she asked if I wanted to grab lunch." My mood lightens when I spot lamb on the menu.

"You don't like Catherine do you? It's fine. She's a tyrant with women. I get it." He grabs a menu and pokes at a few items of interest, tracing the descriptions with his index finger.

"And you think she's hotter than a white-hot inferno." My tone is snarky but I'm so darn sick of shallow guys. It's all about legs, butts, breasts, and oh—did I mention legs? I roll my eyes and sigh.

Don't get me wrong, everyone loves a bombshell,

but isn't there something more? Like intelligence perhaps, or companionship, intimacy, and a real connection? My mood has nothing to do with Rowan and I offer a suggestion.

"I'd get the lentil soup and pork vindaloo." I point to numbers three and seven on the menu and he nods in agreement.

"Good call, Malone." His use of my last name suggests a level of intimacy that doesn't exist.

The waiter brings a pitcher of water and fills tall, red, plastic cups. The whole red cup thing in restaurants is cliché, and it's just one more absurd detail I notice. Our server doesn't have a pad of paper but cocks his ear to the side as if absorbing every word when we order. I haven't eaten lamb in a long time and am curious about New York's version of my favorite dish.

I'm prepared to give my speech on the benefits of Indian spices but think better of it. The academic conversations can wait for Dexter—or Nic if we ever speak again. Rowan doesn't strike me as an intellectual power-house. This is the first time I've had lunch outside the office and it's nice to switch gears.

The restaurant is dark and intimate even in the middle of the day. The walls are painted in shades of burnt orange and gold, with colorful lithographs marking off different eating sections. Most of the art depicts common Indian culture with Buddhist prints from the seventeenth century. Times like this make me realize the importance of Lillian's culture studies. Rowan snaps his fingers in front of my face.

"Hey. You've got company here, you know."

"Don't worry, I'm just taking it all in. So. Lauren from the cafeteria sure thinks you're nice. Are you good friends?"

"I hope so. She's my aunt." He touches his face and glances away. The contradictory body language catches my attention.

"She didn't mention your relation when we talked."

"Aunt Lauren told me about the ad executive positions. She's the reason I applied."

"Oh, that's right. Is the money better than bartending?" I remember when I met Rowan, and how Nic's jealousy ruined my excitement over finding a new friend. Again, thoughts of Nic squeak under the door. Stitches from my gaping love wound burst open and I watch blood spurt across the table. If my imagination ever came to life I'd probably scare people half to death. I return my attention back to the conversation.

"The money sucks, but that should change after the launch. Good bartenders can make bank." I grin at the memory of our silly, hot chocolate date, and his charming theatrical show.

"How could I forget? It was the outrageous tip I left."

"I amuse you. Good, I like that." Rowan is skilled in the art of flirting, and if his interactions with me are any sign, he's already earned his doctorate.

"Actually, I *do* find you amusing. Do me a favor and stay on my good side so I don't have to you kill you."

"Only in your head, I hope." He holds his hands back.

"Eh... depends on the offense." I look up just as the waiter brings our plates.

After an extended lunch with good laughs and inappropriate jokes, we head back to Van Buren, parting ways inside the entrance. His confused look becomes one of understanding when I point toward the lab.

"That's my competition? Never thought I'd have to compete with a science geek, but crazier things have happened."

"You're funny. He's *at least* fifteen years older…and just a friend. I didn't realize you were competing." My purse slides off my shoulder and I push it back up, wondering if he's serious. He's hard to read, and it's frustrating.

"Stay straight Malone." He jokes and I walk the other direction shaking my head.

Dexter is nowhere to be found when I get to the lab. In fact, there's not a single scientist in sight. No one skitters past the hefty desks, Petri dishes and Bunsen burners. I can either rot in my stuffy, isolated office, or snoop while no one is looking. This one's a no brainer.

Dexter's desk drawers are unlocked and I rifle around looking for something he won't miss for a while. You'd think my penchant for snooping would have my craft wheedled to an art, complete with black latex gloves and a Cat Woman suit.

Hushed voices and footsteps filter through the air vents and I can't tell if they're headed this way or the other direction. There are rows of white metal footlockers lining the wall and I rattle each handle until I find one that's open, and crawl inside. Claude's voice is now at Dexter's desk and I let the door mechanism fall into place real slow to avoid detection.

"Where's that Julia gotten off to now? No wonder you had such a hard time with that girl in England."

Frustration raises the pitch of his voice. "That's odd; Dexter should be here."

"There were difficulties after she took the elixir." Lillian's voice is a murmur. "You knew she'd progress at an alarming rate, but what about the others? Their genetic history is sketchy."

"You worry too much, Lillian. Henry sees ahead and everything works out in the end," and as an afterthought, "Julia is so much like her mother."

"And when did Henry become a reliable source of information about the future?" Her bold sarcasm is a departure from the norm.

Through the locker slats, I see Claude searching for something, and keep my thoughts on lockdown to hide my whereabouts. More footsteps arrive and I recognize Dexter's disorganized movements.

"Rowan said she came to work with you. You haven't seen her?"

"Who, sir?" Dexter's absentminded response irritates Claude.

"Julia, you blasted idiot. Who do you think I'm talking about?" His temper erupts and Lillian blanches. He's *always* so controlled.

"Leave the poor lad alone; he hasn't seen her." She

255

turns to Dexter. "Don't worry, dear, we'll find Julia on our own." She sends Claude a wilting look as he turns on his heel and stalks from the lab.

Dexter shrugs and she pats him on the back, clucking with maternal reassurances. She follows Claude although he doesn't bother waiting. When the intrusive higher-ups leave, Dex produces a key from his lab coat pocket, looks around, and opens the locked drawer.

"Hey, Jules, I don't know what mess you've gotten yourself into, but get your butt up here. Claude is on the warpath." Nic's familiar mental tugging is urgent.

"I'm indisposed at the moment—in the worst way possible."

"Think fast because he's scouring the building with a fine toothed comb."

"When I say indisposed, I mean indisposed. I have to go."

"Julia—" I never cut him off, but something isn't right. I'm not sure if I'm in danger or my imagination is in overdrive again.

Dexter pores over weathered notebooks and these are nothing like the ones he shared this morning. They're leather-bound and old, the paper yellowed with time. He deposits the journals into the locked drawer and drops the key in his pocket.

After a moment of agitated shuffling, he disappears through the double doors, giving me time to escape. I lift the inside latch to find an empty room. Claude and Lillian's conversation left too many questions rattling around my head.

"Henry sees ahead and everything works out in the end."

Chapter Sixteen—Truth or Dare

Leopold waits out front and I make a stealthy escape into obscurity. Donned in oversized round sunglasses that swallow my face, I scout through my purse to locate the platinum card. I've learned to treasure it these past few weeks.

He stops at a corner ATM and I withdraw cash, stuffing hundreds in my purse. I check both directions to make sure no one notices and slip into the limo.

"Can you drop me off at The Eclectic Eatery? A friend is meeting me for dinner so no need to wait around." I'm a horrible liar, but the need for solace overrides my inclination toward honesty.

"Yes ma'am. It's no trouble." He studies me from the rear-view mirror, complying without hesitation.

Once on the curb, I duck inside the eatery and wait for Leopold to dissolve back into traffic. I reemerge and hail a taxi, directing my driver to The Plaza. It takes forever to get there through swarms of obnoxious traffic, but I spot the building and relax.

I hand the driver a fifty, step out, and crane my neck to take in the towering New York hotel. This will be home for the next couple days while I regroup. My life is out of control and I don't know who I can trust anymore.

Sometimes, I wonder if trusting my perceptions is wise. My intuition crashed when I took the elixir and everything turned upside down in the aftermath.

A portly doorman bows, and I enter the grandeur of an open lobby, a stark contrast from the grayness of weather and the streets. The hotel's gold and white theme is airy and elegant, chandeliers dripping with crystals while potted palms flank tall windows with rich, goldenrod curtains. High ceilings are gilded, and intricate designs delight the eye. A marble staircase and a wrought iron railing built of golden curlicues winds to the left and ends at a landing with deep burgundy curtains. There are murmuring conversations at the top and seems to lead to a lounge area.

I glance at a vintage chestnut topiary containing a five foot spray of branches that dominates the elegant seating area of the lobby. It's breathtaking and I glance down at the diamond pattern beneath my feet, and an enormous gold and black emblem set into glossy marble flooring.

259

Reception waits under a squared arch, tucked between the grand staircase and a seating area to the left. A man in a black suit before the check-in area greets me. It's intimate, and comprised of dark, lush, woods.

The receptionist asks for identification and then looks me up in their system.

"I don't see you here; did you make a reservation?" She seems perplexed but probably doesn't encounter this much.

"I didn't have time. Do you have rooms available?" The process has me nervous and sweating, and she requests a credit card.

"I'll be paying in cash if that's okay." The receptionist eyes me with suspicion. "It's all I have." No one can track me with paper money, and I don't want Claude, or anyone else, finding me with credit card transactions. She calls her supervisor for approval and I try to act nonchalant. I'd never cut it as a criminal.

After passing her supervisor's scrutiny, the receptionist checks me in and tells me about their accommodations. The only thing I can do is nod after handing her a stack of hundred dollar bills, which were quickly checked for authenticity. How embarrassing.

My room carries the same well-designed theme as

the hotel and is perfect for screwing my head on straight. I'm exhausted and flop on the bed, noticing the arched headboard. It's cushioned in a crème hue and surrounded by gold wood in thick, curling arches. It's medieval in a charming, updated way, and the warm, elegant hues relax my frazzled nerves. Within minutes my lids become heavy and I fall into light sleep, recalling memories of my past.

I'm a small girl standing on the doorstep of our manor with a stranger who appears dark and formidable to my young eyes. It's storming, and raindrops mingle with my tears as I'm delivered to an uncertain fate. I remember Lillian then, thinner and less frazzled, but still the mother hen that took me under her wing. A week later, the same man delivered Nic, Sebastian, and Dutch.

Nic's good-natured charm, Sebastian's intensity, and Dutch's soft demeanor were distinct contrasts to my own personality. I bolt upright in bed, disturbed. None of us knows our real family. There's no blood relation, so what do we have in common? We read minds, emotions, and pick up subtleties of body language and communication. Our gifts in the unseen are what make us a family. Is our benefactor a philanthropist or a nihilist?

I drift over early memories of the manor with my improvised family, our combination of odd mental backgrounds making us who we are. We've always been a complex mismatch of similar creatures whose personalities couldn't be more different. When Lyra and Lincoln arrived, each a week apart, our tribe was complete.

Lillian taught and encouraged us to speak with our minds, and most of our lessons were trial and error. It wasn't often we experienced the outside world, or even classes in the public school system. We tried in our teens but Lillian rejected outside schooling when it didn't work. The boys couldn't seem to control themselves, which makes sense according to the laws of maturation.

It was interesting while it lasted though, the experience both complex and confusing. Even at this age, it's difficult blending in with others. How does *Immortality* complete the picture? Are we aiming to enhance the traits of everyone who uses it? Who will use it? Is it an elite product, or for the masses?

It's doubtful these burning questions have an immediate answer, and my thoughts drift back to friends. I love three of them in different ways, one drives me crazy but I still love her, and the last remains a dark and disturbing mystery.

I remember how that frigid day in October brought a strange sense of apprehension before the first frost. A small-boned, black haired boy with enormous blue gray eyes stood on the stoop, unsmiling. Lincoln's wiry frame seemed unnatural, but it was his demeanor that unnerved me.

His distinguishing attribute was the tendency to hide. Thoughts, emotions, and even his reactions remained buried in an undercurrent of seething rage. That was the only trait I ever sensed. Lyra has a somewhat shallow bond with him.

Lincoln studied us from the sidelines, waiting for the perfect opportunity to eliminate his imaginary opponents. I watched as he observed us over the years, wondering at the wheels that turned in his head. Lincoln was a mastermind always calculating his next chess move. He was a black, emotional void that lacked everything that made us human.

I glance around the hotel room, no idea why I'm hiding. Who is the enemy—my family of unusual orphans, a benefactor wielding an unknown substance, or the inability of humanity to differentiate between right and wrong? Morally, the lines blur at different points for everyone.

Lillian took us to church every Sunday, but never taught us about character; an oversight on her part. She allowed each of us to develop according to our own unique temperaments and genetic dispositions.

My independent streak is legendary so why am I hiding from anyone? I'm my own person, not Lillian's ward, Claude's puppet, or even Nic's girlfriend. I'm Julia Malone, and I shouldn't *have* to run. This new burst of realization leads to another one; I'm starving. I call room service to order, and they inform me it's already on the way.

"You must be mistaken. I didn't order food." I move the phone closer to my ear.

"Ma'am, I'm sorry but there's a card with the order. Your waiter should be there any moment. Is there anything else I can get for you?" She waits at the other end.

"No, I guess not. Thank you." Either Claude had me followed, or my phone has a tracking device.

A moment later, a butler arrives and wheels his cart in my room. I'm reserved and suspicious but hand him a twenty, thanking him for the service.

"Thank you, ma'am. Enjoy your dinner." He nods and departs. I pluck the card from between a metal dome and a flower vase.

Dear Julia,

I hope I'm not butting in where I don't belong, but I

264

didn't want you to be alone.

Love, Nic

My face heats with humiliation and I hustle toward the peephole in my door after a second knock. Nic's on the other side. I whip the door open and grab his arm, darn near tearing it from the socket.

"How in the heck did you even find me?" I turn my back to him, crossing my arms. If there were stones on the carpet, I'd kick every one. *The nerve.*

"Really, Jules? You're gonna ask how I found you?"

"How did you get past my blocks?" I turn back with an accusing glare.

"For the love of God, you were wide open!" He throws his hands in the air. "A neon sign reading *'here I am'* would have been less obvious."

"This is a total disaster." I cover my face with both hands. "That's the hardest I've blocked in my life." My head is spinning and I flop to the bed, recalling how Claude and Lillian pretended they didn't know I was in the locker. Nic sits beside me.

"How long? And just so you know, I officially hate my life."

"How long, what?" He uses both hands to crack his

neck to the left, and then the right.

"How long have my blocks been useless?" The thought of Sebastian privy to my fantasies that night has me recoiling with nausea.

"I read you in the cab. Your thoughts were frantic, but I slowed them with my own mind to see if you were in any real danger. Then I recognized the hormonal shift, took a deep breath, and ordered you dinner." He won't look me in the eye, and waits for me to figure it out. I'm mortified when his explanation registers.

"It would serve you well to elaborate, Mr. Maye."

"Your mental guards are compromised right before…um…" He stutters, his cheeks flaming.

"How long have you known this fact?" My tone is murderous and so is my expression.

"Since forever?" He chews his lower lip and adds, "I noticed when you were twelve. Sorry I didn't tell you." At least he has the courtesy to look ashamed.

"You didn't think it was something I needed to know, or might save my life someday?" My voice cracks.

"Goose, calm down; it's not a big deal."

"I can't use my mental blocks at certain times of the month but that's not important enough to share?" I take a deep breath so I don't choke him. "Claude and Lillian came looking for me and I was hiding in a stupid foot locker for God's sake. Do you know how humiliated I am?" The urge to swat him silly makes me jump up and pace the room.

"See what I ordered before you go all nuclear on me." He points to the silver domes. "I'm sorry, it was selfish. I love knowing what's going on in your head but I shouldn't have kept it from you."

"You think? Was that a *real* apology? Hang tight. I need to regulate my heartbeat here." I throw my hands in the air and stalk over to the dinner cart.

The largest dome has a plate of steak, grilled asparagus, and cheddar mashed potatoes. The second dome holds a slice of triple-layer chocolate cake. A steaming silver decanter of hot water sits beside a cup and an assortment of teas.

I want to dig a hole in the carpet and hide when I find a packet of Midol and a feminine product sitting behind the hot water decanter. Then the cramps hit and I rush to the bathroom with my supplies.

"You think you're so smart, don't you?"

"Well you have to admit..."

"Thank you."

"No problem."

"No, thank you. It taught me two things."

267

"What's that?"

"Trusting you to have my best interests at heart—and to tell you what my best interests are. I could have used this information a few years ago."

"Don't worry; I'm the only one who can break though."

"You have no proof of that."

"I'm almost positive."

"I'm such an idiot. Now I have to re-train all over again."

After swallowing two pills and taking care of business, I return and find him salivating over my food.

"Sit your butt down. We'll share since you were kind enough to order it for us." I take a deep breath and let the air hiss through my teeth. Then I repeat the process two more times until I'm no longer aggravated.

"I didn't order it for us, I ordered it for you." He's drooling down the front of his shirt and I'm supposed to believe him.

"Well, you're here aren't you?"

"Yeah, I guess I am."

I cut the steak and alternate between taking a bite myself, and feeding him a bite, our familiar and intimate way with each other.

When we get to the chocolate cake I shake my head. He's not getting any of it. It's embarrassing to admit that even I, Julia Goose Malone, am a slave to monthly hormones. I stuff my face with cake.

"You want to get out of here? No one has to know this ever happened." He grabs me under the shoulders and pushes me out the front door as I dig in with heavy, reluctant steps, snatching my purse on the way out.

"Stop dragging me; I got it." He lets go and I follow him down to the lobby.

Older women in expensive dresses and business suits stare as we leave the building. I'm sure they assume the worst for as young as we are, but who cares? I pity their shallow way of existing, judging and mocking others to feel superior. You'd think human beings had better things to do with their lives, but apparently not.

Taxi drivers ignore us for twenty minutes before a shiny new cab answers our hail. We slide into the back seat and Nic gives the driver our coordinates while I slump to the side, feeling ridiculous for running away from home. When the driver misses our turn, I realize we're headed the wrong direction and elbow Nic.

"Sir, you need to turn around," and he repeats our address to the driver. The doors automatically lock and Nic grabs my hand.

"Don't worry, you're safe. I'm bringing you back to Claude." The cab driver's thick accent is far from reassuring and I reach for my cell after noticing Nic's jaw tic.

"And Claude sent you?" Nic asks.

"Yes." He adjusts his rear-view mirror to watch us.

Dutch answers the phone, and my heart skips a beat. I'm relieved they're safe, but the underarms of my shirt are already soaked.

"Hey, you guys okay?" There is unusual noise in the background and I glance at Nic. His body is rigid, as if preparing to fight, and I struggle to keep my voice steady.

"Yeah, we're just waiting for you and Nic to get here. We got back from the tour this afternoon and expected you home by now. Is everything kosher?" Dutch sounds cheerful and I don't want to alarm him.

"We're fine. Is Claude there?"

"Everyone's here, the whole group." I put my phone on speaker so Nic can hear.

"So Claude's at *my* penthouse with you?" My heart thunders in my chest.

"Yeah, Lillian's making her famous beef stroganoff. She put Claude to work in the kitchen and he's a total duck

270

out of water." He laughs. "I've never seen anything so funny in my life."

Nic's eyes widen and I shake my head back and forth. "Listen, can you get Claude on the phone for me? It's important." The driver glares at us in the rear-view mirror, knowing he's busted.

He slams on the brakes and Nic kicks at the window with the heel of his shoe until it cracks and shatters. The driver rams a car in front of us, and then throws the cab in reverse, slamming into another cab. Nic kicks the remaining glass from the window.

With no alternative, the driver opens his door and flees into traffic, zig zagging through stopped vehicles and pedestrians while several people step from their cars to call for help. Nearby officers spot the commotion and race toward our taxi. Nic scrambles through the back window tearing his pants, but officers unlock the door before I do the same and cut myself. We stand in the middle of traffic with dozens of onlookers as people lay on their horns or point.

I put the phone to my ear and Claude's voice is panicked, but Lillian sounds downright hysterical in the background. Men and women on the sidewalks hold their cells midair, while others stand outside their vehicles, leaning against opened doors to get a better view.

The shorter of the two officers, a Mr. Jenks, gestures for me to hand him my phone. He talks with Claude and asks him to meet us at the station. Officer Jenks returns my phone, directing us to the back of his squad car. He helps Nic and me inside before closing the door.

Nic and I slink into our seats feeling conspicuous while people stare at the crime scene. An unknown man in a grungy jacket and grime smeared face taps on my window and grins. He taunts us with a toothless smile, grabbing his belly and cackling as if insane.

Sirens from the squad car blare and traffic slowly moves aside until we're on the outskirts of the heavy congestion.

"This is the worst day of my life." I whisper to no one. The city slides by, the fast pace of New York slowing the further we drive.

"It's not over yet." Nic whispers from the corner of his mouth, locking eyes with the heavy officer who turns to appraise us in the back seat.

"Are you both okay?" He shoves half a glazed donut in his mouth in one bite.

"We're fine, officer, and thank you." I wrap my arms around my midsection and turn toward the window.

Officer Jenks heaves his extra weight around to face forward and I hear his loud chomping from the back seat, which causes my dinner to make its way up my throat. A lunatic tried to kidnap us, but to the officer, it's just another day at the office.

The ride to the police station is eerily quiet and there's nothing but calm silence in our heads. Our police escorts usher us inside the station. There's a dilapidated waiting room with worn blue seats arranged in haphazard rows. We're greeted by hideous yellow paint, and appears as if people scraped objects across the walls to make their point. I expect to see Claude and Lillian in the waiting room, but they're nowhere in sight.

"This way, please." The tall officer gestures toward room number five. Once inside, we find Claude and Lillian at a long rectangular table. The wood is marred by circular coffee stains further adding to the ambiance of wear and graffiti.

We sit, flanked by New York's finest at opposite ends of the table, and officer Jenks prepares to speak. Claude interrupts.

"As explained earlier, security was compromised at Van Buren Industries this afternoon. We believe the intruder was after a trade secret. It's possible the attempted

273

abduction relates to this breach." It's obvious to everyone in the room that Claude is the man in charge.

"Why would a cab driver abduct a couple kids? Why are they significant to a trade secret?" His eyes narrow.

"Julia is the vice president of product development for a new line of skincare. She has firsthand knowledge of our patent, and she's far from a kid." His response is stiff and formal.

"How did the cab driver come in contact with your employees?"

The officers, Claude, and Lillian shift their attention.

"I went to The Plaza to get away for a few days." My cheeks fire up and if I could blend into the furniture, I'd surely try.

"And what about Nic?" Lillian studies our faces.

"Found me." I stare into my lap, nibbling at my lower lip. Claude's anger is palpable, and the officers let out an exasperated sigh. It's obvious their interrogation is going nowhere.

"Julia, can you tell us what happened, and please start at the beginning." The tall officer taps his pen on the table and glances up, preparing to take a statement.

I recount the story, leaving out a few minor details to avoid further humiliation, and the officers seem satisfied—but not motivated to take the case further. We didn't get a good look at the cab driver, and they don't bother calling in a sketch artist. It's an open and shut case as far as they're concerned. The only practical motive is the one Claude provided.

"If that's it, can we take them home now?" He stands, smoothing his suit and the officers dismiss our case.

Claude stiff arms me from the building and then urges me into the limo. Nic and Lillian file in behind us.

"Are you both okay?" His concern startles me because I assumed he was furious.

"I—yeah, I guess. Thank God for Nic though." The thought makes me shiver because it happened so fast.

"An intruder compromised the lab this afternoon. I'll need you to look at surveillance tapes tomorrow morning." His intense expression has me avoiding eye contact and I turn to Nic for reassurance.

"What do you think is happening?" My gaze remains downcast.

"Are your blocks in place?"

"Yes, why?"

"Because I can read you like a book. Are you

275

sure?"

"Nic, I'm positive!"

"Just checking. Claude makes less sense the more I know him."

"What do you mean?"

"He was furious when he went looking for you in the lab."

"Just furious—or furious with me?" I keep my expression neutral.

"He was mad about something you and Dexter discovered and didn't tell him."

"I wasn't working with Dexter. He wasn't even in the lab when I went looking."

"Did he change the formula based on something you said?"

"Well, yes, but wait—how did you know?"

"Just plucking thoughts again Julia, it's what we do. Does Rowan know about it?"

"Why would he know? What the hell is going on here? You act like I invented a nuclear bomb or something."

"You did."

The limo arrives and Claude opens the door for us to step out. He blocks me as I'm ready to exit, and whispers in my ear.

"I knew you were in that locker. Don't hide from me again." The arm lifts, and he allows me to pass, followed by Nic. Claude shuts the door with a crisp click and they merge into the left lane.

"What did he say?" Nic demands.

When I don't respond he nudges my arm.

"Julia, what did he say?"

"He got through my blocks and knew I was in the locker."

We stare into a haze of electric lights and slow moving vehicles as a blur of dizzying New York City traffic swallows the limo.

Chapter Seventeen—Insider

Dutch and Sebastian greet us at the elevator, but I storm to the bedroom with Nic on my heels. I slam my door and turn the lock.

"Why didn't Claude simply lift the handle on my locker? What's with his mind games?"

"What happened in there anyway?"

"When Claude and Lillian left, Dexter came back a second time and unlocked a secret drawer. The other drawers aren't locked, and this one is hidden below his desk. Dex checked on the notebooks and that's it."

"Then what?"

"Then nothing. He locked the drawer and left the lab." I replay the entire scene and didn't miss anything as far as I can tell.

"So what did you say that made Dexter reformulate *Immortality*?" Nic grabs my shoulders to stop my angry pacing.

"I asked about the base. He couldn't stabilize substance X in the facial cream and didn't know why."

"What was the brilliant scientific suggestion?"

"You're being sarcastic?" I pull from his grip and continue pacing.

"Yes, Julia, that's sarcasm. What did you tell the *experienced* scientist to cause so much trouble?"

"You're a jerk." I barge toward the window but Nic catches my coat and spins me into his arms. I struggle but it's no use.

"Who gets all the attention?" He lets go and rakes a hand through his hair because it's sticking up in different directions.

"Right. Is this a jealousy thing?"

"Are you kidding? You figure everything out before anyone else even gets a chance. It makes us crazy."

"That's funny coming from shiny, golden, halo boy."

"Don't even want to know what that means." Nic crosses his arms.

"Get over your fragile male ego. We're in over our heads and you know it."

Nic nods in agreement and we stare out the window at hectic traffic, focusing on the masses of unsuspecting people. The men and women resemble ants from the twentieth floor and I feel alienated from the rest of society.

"I want to go back to England. This life isn't worth

it."

Nic's presence is reassuring even though I still want to sock him in the eye. Maybe my definition of love is too rigid. One minute I want nothing more than to wrap myself in his arms, and the next minute I want to knock him upside the head with a blunt object.

"Dexter stabilized *Immortality* with your help so how can we go home now? Van Buren Industries is launching with or without us."

"Correction—the company is launching without long-term studies on safety."

Put in those terms, it's not so black and white anymore. Experimenting on kids in a controlled environment is one thing. Too many variables exist with ordinary people.

"Claude *must* realize Lincoln's not right in the head. Lillian knows. The rest of us know." Nic admits.

"The wealthy don't think about casualties. And Rowan was dangerous?" My jab was long overdue.

"Rowan wasn't in today, but you don't think there's anything suspicious about his absence?"

"No. Why would I?"

"The day Van Buren is infiltrated, you take off, and we're abducted by a taxi driver. Rowan just happens to be gone? Not buying that ocean-front property in Arizona, Jules."

"Who is the acting vice president of product development at Van Buren? I've been here a whopping seven weeks and I'm eighteen years old. What does that say?" Nic's so focused on Rowan; he can't add two plus two.

"Not following."

"Well, start. We're figureheads and nothing more."

"Settle down. You need chocolate."

"While you learned sales tactics I read the chemistry and science behind the product. Want to know what I found?" He shrugs.

"No one can identify substance X. Nothing similar appears in any of the world's scientific journals. They wouldn't know the difference if it came from Venus. Dexter is the lead scientist on this project and still doesn't have a clue."

Nic cocks his head to the side and stares long and hard.

"What?" I snap.

"You don't see it?"

"See what?"

"How much smarter you are. You've always been

smart, but the changes are different. We're still evolving and—"

I cut him off short. "There are six people in this group. Not everyone got the long end of the stick."

No one's had time to observe Lincoln and Lyra because Claude and Lillian keep them under wraps. Dutch's enhancements are positive, but his traits were wonderful to start with—at least in my eyes. Nic hasn't shown any changes at all these past few weeks.

"You noticed my increased intelligence, but how are *you* changing? There's nothing out of the ordinary unless you're hiding something." My legs feel rubbery and I sit. Nic stands there dazed.

"I *am* a man for jolly sake."

"You *wish* you were a man. Okay; your head's a little bigger maybe."

"You're a funny girl. I better add that to a list of notorious observations for the goose." He hoists me from the chair and tosses me onto the bed. In one second flat, I'm pinned into something resembling a pretzel.

"Stop!" My squealing attracts attention and there's a knock at the door.

I bust out of Nic's half-nelson and race over to let Sebastian and Dutch in the room. We pile drive Nic and it's an all-out wrestling match on my bed. For the first time in weeks, there's normalcy again. Not that anyone could call narrowly escaping the hands of a kidnapper, normal.

***

My alarm clock shocks me out of bed before the break of dawn so I grab a quick shower and slip into a black pantsuit. The boys are already in the kitchen and inform me that Catherine has everyone's offices ready. Sebastian follows my every move while we eat breakfast and drink coffee, and Dutch senses the unspoken friction between him and Nic.

Leopold rings to let us know he's out front and I grab my coat and briefcase. The ride to Van Buren is quiet and Catherine is waiting on the fourth floor landing, ready to show everyone the new offices. Lincoln studies us, but I don't have the time or patience for him this morning.

"Okay, guys, it's the big day. Are you ready?" Her voice is high-pitched and as irritating as a cheerleader.

We follow Catherine and she deposits the boys into offices as lush as Nic's. When we arrive at Lyra's office, Catherine remained true to form. It's not as horrid as mine was—it's worse. I slap a hand over my mouth, pretending to sneeze, and turn to avoid laughing. Once it starts, I can't stop. *This spat won't be pretty.*

"What do you think?" Catherine beams at Lyra as if she single-handedly created an architectural masterpiece.

"I think you're a freaking nut job. Not happening." Lyra's response causes Catherine's smile to fade real quick. It takes her a couple seconds to recover from the insult. I've never cared for Lyra, but even I'm not stupid enough to mess with the girl.

"This is your new office, Lyra" and then adds, "Julia, you may go now." Her flippant dismissal isn't happening.

"That's quite alright. I'll help Lyra unpack. Don't want to miss this, trust me." I can't tell who wields the deadlier glare because both of them could burn the skin from someone's face. Everyone pauses, waiting for Lyra's reaction. I walk into her new nightmare and stop short. Catherine certainly has a death wish.

"I'm not working in this revolting office, you corporate cheese-head. How about you try this again," she snaps and adds, "Did your mum drop you on your noggin when you were a wee little monster?" Lyra's comebacks are brutal.

She and Catherine are locked in a seething battle of wills so I leave the cats to their litter box. By the time I reach my office, shouts from the other end of the hallway are loud enough to draw attention from another floor. I race back to find a scene nothing short of spectacular.

Lyra and Catherine are battling it out on the floor, pulling hair, scratching faces and cussing like sailors. A group of shocked spectators stands by, but no one breaks up the fight. Lyra emerges with a handful of blonde hair in her fist.

"You witch!" The blonde dictator shouts.

Another round of grunts and Cruella's skirt rips to the waist. Lyra stands and takes the title, knowing she's the victor. Catherine squawks and thrashes on the floor before realizing she no longer has an opponent.

Claude marches around the corner with a furious expression, and his employees scatter like rats. I stand there with *dukes-a-hoy* by my side while legs-a-hoy regains her composure on the floor.

"What the Sam Hill is going on in here?" His eyes are bloodshot, and an enormous vein bulges at the side of his neck. Claude's heartbeat is visible and I avert my gaze, trying not to gawk at the artery getting ready to explode.

"This hell hound thought she would cram me into that repulsive office and I wasn't having any part of it." Her glare staples Catherine to the floor but Claude helps the frazzled mess to her feet.

"Julia, did you see what happened here?" His expression is one of disgust.

"Yes sir, I did." My vague response doesn't impress him and he scowls.

"She painted our offices like this on purpose, temporary or not. Check for yourself. It wasn't only me." He takes a peek.

"What the—" He can't even finish his sentence. It's the size of a linen closet, and painted in shades of hot pink, green, and mustard. Catherine shrinks from his contemptuous glare.

"Is this your handiwork?" His lips press into a thin line.

She nods and stretches the torn skirt over her exposed thigh.

"I'll deal with you later," he promises, and adds, "Settle in for now. Julia is also waiting for a permanent office, but an employee repainted hers beforehand. I didn't get to see the previous design of my *trusted* executive assistant."

Lyra pouts and barges in her office as Catherine skitters the other direction, beaten at her own game. Claude catches up to me, taking long strides.

"I'm sorry about all this. Was *your* office that

bad?"

"It was hideous."

"That Catherine is something else." His tone is chipped.

"Let's just say she gives new meaning to the phrase, *piece of work.*" I unlock my office, gesturing for him to sit in the worn out chair next to my desk.

"Don't worry; I have grand plans for your permanent office. Why didn't you complain?" He sits, a frown disturbing his line-free face.

"I'm easy to please but if not for my friend Rowan repainting my office in an act of mercy, I would have complained."

He waits for me to seat myself. "Remember, I need you to review security tapes this morning."

"It's all I've thought about since last night. I'm ready when you are."

He takes me by service elevator to the tenth floor where we step into a giant black and white space with video equipment lining every conceivable corner. The exterior wall is solid windows and we can see the entire city of New York from this vantage point.

"The whole floor is security?" There are monitors with split screens everywhere, and the room is filled with so much light it gives the illusion of being outdoors.

"Yes. I dedicated the tenth floor to security. Nothing in Van Buren Industries is unmonitored, but I didn't need surveillance equipment to know you were hiding in that locker."

Ouch.

He leads me to a glass encased cubicle with an overweight bald man watching six monitors at the same time. The man has huge fleshy wrinkles stacked on his neck and sweat drips into the collar of his shirt, creating an enormous wet spot on his back. The man doesn't bother with a greeting, but Claude makes introductions.

"This is Plato. He's the eyes and ears of Van Buren and takes his job seriously." Claude pats him on the back and he grunts to acknowledge our presence. He zooms in on camera number five and removes his sunglasses, squinting at the screen. I shake my head, thinking the man quite rude, but Claude doesn't notice.

We leave Plato to his work and walk to a sectioned off table where a gray haired man with a wiry body greets us with pleasantries. Round spectacles make his eyes appear too close together and I wonder if square frames might have suited him better. His high-pitched voice reels me back, reminding me of when the boys went through puberty.

"Mr. Van Buren, I have the tapes you requested. This must be Julia." He thrusts his hand into mine and rattles my arm all the way to my neck. Did he *not* notice my super thin frame? Good grief, it's not as if I need to use that arm anytime soon.

"Yes, meet our Julia. She needs to understand I'm not the villain around here, but we have an intruder inside our walls. Take a seat beside Mr. Callen." Claude instructs. "Please call me Jim, everybody does." He points to a gray, plastic chair so I sit, scooting in tight. Mr. Callen hits play on the first tape. Then he fast-forwards until I see people moving into the picture. He hits the stop button when a female appears near the lab doors.

"That woman is trying to infiltrate the lab—" He zooms in closer. "Do you recognize her?"

"Can you zoom in more?" I narrow my eyes, trying to focus. I'm shocked when I recognize her face.

"You're acquainted with this woman?"

"It's Lauren from the cafeteria." She glances both ways before holding a security badge to the automated doors, trying to gain entrance. After failing she hurries back down the hall.

"We have her on other cameras but they show her

leaving the building. What can you tell us?" Jim shoves an e-cigarette in his mouth and puffs as if his life depended on it, his eyes wide and excited. It doesn't get much more comical than this, but I bite back the urge to laugh.

"Not much. I go to the cafeteria for coffee and she makes great breakfast sandwiches. She seemed normal but—" Then I recall the lunch conversation. "She's Rowan's aunt."

"I knew it!" Claude shouts and I jump in my chair, almost tipping Jim's coffee.

"Has she worked here long?" I'm recovering from my benefactor's reaction while my heart returns to its normal rhythm. This is the second time I've watched him come un-glued.

"Julia, meet my ex-wife. Her name is Claire Underwood. She's wearing a wig and I can't believe I didn't recognize her—plastic surgery no doubt."

"A wife?"

"Our six month marriage was a colossal mistake; long story. She used to talk about her nephew Rowan all the time. When I found out she was a raving lunatic, I had the marriage annulled. Rowan is her son. I didn't want more children, so she hid his existence." His expression is murderous and I hope I'm never at the receiving end of it.

"Okay." I prod. "Wait…*more* children? You don't have any children."

"I misspoke, sorry. At any rate, he stayed with her brother Sam, the cab driver. It's amazing what private investigators can unearth." He points to camera number four and nudges the arm-rattling gray haired man named Jim.

"Check Julia's floor. That little rat better not be in my building." Claude leans over Jim's shoulder.

He scans the fourth floor and Rowan's cubicle is empty for the second day in a row. My stomach sinks. Nic pegged him from the beginning and I wouldn't listen.

"You know Claude; I didn't take you for the marrying kind."

"There's much you don't know, kiddo." He pats me on the back. "You can go back to your office if you wish."

I leave Claude and Jim to finish their detective work, but my heart hurts. The first person I meet in New York turns out to be a con artist, and Nic knew it the entire time.

"Such is life," I mutter to myself, paying no attention to my surroundings. The glitchy service elevator let me out on the wrong floor and I'm startled by a voice I didn't expect to hear.

"What's up?" Rowan asks, leaning against a wall. I jump back, unprepared for the chance meeting.

"Remind me to get my peripheral vision checked. Good lord." I say, noticing his casual attire. He looks nice in jeans and a sweater but that's not the point and I take a second to gather my thoughts.

Rowan acts the pillar of innocence, and I want nothing more than to knock him senseless for making me look like an idiot. I'll let Claude dole out the justice on this one; a newfound sense of loyalty to Van Buren Industries rears its head.

"Where have you been the last two days?" My stomach does a somersault and acting normal proves unsuccessful. He knits his brows for a second and just as quick his facade changes.

"I've been flat on my back with the flu. Company would have been nice." He shoves his hands in his pockets and grins, the insinuation making me sick.

"Nah—big tough guy like you?" I hold him off in the hallway, hoping Plato or Jim is paying attention and catches up with us. My search for Claude's mind proves difficult.

"Yeah, I threw up for hours. I shouldn't be here but needed something from my desk." He glances over my shoulder as if something has him spooked.

"What would that be?" My ghost of a smile feels plastic.

"I need a few papers for a presentation this week." His demeanor changes, knowing something is off between us.

"Claude, I have Rowan in the hallway. Get down here now."

"Can you hold him?"

"I'll try, but he already knows something isn't right."

Acting normal under these circumstances is beyond my repertoire of skills and I stop blinking, my smile frozen.

"Listen, I have to get going but I'll see you tomorrow. Stay straight." He hits me with a megawatt fake smile and I offer him a halfhearted one in return.

"Wait!" I touch his arm and he stops. "Did you hear about the fight between Catherine and Lyra this morning? It was hilarious."

"No, but you can tell me about it tomorrow. Sorry, gotta run." He jerks his chin upward and walks the other direction—fast. By the time Claude arrives, he's already gone. I bang my forehead against the wall at our dumb luck and poor timing. One minute more was all I needed.

"If he comes back tomorrow I'll have a surprise waiting for him in the form of handcuffs. Go see Dexter. He's been waiting for you." Claude squeezes my shoulder and walks the other direction.

Chapter Eighteen—Launch

The long walk back is the saddest road possible and I replay everything in my head I ever missed about Rowan. My first clue, should have been the *too good to be true*, charm.

Tonight, I need to sit with Nic and go over everything I didn't catch, but for now, it's time to dance with Dexter on science. I find him in the lab dressed in a black business suit instead of his usual lab coat and scrubs. At first glance, he's almost unrecognizable. My favorite science geek underwent a metamorphosis.

"Contacts?" I point and circle him like a predatory cat. He looks amazing from head to toe, but his body language screams *unsure*.

"I guess it was time for an upgrade. Chicks don't dig blind guys." He blushes and kicks at the floor with his new black shoes.

"So what's the big occasion? Claude said to come see you." I glance at the scuff mark his shoe left and notice we're both staring at it. Obsessive compulsive disorder isn't fun unless you have someone who understands. We both laugh.

"This is why I love you so much." I say.

Dexter straightens his shoulders and clears his throat as if preparing for a commencement speech. "I stabilized *Immortality* thanks to you." He fidgets.

"That's wonderful." I draw him in for a hug, and he rests his head on my shoulder. My annoying title is an invisible barrier—still.

"We go into production soon, and I wanted you to find out from me." He glances at his shiny black shoes, unable to contain his excitement.

"Where are you headed looking as if you just stepped off the cover of a men's magazine? Dex, you clean up nice." I adjust his lapels and smooth my hands over his shoulders twice.

"I'm meeting with the board of directors for final approval."

"How long before *Immortality* hits stores?" The walls of the lab seem to breathe thinking about the impact of our product on store shelves. My heartbeat picks up, making me dizzy and anxious.

"That's up to Claude. He has new people in marketing. Your brothers and a sister I believe." He studies my reaction, but I already knew.

"Well, hop to it, mister—knock em' dead." He dares to hug me and I hold our embrace for good measure.

Dexter strides toward the exit with newfound confidence. I'll sit with him this week and discuss the reformulation. He hasn't yet shared his results from the testing and implementation.

My walk to the fourth floor yields nothing new, but I'm greeted by a yellow sticky note on the door that reads, *Walk until you find your nameplate.* Claude pulled through and my new office must be ready.

I check each door in passing until I spot my name in gold. It's two offices up from Nic, and I'm relieved to discover an enormous space with floor to ceiling windows.

A massive cherry desk and matching bookshelves dwarf an ultra cushy executive chair. The new office is bare, but it's a nice blank canvas awaiting my touch.

"Well, there you are. Do you like it?" Claude is cross-armed leaning against my door.

"Do I like it? You gave me the conference room. It's beyond awesome." Weeks in that cramped, windowless office took a toll on my personality and outlook.

"This is the office I had in mind for you. Once it's furnished, Catherine gets your old one." He smiles and my sense of justice is appeased.

"Dexter left for a board meeting. Is it true that *Immortality* is going into production soon?" The tone of our conversation takes a serious turn.

"Yes, it's true, but I can't say how long before we're ready to market."

"Speaking of marketing—"

"The answer to your question is *yes*. Dutch, Lyra, and Sebastian are in marketing. I chose Nic to lead up sales because he's a charmer." The word makes me cringe and brings Rowan to mind. "But you already know this."

"I figured Nic out years ago. And Lincoln—where did you put him?" Claude's mood shifts at the mention of Lincoln but I resist the urge to sweep his thoughts.

"I'll wait awhile on him. I'm not sure where his talents lie hidden just yet." He stares out the windows at a breathtaking view of New York City, his demeanor contemplative.

"Well, if it's any consolation, we've never been able to get a read on him either." I stand next to Claude and gaze down at passing pedestrians. People aren't as small from the fourth floor as they are the twentieth. From here, I can enjoy their idiosyncrasies. The women who walk New York City streets wearing stilettos stand out the most. Our

298

sidewalks are obstacle courses rather than a means to an end. I can even count how much money is in the guitar player's hat. I'm sure security will chase him off by noon. Claude's voice jolts me back to our conversation and away from the visual distractions.

"Tell me, Julia, what do you see when you look at people now?"

The question takes me off guard because it's not straightforward. I'm honest to a fault, but his inquiry is loaded. When I glance back, he's behind my desk, studying me for signs of recognition.

"I'm not sure what you mean by that."

He taps a knuckle on my desk and turns to leave. "I'll have movers bring your things tomorrow. Why don't you go home for the day? It's been a crazy week. In fact, why don't you take a vacation?"

"I've never been on a vacation. Well, not really." The mention of it holds intriguing possibilities.

"You just leave everything to me. Leopold can take you home." He walks out with a curious expression on his face.

I melt into my executive chair, swivel toward the windows, and watch hundreds of people moving in different directions though life. My time at Van Buren

Industries is spent reading and researching, but when I stop to watch life in action, I wonder if their lives are as complex as mine. I'm sobered by the idea of vacationing alone.

"Are you in your office?" Nic's been quiet all morning.

"I'm right here studying. I meet with the sales team in a few minutes though. What's up?"

"Come to my new office."

"When are you going to learn I'm one step ahead of you? I'll be there in a couple minutes."

"Okay."

When he says a couple minutes he means a couple seconds, and his booming voice makes me jump.

"Nice office!"

"Nic, you scared me."

"It's like mine, but twice the size," he glances around the room. "I'm happy you're right next door though." There's a hint of jealousy in his tone and I never took him for the type.

"Did you hear what Claude did to Catherine?" It's hard to hide my amusement and don't even try.

"I'm always in the know, brainiac. Lyra's office is four doors beyond yours. Check where your favorite people are located." His smart-assed grin is maddening.

"Fabulous."

"I hear you have things to tell me." He stretches his arms behind his neck and waits.

"Are you tinkering with me, Mr. Maye?"

"Maybe, who's asking?"

"You're hopeless but cute. Claude thinks I need a vacation but going alone sounds dull. Did he mention anything like that to you?"

He rolls his eyes and gives me a dramatic sigh. I look around for something to throw at him and much to my annoyance the new desk is free of blunt, heavy objects.

"Grab your things and get gone, I'll see you soon." He struts from my office but the smile is a dead giveaway.

Nic was right, and Leopold is waiting at the curb when I burst onto the street, free at last. I'm starving so he doesn't waste time in traffic and weaves through every available opening. At home, I throw together a turkey sandwich and unwind in my room.

Other than Sebastian, everyone else moved into their new places on Saturday. The group is headed in different directions, and it makes me sad. A curious packet of materials sits in the middle of my bed and I wander over to inspect the envelope. I rip the cardboard zipper and pour the contents out while the sandwich hangs from my mouth. It's an itinerary, plane tickets, and a map of Mexico. Nic's name is on one of the tickets.

"Yesh!" Turkey flies everywhere as I squeal, hop up and down, and forget about the sandwich dangling from my mouth. "That was brilliant," I kneel and pick scraps of meat off the floor.

I'm ecstatic Nic's coming along, but Claude's motive for our trip is questionable. Cancun isn't far from Chichen Itza, where Dexter said Henry discovered the elixir. If the destination was Acapulco or Puerto Vallarta, there'd be no suspicion. I run a hot bath and ponder the possible motives behind our upcoming trip.

Steam swirls up around my head and I contemplate Claude's question from earlier. *Tell me Julia, what do you see when you look at people now?* It's a riddle, but not one I'm prepared to solve just yet.

The faint echo of our elevator vibrates the walls and I wonder if Nic came home early to discuss our upcoming trip to Mexico. I reach for a blue towel just as Sebastian barges into my bathroom unannounced. He stands there stunned and unmoving while I scramble to cover myself.

"Are you bloody daft? You can't just barge into a girl's bathroom without knocking!" Water drips from me to the floor, forming a puddle around my feet.

"Dang, I mean…okay, wow. I'm sorry, I wasn't—"
He flees without finishing his sentence. That's darn near
perfect. If his imagination wasn't dreadful enough, I just
provided him with a visual.

*Focus on vacation, Julia. You're going somewhere
warm and tropical, and no one in Mexico will have
firsthand knowledge of you naked.*

"You're going to Mexico?" His swift response
makes me realize I didn't guard my thoughts—again.

"Do you mind?" I wipe myself off and throw a
towel on the floor to soak up the mess.

"Sorry for eavesdropping. Can I come with you?"

"No!" Yoga pants and a sweatshirt lay nearby on a
chair and I tug them on, the fabric catching on my still
moist skin.

Telepathic blocking is now a new sore spot. This
vulnerable, wide open crap is for the birds. We spent a
lifetime mastering our telepathy and controlling who can
and can't read our thoughts. Now I'm aware everyone has a
front row ticket to my thoughts every month. My abilities
weren't so foolproof.

The next three hours drag as I avoid Sebastian like
the plague, but I'm up and running when I hear the

303

elevator. Nic and Dutch talk in animated voices and neither of them notice my presence. Sebastian stares from the other side of the great room, refusing to avert his gaze.

I imagine the cad is visualizing me naked.

"Hi, guys." They startle when I place myself in their path, stopping short as if I appeared from thin air. I'm well aware I don't light up a room, but I certainly don't blend in with the furniture either—what the hell?

"Julia, I didn't even notice you standing there." Nic looks from me to Sebastian.

"I needed the power of invisibility today," I admit and then add, "Why are you and Dutch so excited?" Sebastian won't stop staring and I blurt. "He saw me naked."

"Who saw you naked? What are you talking about?" Nic's voice falters and Dutch takes a step back.

"Sebastian. He barged into my bathroom without knocking." I scowl at the guilty party, and he has the audacity to smirk.

"It was a total accident—one of my better accidents, but not intentional." He leans against the wall, unable to hold a straight face.

I'm enraged and charge him from across the room. Dutch grabs my waist and spins me around before I reach his dirty rotten brother. He's not sorry and there's no way it was an accident.

"Someone needs chocolate. Isn't that *your* forte, Nic?"

That man poked at the wrong lion and I charge again, but Dutch tackles me to the floor, taking the brunt of our fall. You'd think we were ten again.

"He's trying to get you riled up so quit falling for it." He whispers in my ear, helping me to my feet.

Nic is staring Sebastian down, but I can't tell whether he's furious, indifferent, or feels nothing at all. His demeanor gives nothing away. Then he snaps out of the daze and addresses my question in an even voice.

"Dutch and I were chatting about the launch." Nic crosses his arms, mirroring Sebastian. "We met with Dexter and spoke to members of the board. Dutch and I were excited because we're part of something revolutionary. Claude doesn't treat us like kids and his staff respects us." He takes a breath and adds, "I'm glad you and Sebastian had fun today. But if you'll excuse me, I need to shower." He stalks down the hall and I follow, demanding to know why his anger isn't directed at Sebastian. His shuts and locks his door, and I press my cheek against the wood.

"I never should have told you."

"Wise idea."

His back slides down the door and it breaks my heart. Then I feel years of his pent up emotion at once, and it leaves me breathless.

"My brain is faster than my off switch, but I didn't want you thinking I hide things from you... because I don't."

"He needs to move out."

"I'll take care of it. Do you know about Mexico?"

"Yeah."

"Are you excited?" My cheek is still pressed to the door.

"I guess."

"Will you please let me in?"

The door unlocks, and he walks toward the bed with his head lowered. We sit in silence, not knowing how to make it better. Words don't seem to exist when you need them most.

"Can we forget all this and start over? I'll talk to Sebastian when we get back from Mexico. Until then, stay away from him." Nic orders.

"That won't be a problem. Are we still friends?"

"Don't get weird on me, we'll always be friends. It took me off guard; what did you expect?"

306

"You're right, if I had a brother…or someone I considered a brother, I'd react the same way."

"What do you mean?"

"You know."

I'm surprised he never put it together. Either their mothers are miracle workers or we aren't the same age. He frowns, a deep line forming between his brows.

"You can't *all* be eighteen. It's impossible and you're nothing alike." He stares at the walls, silent for a few moments, and finally speaks.

"It's not as if I haven't considered it. Who wants to admit they're all alone in the world."

"You've never been alone in the world—ever." I wrap my arm around his shoulder and he slumps into my embrace, sad and defeated.

A bang at the door jolts him off my shoulder, and we notice the now charcoal-gray sky. The last sliver of sun melts behind a New York City skyline and we watch it disappear together.

"Dinner!" Sebastian calls from the hall. He cracks the door to find us side by side on the bed and waltzes in not having learned his lesson from the last time.

"I'm not hungry." I glare.

"Lock my door on the way out." Nic's tone is

territorial and Sebastian catches my eye before closing the door.

We stay quiet for a few minutes, unsettled by a host of convoluted emotions.

"Are you stoked out of your mind?" It's my first real vacation and I can't imagine taking it with anyone other than Nic. I hope he feels the same way, but it's possible he doesn't. It's not as if I can force him to love me.

"A whole ten days with my favorite goose? *Sheck-yeah*."

"Be back in a minute." I squeal, racing to fetch the vacation materials still on my bed.

I grab the envelope and turn off the lights. My eyes are still adjusting to the darkened hallway and I crash into something solid. One second I'm gazing at an envelope, and the next moment I'm pressed against Sebastian.

Before I can apologize, he frames my face with his hands, and presses his lips on mine. I'm too shocked to react. In a blur, Nic's fist slams into the wall beside our heads. He read Sebastian's intent long before now because it's impossible to respond that fast.

"Get out." Nic demands between gritted teeth, his rage lethal.

"It's her call to make brother, not yours." His defiance is unbelievable and I envision bloodstains from one end of the hallway to the other but it never happens.

"You need to go, Sebastian." My eyes fill with tears. "Call for Leopold." I rush to my bedroom, slamming the door hard enough to make the walls rattle.

He packs, and I sense his every emotion as if my own. Sebastian's overwhelming sadness is a hollow ache, and when it's time, I meet him in the hall. He pauses before zipping the generic black suitcase, peering around the guest room one last time. I walk him to the elevator and push the down arrow. With a parting of doors, he steps inside and turns around, but not before a tear hits the floor. I'll never forget the sharp mechanical scraping of elevator doors; its lurching sound would haunt my dreams for a long time to come. I now associate the sound with an emotion— pain. That night became a pivotal moment in my life and I didn't even realize it at the time.

It might be weeks before we see each other again, and it's a sobering thought. As much as I love to hate Sebastian, I love him even more. Thinking, explaining, or even talking about it with anyone is out of the question. In fact, I don't want to look at another human being until we're on a plane to Mexico. If it's even possible to turn off my emotions, I just did. Sometimes, too much is just too much.

I'm in love with Nic, I remind myself—again.

Chapter Nineteen—More

Nic follows me up the steps of Claude's private jet with heavy feet and I wish the tension between us wasn't so obvious. Two days ago, Sebastian crossed a line, but no one identified which line he crossed. Technically, Nic and I aren't dating. If we don't put the incident behind us, we never will.

The Van Buren Industries jet is plush with light gray walls and flooring. At first glance, I spot oversized black leather seats, a sofa, and a mini-bar. The galley is much bigger than most commercial planes. Nic and I sit opposite each other with a speckled granite table separating the dark gray seats.

Anxiety makes the sun-filled day seem cloudy, but I'm determined to make the best of it. I won't allow the incident with Sebastian to overshadow my first real vacation.

"This is it," I glance around, impressed with the cabin.

"Yeah."

"Do you think we'll get snacks and a drink?"

"It doesn't matter."

"You don't want to go, do you? With me, that is."

Nic seems impatient with my small talk and turns his attention to the window next to his seat. He takes a deep breath before responding. "It's not the vacation. I don't understand why you didn't hit him, scream, or run away." His tone is controlled but angry. I don't have the answer he wants.

The door closes behind two pilots and an attendant, and I'm distracted for a moment. Then I consider the question.

"Reactions happen or don't happen for several reasons. He shocked me." I direct my attention to the flight attendant and she finishes her canned announcement. He studies my face.

"Most people react by resisting. *You* kissed him back."

"Nic." The air-conditioned cabin is much too cold and I tremble. "I didn't have *time* to kiss him back. Your fist hit the wall the second it happened." I rub my temples, resisting the urge to cry; I should've known we'd never get through this trip without rehashing that stupid incident.

"Yeah, well." He crosses his arms over his chest.

312

"It's not what I saw."

"You saw wrong. A person can run, fight, or freeze. I froze." The plane moves and I look out the window. The first thing I notice is the contrast between private and commercial jets, which take forever to taxi down the runway and take flight. "I'm sure he's sorry it happened."

"I don't care how he feels," Nic snaps. "I need to know how *you* feel." The plane takes off and cabin pressure increases, pinning me to my seat.

"What do you mean?"

"How do you feel about Sebastian kissing you? His feelings are pretty obvious, but yours I can't read."

"Thank God for small favors. My ability to block is back." When he doesn't laugh, I apologize. "Sorry."

"Just answer the question."

"There you go again. I get in trouble for trying to be funny, but you act the same when you're uncomfortable. Guys are exasperating; I swear to God."

"It doesn't matter, you're stalling." He nails my motivation and I realize he's right; I *am* stalling.

"I don't like what happened if that's what you're asking."

"That tells me nothing."

"What do you want me to say? He's your brother.

We grew up together."

"I want you to name your feelings. Spell it out for me."

"Shock, he took me off guard. And humiliated you had to stop him. Not to mention angry I didn't know to react or make everything better. Shall I go on or is that enough for you?" I hop up and storm to the back of the plane, locking myself in the bathroom.

After twenty good minutes of stewing in silence, I lumber back to my seat.

"Are we good?" I ask.

"When have we ever not been good?"

"I've been tiptoeing around for days. It's exhausting."

"You're on my good side for now. Try to stay on it." He thinks he's funny using my lines.

I wave at the attendant to get her attention, and she jumps up from her pristine perch near the cockpit to see what I need.

"What can I do for you, Julia?"

"If it's not too much bother, can we get a glass of wine?" She looks to Nic, and he nods. Her nametag reads Jeanine.

"You sure can."

"Thank you, Jeanine, we appreciate it."

She strolls toward the galley and busies herself in the fridge, her movements quick and efficient. We hear a loud pop, pulling our attention back to Jeanine. She slips a silver corkscrew back in the drawer and then balances two wine glasses in the crook of her hand. No twist cap means it's from a decent winery and I'm relieved. The cheap stuff gives me headaches. We sip in silence for most of the flight, quietly gazing out the window or flipping through magazines.

When we touchdown in Cancun, Nic steadies me down the ramp because my legs are stiff and rubbery from sitting so long. A black, sport utility vehicle waits on the runway and we hesitate when a tall man greets us in a foreign accent. He has graying hair on the sides.

"It nice meet you." He extends his hand. "My name Sanchez. Come please? Don't worry bags." He's professional and polite, but we soon realize he's not fluent in English.

"Can you get inside his head?" I nudge Nic and we follow him to our awaiting transportation.

"I'm trying but he's deadlocked." Nic turns and waves at our flight crew, trying to appear as if everything is fine.

"Interesting, I'm hitting the same thing. Do you think we're safe?"

"The guy is okay. Try to relax, goose."

"I thought I was your brainiac."

"You can be whatever you wish, Mistress Malone."

"Now that I like."

Nic elbows me, so I pay attention. Unable to read Sanchez, we're at a disadvantage. I swear I'm taking up martial arts and getting my concealed weapons permit when we get home. For the moment, I put my hesitations to rest and enjoy the ride. Claude wouldn't put us in danger, but it's his style to keep us in the dark until the last minute.

Sanchez opens the right passenger door and we slip inside, nervous but energized. The firm hitch when he closes our door seems final, and he slides in the driver's side of the vehicle. Once we're well away from the private landing strip, he pulls into an alcove off the road.

"If excuse please. Mr. Van Buren want you wear these." Sanchez holds up two sets of black blindfolds. The man would have killed us by now if he meant any harm so we comply.

"Gracias." The polite response in his native tongue is reassuring, but I'm anxious without my sight.

Nic and I use telepathy, but there's an undercurrent

of uneasy tension between us. It seems like hours before the vehicle comes to a stop, but when it does, Sanchez allows us to remove our blindfolds.

The mid-afternoon sun stings my eyes and I'm not sure what I'm looking at until my vision refocuses. In front of our vehicle is a red and white Cessna plane with floatation devices attached to the landing gear. We're next to a man-made body of water in the absolute middle of nowhere. The lake is too round and level to be a natural occurrence. I spot cactus and dried-up brush, but nothing beyond that.

"Excuse me, Mr. Sanchez, but where are we?"

"The location be so secret, can no tell." His soft tone and relaxed facial expression puts me at ease. Although English isn't his native tongue, I'm impressed by his effort to make sure we understand what's happening.

"Thank you." I nod.

Our doors open at the same time and two men dressed in khaki uniforms appear from nowhere to guide us on the next leg of our journey. We walk to a small paddleboat held in place by a stake, and they instruct us to step into the craft. It's a wobbly endeavor at best, and I look to Nic for reassurance.

"I checked their thoughts. Everything Sanchez said

317

is true, and it's standard procedure for confidentiality reasons."

I exhale; relieved we aren't headed to our own execution. The two men are patient as they guide us into the paddleboat and take their seats at the stern. We come to a stop beside the plane, and our footing is awkward as we step up to the guardrail. An obese pilot grabs my hand and jerks me into the plane, followed by Nic. The small, single engine craft seems as if it's made of tinfoil and does nothing to ease my fears.

"The name's Jerry," he grunts. "Buckle your seatbelt and put these over your eyes." Jerry reaches around and hands us another set of blindfolds. We follow his instructions but Claude could have at least warned us about this guy.

What's the cost of a simple warning? Our grumpy, sweaty, pilot orders us to settle in for a long flight. He mutters to himself about the heat and our plane roars to life. The flight is excruciating, nerve wracking and uncomfortable. There's nothing about this experience that screams *vacation of a lifetime.*

By the time Jerry informs us of our imminent arrival, my stomach has darn near chewed through my backbone. I'm starving, disoriented, and find it difficult to

318

concentrate on conversation. The roaring engine rattled my body the entire flight. I'm numb, and the earphones did nothing to drown out the constant buzzing in my head and bones.

Exasperated, I take my blindfold off and Jerry scolds me in his native tongue. I'm certain he's cussing me out, but I don't care. It's been a long day and I just want him to land this rickety old plane already. I grab Nic's blindfold and yank it down around his neck. He blinks a couple times to adjust to the light while Jerry cusses even louder.

Based on internet searches before our trip, we're not in Mexico. It's obvious as we fly low over thick, lush vegetation indicative of a jungle environment.

"Where are we?" I shout over the roaring engine.

"I can't tell you." Jerry's attitude is downright unreasonable, and he has the personality of a donkey. Our pilot is nothing like Sanchez.

The plane circles around to land in swampy marshland, making the perfect backdrop for a horror movie. The setting sun makes it doubtful we'll see anything before dark. Jerry cuts the engine and my ears continue ringing long after we remove our earphones. Now we wait.

"Where do you think we are?" I peer out the

window and see nothing but trees.

"I have no clue but we're not in Kansas anymore, Dorothy."

Jerry is dead silent and our predicament gets weirder as time passes. I notice movement in the trees followed by dark skinned men lowering a man-made canoe into the swampy, muck-covered water.

"I guess that's our ride, Tin Man."

"Now that's creepy."

The men slice through the water with wooden paddles until they reach the plane. Their movements appear stealthy and predatory, but anything is better than hanging with Jerry all night.

They open the door, motioning for us to step down into the canoe. We do as instructed, almost tipping us into the stagnant, loamy water. Once settled, the men paddle back to shore, and we step into marshy soil before hitting dry ground.

"Are we on vacation yet?" Our shoes are ruined.

"Why do I hear 'Welcome to the Jungle' playing in my head?" Nic asks, bobbing his head like an idiot. Yep, he's lost it.

"It's because you're intellectually challenged. You have to admit, this is a messed up trip. Claude puts the

creep in creepy."

An older man with a silver beard steps from behind jungle vegetation and greets us in perfect English. Although it's dark, I make out his khaki trousers, crisp white shirt, and hand-woven hat. He's carrying an old-fashioned lantern that sways back and forth.

"Welcome. I trust your journey wasn't *too* traumatic." His tone holds an amused titter. He must know the routine well.

"Uh—hi." My reluctance and lack of manners must be due to travel weariness, but Nic is quick to recoup and shakes the man's hand.

"I'm Jack Perriman and you must be Nic. I hope you're both hungry because we have a feast waiting for you at the tree house." He turns and leads us through a clearing and I see twinkling amber lights somewhere in the distance.

"Perriman…do you know *Lillian* Perriman?" I ask.

He grins over his shoulder and I assume there's a relation. Nic elbows me for being nosy and presumptuous.

"Ah, Julia. Your reputation precedes you I'm afraid."

"How so?"

"I've heard you're an intelligent and curious girl— one for figuring things out, yet missing the finer details.

Don't be disheartened, dear. We have minions who take care of the details. We need thinkers who see the big picture, and you and Nic are a pair to be reckoned with I imagine."

"What do you mean by that?" I ask, wondering if I can trust this man.

"You complement each other's strengths and fill in for the weaknesses. It was a perfect pairing." I'm ready to question his coded statement, but stop in my tracks at the breathtaking sight ahead. I've never laid eyes on anything like it in my life.

"Whoa." Nic rams into the back of me.

A complex of interconnected tree houses lights our dense surroundings with the incandescence of a thousand shimmering lanterns. I can't imagine a more beautiful sight in the entire world that compares to this magical anomaly in the middle of nowhere.

"What do you think? We named it Enchantment. It's the perfect name, no?"

"What are these trees?" Their massive structure is unreal.

"They're banyans. Incredible aren't they?" Jack muses, a smile playing at his mouth. He taps his chin, proceeding forward after a cursory nod.

"They sure look prehistoric." I say loud enough for him to hear.

Although the air is thick with humidity, another scent catches my attention and I glance toward the source. It's possible I'm drooling but I don't bother wiping my mouth.

"Holy Hannah, what is that smell?" I'm so tired, hungry, and overwhelmed; my manners seem to take a vacation of their own.

"Her circuit breaker is malfunctioning. It's a chick thing. You'll get used to it." They laugh while I ignore them and walk toward the source.

I stop at the base of the primary tree house, close my eyes, and inhale. Whatever is cooking, Jack didn't exaggerate. If scents were flavors, I'd be salivating on my ruined shoes. A quick perusal of my ruined shoes has me sulking again. They were my favorite penny loafers.

"Ha—you worry too much, dear girl. We have everything you need, even without such curious things as luggage. You should know Claude by now. He's a control freak."

Jack leads us up graduating wooden steps that wind around an elegant resort built into massive trees. From the outside, it looks like an adult-sized playhouse for the wealthy, but once inside I'm surprised to find the atmosphere cozy and quaint.

Wicker furniture sits in intimate groupings on dark, stained, hardwood floors. Banana-leaf fan blades whirl high above our heads, and the breeze is a relief, but I can't figure out the source of the cool air. Gauzy white fabric hangs between huge wooden beams of teakwood, and dozens of solid shutters flank the sides of each opening. There can be no air conditioning in an open structure such as this. Then I spot swamp coolers hidden beneath the clever disguise of slatted wood. The mystery is solved.

A buffet table lined with silver domed platters rests against the furthest wall to our right. I count out ten domes, and the scents both captivate and distract me.

"Are there bathrooms here?" I step from one foot to the other.

"Where are my manners?" Jack points the opposite direction and I'm confused. After several seconds I focus on the faintest outline of a door that blends into the walls as if camouflaged. He leads Nic to the men's bathroom on the other side.

We take care of business and Jack escorts us to a table near the buffet. A fine linen cloth covers our table and a single red rose sits in the center. The silver vase is constructed of candle votives and has me marveling the artisan's craftiness. We sit, travel worn and exhausted.

A server opens a door I couldn't see until the wood moved away from the wall. She floats to our table on bare feet carrying a decanter of ice water and offers us a gracious smile. She's in a white tunic, free of embellishment and I long for the simplicity of what this lifestyle entails. That means no cell phones, computers, traffic, or deadlines. Nic and I look at each other, wondering if she speaks English, but she answers our question in a docile voice.

"Please help yourself. My name is Anya if I can aid you further." She gestures to the buffet table, floating back through the cleverly disguised door. It's as if she disappears into nothingness.

No one has to tell me twice; I'm starved. Jack is chatting with a small group of employees at the other end of the palatial room. He points our direction several times and they nod.

I lift dome number one to find the source of that luscious scent and jump back before the steam burns my face. It's meat and potatoes in a brown sauce and it takes everything I have not to dive onto the platter. The next dome has rice and vegetables and Nic heaps his plate.

325

There is also broth soup with strange objects floating on top and I pass. My plate is loaded so I retreat to the table and start eating.

"Oh my gosh." I sputter through a mouthful of food, forgetting I have telepathic abilities.

"What's the meat?" The texture is like silk in my mouth.

"I don't know, but it's delicious. Just enjoy your monkey kabobs, goose."

"Monkey kabobs? You're a dork." I stuff another forkful in my mouth and close my eyes, trying not to think of monkeys. It proves impossible.

We find sweet breads, quinoa, chickpeas, tropical fruit medleys, and a buttery bread pudding with cinnamon and plantains. My stomach is close to exploding, and it's difficult to breathe so I put the fork down and throw my napkin on the table. Jack stops by to check our progress.

"What did you think of the buffet?" He clasps his hands in front of his belly and winks.

"You weren't kidding about the food; it was amazing. Thank you."

"It's my pleasure. Claude and I have known each other forever and his friends are my friends. Welcome to Enchantment." Jack has a flair for the mysterious, but his

326

genuine charm and warmth is refreshing. "Are you ready to see your quarters?" He claps his hands together, signaling the end of dinner. We wipe our mouths one last time and push our chairs out from the table.

It's clear he wants to make our stay extraordinary, and so far, I've never seen anything that rivals the mystique of Enchantment. A native couple in plain cotton shifts and flip flops greets us at the table. The woman's hair is held back with a white bandanna and she's missing her two front teeth.

"Julia, meet Anya's sister, Aykay. She'll help throughout your stay, clean and bring whatever you need including room service and whatnot."

"Nic, meet Xande'. He'll provide the same for you." We smile and nod, thanking Jack for the hospitality. Aykay leads us outside and to the first bungalow, gesturing for me to ascend the stairs, while Xande' and Nic keep walking.

"See you later?" I shout after them, but he's already yawning.

"You got it. I'm crashing." He walks up the stairs of his own bungalow and waves before ducking inside, followed by Xande'.

Once inside my own tree house bungalow, Aykay

switches on a lamp, illuminating the room in a subdued yellow glow. Against the furthest wall is a four-poster bed draped in mosquito netting. A wicker table and chairs with cherry red cushions sits against the opposite wall.

"Is this the bathroom?" I peek around a tri-fold divider to find a tiny porcelain tub and pedestal sink. My lower half might fit—maybe.

It's primitive luxury, a design concept I can appreciate thanks to Dutch. I thank Aykay and she leaves me to my own devices, never a good idea by anyone's standards.

It would be nice to crawl in bed and pass out, but I don't want to be alone. We're still in the middle of nowhere and it's no less creepy than before we relieved ourselves and ate. I snoop in a closet behind my bed. Sure enough, two weeks' worth of clothing in my size. Jack's assessment of Claude couldn't be closer to the truth—total control freak. He took care of *everything*.

I toss my ruined shoes in a nearby trashcan and slip on a pair of leather sandals. It's time to check with Nic, so I wind my way around the steps and over to his bungalow to find identical accommodations. He's sprawled on the bed bare footed and his eyes are closed. Is he snoring? His mouth is hanging wide open and I hear a deep throaty rumble followed by several quick snorts.

It's impossible not to laugh because he looks hilarious and I wish I'd brought my camera. He'd have unwelcome friends taking up residence in his mouth if not for the mosquito netting surrounding his bed. I kick my shoes off, spread the netting, and crawl in for the night. My eyelids close, and the thrumming buzz of millions of insects' lulls me to sleep.

Chapter Twenty—Impossible

Water trickles down my back and I crack an eye, realizing I'm covered in sweat. The sun is up, stagnant humidity making it difficult to breathe and I'm thirsty. I nudge Nic and he's hot to the touch. His chest barely rises and falls, and I've never seen his skin this pale.

"Nic, get out of bed." I slap at his cheeks, rolling him from left to right. He groans but doesn't speak. "Your skin is on fire. Come on big boy you need to get up." I shake his shoulders when he doesn't respond.

"Come on Nic, don't do this." It feels as if I'm having a panic attack, the tightness in my chest a good indicator. His body is still limp so I run for help. When I reach the bottom of the bungalow, Aykay and Xande' smile, ready to serve us.

"Run and get Jack! Bring as much fresh drinking water as you can carry and hurry." I race back up the stairs and find a cup in the bathroom. Even though the water is tepid, it's better than nothing.

"Nic, you have to lean forward and drink; you're

sick." I push against his shoulders to force him into a sitting position, but it's no use because he flops to the side like a rag doll. I trickle water into his mouth and it runs back out.

Come on Jack!

My ears perk at the sound of running footsteps and gravel crunching under several pairs of shoes. Panicked whispers and thundering footsteps shake the entire tree house. Jack rushes over and covers his mouth with a hand.

"He's pale and sweaty," Jack touches Nic's forehead, "Aykay, call Doctor Reiner and tell him to bring intravenous antibiotics and five bags of saline."

"What's wrong with him?" I make my way to Nic's side, pushing back tears.

"I don't know honey. How long has he been this way?"

"That's just it, I don't know. Nic was sleeping, and I thought he was fine. When I woke up he wouldn't move."

"It could range from food poisoning to nasty bugs In these parts. We won't know until Dr. Rainer arrives." Jack touches my arm and adds, "You need to get back to your own bungalow though."

"I'm all he has." The tension in my jaw is making my head pound and my feet refuse to move.

"Julia." He attempts patience. "There's nothing you

331

can do here. Go get breakfast and relax."

Aykay places icy, wet cloths over Nic's body to reduce the fever. I've known Nic for fifteen years and have never seen him sick.

"Can you hear me?" Tears burn the back of my eyelids. When he doesn't respond, I rush from the bungalow and wait on the stairs for Doctor Rainer.

After what seems like forever, a dark skinned man wearing tan pants and a black t-shirt pulls up in a jeep, raising clouds of dust. He isn't what I expected, and two of his assistants struggle with supplies. I rush over, but the doctor addresses me in a stern manner.

"It's not safe for you just yet. Please return to your quarters, miss." He jogs up the stairs and I stalk off, feeling helpless.

I'm exposed already, you idiot.

Aykay brings me toast, cheese, and coffee and I doubt my stomach could tolerate much more. The sound of footsteps and voices alerts me to the doctor's departure and Jack keeps pace by his side. They get into the jeep, disappearing into a thicket of dense jungle. When I'm positive they're gone I run next door.

"Your friend be okay, but he do need rest." Xande' looks to the bed and my eyes follow.

The doctor has Nic hooked to an I.V. and covered with a thin cotton sheet but I'm relieved to see his color improved since the last time I was here.

"How long before I can see him?"

"The doctor make him sleep. His body need much rest." I nod and he offers me a weak smile.

On the way back to my quarters, I meet Jack on the trail and he's sporting a cheerful smile, despite our present circumstances.

"Not to worry yourself, my dear. He's on antibiotics and should be better in a few days. We need to let him rest and regain strength. Nic had a nasty bug, but we caught it early thanks to you."

"What kind of bug?"

"Mosquitoes and other insects carry sickness in the jungle. You wouldn't have had previous exposure to these strains in the states."

"I see. Is this *really* a vacation?" I study his body language, looking for signs of deception.

"Of course it's a vacation. We'll have Nic up and running in a few days. In the meantime, I have an excursion planned for you. It's like nothing you've ever experienced. Nor will you experience anything like it again." His words carry a cryptic undertone, making him seem less mysterious and more diabolical.

"Not until Nic is okay." How can I leave when he's so sick? I glance over at Nic's bungalow, doubtful Jack's suggestion is a good one.

"Nonsense, he's fine and resting. I'll arrange for the jeep to take us this afternoon. Have you eaten?" He eyes my tiny frame and clucks his tongue as if preparing to lecture me.

"I had a bite or two."

"You need more than that. I'll make sure Aykay brings you the works. Now go. Explore the grounds but don't leave camp." He waves me off and I thank him for the hospitality, but with unsettling doubt clawing at my insides. When he's out of ear shot, I kick a stone to release my frustration. This is the vacation from hell, or maybe I've died and gone to hell—I don't know anymore.

The back of Jack's red shirt disappears inside the primary tree house so I explore the grounds. In the light of day it's much less magical than the night we arrived.

There are smaller bungalows set behind the main ones and I figure they must be servants' quarters. Jack's quarters are three times the size of ours; the wood stained a rich mahogany hue. A porch area with a hand hewed wooden table and chairs makes the space inviting even though he never bothered clearing the vines creeping up the sides of his tree house. Dense vegetation hides his quarters from the rest of Enchantment, and it's a curious, hidden space.

Aykay is balancing an enormous tray of food high above her head and I rush over to help before she drops everything. We both take one side of the tray, snaking our way up the staircase of my bungalow.

"Thank you Miss Julia." She excuses herself after we set the tray down, leaving me with an obscene amount of food. There is oat cereal with dates and other dried fruit, plantain pudding, and dense sweet bread with cinnamon butter.

After polishing off my last cup of coffee I roll over and groan, and the rest of the food goes uneaten. My eyelids grow heavy and I fall asleep only to be awakened by the thud of heavy footsteps. Jack is standing in the doorway.

"Are you ready?" He's grinning like a lunatic.

"Uh... ready for what?"

"Our excursion, silly girl."

"I'm sorry, I fell asleep, and...what the heck are you wearing?" Not only is he grinning like a lunatic, he's dressed in yellow rubber pants, a matching rubber vest, and mammoth boots comprising the same yellow rubber.

"You'll find the same gear in one of your closets. It can be mushy where we're going and not proper for a lady, but you'll love it. Trust me."

Sure enough, I open an uninspected closet to find a similar rubber get-up in pink.

"Go on," He urges, pointing to the gear, "It's lightweight and designed to deflect heat."

That's good to know since we're in the middle of a boiling hot jungle.

I peer over at Jack and then down at my own ridiculous outfit and pinch the bridge of my nose. He's nothing but an excitable, overgrown kid and how I got sucked into this nonsense is beyond me.

"How's Nic?" I duck from behind my bed looking like a professional clown in head to toe, pink rubber.

"Nic's doing much better and opened his eyes a couple hours ago. He said don't worry and he'll see you when we get back."

"Well…okay then. Is it safe to assume we're going somewhere wet?" I take a deep breath, realizing I've been breathing shallow ever since Nic first got sick.

"You're assuming correct." He bends to look at his boots, pops back up and gestures to the door. We look like members of the Insane Clown Posse but I'm rolling with it just this once.

"Do I need anything besides this ridiculous rubber get-up?" I point at myself, and then Jack. At least we can acknowledge how crazy we look.

"Nope, everything else is loaded in the jeep."

"Ok then—groovy." I give him thumbs up, and he laughs at my use of slang from the sixties. This man is Lillian's brother as sure as I'm standing here because I'd recognize that cavalier smile anywhere.

Once outside, I call shotgun and Jack takes the wheel. Two of his assistants are in the back squirming with excitement so I embrace their enthusiasm. Wherever we're going, it must be fun.

The terrain is nowhere near roadworthy, and food sloshes in my belly to the point of nausea after a half hour of driving. Jack stops our jeep at the base of a tree that's almost impossible to comprehend with my current knowledge. It looks like a species from another planet. There is no end to it, at least in my field of vision. The base is as big as a house. The gray wood seems to have dozens if not hundreds of tentacles curving around the smooth trunk, reaching for the sky. There's a sharp pain in the back of my neck and I realize I've been staring upward too long imagining *Jack and the Beanstalk*. We hop from our perches in the jeep and I land in thick soggy soil, which explains the need for the pink rubber boots.

"Jack, that tree can't be real," I state, and ask, "Do people know these exist?"

"It's real, and no one but us knows this species exists."

"I'm thinking it would freak people out; my God, it's unreal." I try to move my boots.

This goop we're standing in makes it hard to walk and the quick snap of branches catches my attention. I look up, distracted from the slurping noises my feet make every time I lift a boot. The God-awful stench is something I never want to experience again after we leave. It's putrefied and stinks of sewer. I stare past the mammoth tree but see nothing but a thick wall of vines covering an outcropping of rock.

"That's where we're going," he announces with a victorious grin.

"Where are we going?" I scan the jungle, trying to figure out what he's referring to, and he points to the benign wall of vegetation. "And what was that sound we just heard a minute ago?"

"We kicked up a baby javelina. As long as an entire

338

herd or angry mother isn't nearby, we're good." He pats the side of his jacket and I notice the outline of a gun. I exhale, somewhat relieved.

Jack gave no clues and I'm curious what kind of excursion he has in mind here. I considered zip-lining and waterfalls, but I wouldn't have expected mushy swampland. When we arrived two nights ago, I tried reading Jack's thoughts but met resistance. Since then, I've tried two other occasions and hit the same block. It isn't a shield to protect his thoughts from intrusion, but a wall placed there by someone unknown. It's the difference between hitting mesh and a brick wall.

We stop in front of the thick and almost impenetrable wall of vines, and I notice the walls curve downward on both sides. It's a cave with no discernible entrance. His assistants kneel in the mush, grabbing the vines with both hands, and they pull upward.

It's enough of a hole for us to slip through and we squat. I follow Jack, expecting darkness, but flecks of neon green embedded in the cave walls throws off an eerie illumination. We're going spelunking? I've heard of people getting lost and never finding their way back out. I don't want to become a statistic.

"I hope we aren't going in too far." My nerves pitch

a quick fit along with my voice.

"It's just a ways in and I've been here hundreds of times. Don't worry; you're safe with me."

"Nic would have loved this. It's a shame we didn't wait for him to get better."

"I wanted you to see it first." His voice quiets for no obvious reason, but I imagine it's because of the echo in the cave. I'm sure it's filled with bats, and tangling with thousands of them doesn't appeal to me on any level.

We make our way farther into the cave and I keep glancing down at my feet to avoid slipping. Sheen on the slick, black, bedrock catches my eye. There's intense, stagnant humidity the farther we descend into the belly of the cave. I follow Jack with my gaze on the ground, touching his back every few seconds to steady myself. We stop.

"Julia, look." I glance up from the cave floor and we're standing inside a colossal cavern and it's glowing from the center of the earth. It looks to be the size of a small city in shimmering shades of cherry and emerald.

"Isn't she gorgeous?" Jack's eyes gleam brighter than the cave. I'm somewhat freaked out he refers to the cave as *she*, but who am I to argue with indescribable natural beauty.

He leads us down a walkway carved into the side of the cave, and our surroundings look more like a magical oasis than anything I've ever seen in a movie. Tranquil pools of pale pink water shimmer and appear lit from deep below the surface of the cave.

Next to the larger body of water, are several small cenotes with the same glowing liquid. The light ricochets off the cenotes to the green-flecked walls, and bathes the jungle flora in vibrant color. I marvel that trees and vegetation exist in a cave without natural sunlight but don't bother thinking too long on the impossible.

"Oh, Jack," I murmur, "This is magnificent." My feet move forward of their own accord, and I couldn't stop them if I tried.

All four of us peer into a shimmering pool of glowing, reflective liquid and the familiar amethyst hue, deep below the waters. I'm looking at the source of the elixir and find it impossible to take in air for a moment.

A thousand questions race through my mind but Jack stares into the pool, transfixed and unmoving, as if mesmerized into paralysis.

"Isn't she beautiful?" When he glances up his expression has changed. He looks like someone in a hypnotic trance.

341

I detect movement scurrying through the trees, but can't locate the source of the noise.

"What the heck is *that*?" I turn to Jack's assistants and find them mesmerized, and unaware. Their strange behavior makes me want to run because I no longer feel safe, but my feet won't budge from the sleek, black bedrock.

"Shh—you'll scare them. Don't move an inch." Jack shushes me, his tone intense.

"Scare what? I don't see anything." I whisper, noting nothing unusual.

"You'll see, now hush." Jack faces forward, standing as still as a statue. We mimic him for a long time before I capture more movement ahead.

Two creatures, impossible to identify based on my knowledge of the modern world, walk out on four legs toward a distant cenote, and drink. Their long, narrow bodies should make it impossible to walk on four legs without their bellies scraping the floor.

They resemble meerkats but their odd shape and slow, rhythmic cadence makes no logical sense. The water ripples, and in my astonishment I gasp when both creatures stand and stare our direction. I'm frozen in place and swear my heart stops for a second.

One creature turns to the other, motioning for his companion to stay put. It walks toward us on two legs, stopping in front of Jack. His mouth is set in a grim line as if he's displeased.

"Why do you disturb us this evening, Mr. Jack?"

***

"Julia!" someone slaps my cheeks, "Julia, are you okay?"

My eyes refocus and several faces stare at me with concerned expressions. Disoriented, I realize I'm on the bed in my own bungalow.

"What happened? Why aren't we in the cave?" I bolt upright.

"We had to sedate you, dear. You're one of the rare people who panic inside expansive closed spaces. We thought you were fine and then you weren't. I came prepared for such an event." He taps a hypodermic needle in his side pocket and dismisses it just as fast.

"*Luckily* you came prepared? *Right*. That animal *talked* to us."

"Julia, there weren't any animals in the cave. You had a panic attack." He glances up at the others for effect, and smiles. Then he stares down at me, feigning concern.

"You sedated me? Who does that? I'd call it much

343

more than sedation if I have no recollection after that…that *thing* talked to you." I slap his hands away when he tries to calm me and kick the covers off my legs.

Jack looks to his assistant and motions for him to pour me a glass of water.

"What did you think of the cave though?" He peers in my eyes and pushes at the edge of my mind. I resist.

I snatch the water from his hand and guzzle it in one, long gulp. He doesn't want to know what I think. I lie back and close my eyes, wanting nothing more than to go home. Not back to New York, but to the countryside of England where I belong. No one should have to cope with benefactors, elixirs, sociopaths, and evolutionary anomalies once considered animals.

"Nic, I'm done." I grit my teeth. "I'm done with everything."

No one says another word, and the bed springs back when Jack rises.

"She needs time to process something we know nothing about," he says in a hushed tone just loud enough for me to overhear, "Julia might need psychological care back in the states." He shakes his head, but Nic's not buying it and I can tell from his skeptical expression.

"Just get us home." Nic stomps down the stairs. I

hear gravel crunching under his shoes outside the window and everyone follows, shaking the foundation of my bungalow.

Someone has a lot of explaining to do when I get back home and if they think I need psychological help, they'll have one hell of a fight on their hands when I return.

~The End~

Continue Julia's story in Book II of The Van Buren Series:

Rewind

About the Author

As a published author, Katie St. Claire began freelance writing in 2008, and writing fiction novels since 2013, when she published her first two books in the series as a beta run to determine interest. She has degrees in social work, psychology, sociology, and human resources. This allows her to develop characters with real human quirks, realistic dialogue, and thoughts & feelings we all recognize. As a long time lover of paranormal romance and urban fantasy, she set out to write about something unique and fresh.

Although passionate about vampire books, movies, and television series, she wanted to concentrate on the paranormal as it relates to *real* human traits. As usual, she writes a few steps further and takes it into the realm of fantasy. Her goal was to make the series *almost* believable, bringing elements of science fiction and apocalyptic events into play.

Her extensive study of psychology and character disorders allowed her to write about sociopathic traits and behaviors associated with those behaviors. This coming of age series, with a paranormal twist, will have you wishing you were Julia or thanking God you're not.

Katie St. Claire incorporates a little of herself into her characters, and writing, using both character traits she has, would love to have, or experienced with other people. Her plots are as vast and varied as her own imagination, which tends to get a little wild sometimes. She walks with the notion that nothing is impossible. This is Katie's first Urban Fantasy/Paranormal Romance series, and she named it after a mysterious family, The Van Burens.

In addition to writing novels we love, Katie is a hardcore gardener and chrysanthemum cross-breeder. She owes her extensive gardens to her imagination, constantly planting, re-planting, dividing, and arranging in order to paint her world with living things. Many of her passions appear in the books.

Affiliations: Fiction Writers Guild, Paranormal Romance Guild, Romance Critters

You can contact Katie St. Claire on Facebook, Pinterest, Instagram, Twitter, GoodReads, or by emailing authorkatiestclaire@gmail.com.

~The Van Buren Series~
Second Hand Stops
Rewind
Fast Forward

CPSIA information can be obtained at www.ICGtesting.com
Printed in the USA
LVOW11s1716160415

434890LV00001B/83/P